PRAISE FOR H

"These mesmerizing stories of disconnection and detritus unfurl with the surreal illogic of dreams—it's as impossible to resist their pull as it is to understand, in retrospect, how circumstance succeeded circumstance to finally deliver the reader into a moment as indelible as it is unexpected. Janet Hong's translation glitters like a blade."
—Susan Choi, author of *Trust Exercise*

"*Flowers of Mold* shows Ha Seong-nan to be a master of the strange story. Here, things almost happen, and the weight of their almost happening hangs over the narrative like a threat. Or they do happen, and then characters go on almost like they haven't, much to the reader's dismay. Or a story builds up and then, where most authors would pursue things to the last fraying thread of their narrative, Ha elegantly severs the rest of the story and delicately ties it off. And as you read more of these stories, they begin to chime within one another, creating a sense of deja-vu. In any case, one is left feeling unsettled, as if something is not right with the world—or, rather (and this latter option becomes increasingly convincing), as if something is not right with *you*."
—Brian Evenson, author of *Song for the Unraveling of the World*

"Brilliantly crafted with precision and compassion, Ha Seong-nan's heartbreaking collection dives into the depths of human vulnerability, where hopes and dreams are created and lost, where ordinary life gains mythological status. A truly gifted writer."
—Nazanine Hozar, author of *Aria*

"Ha Seong-nan's stories are familiar, domestic, and utterly terrifying. Like the best of A. M. Homes, Samantha Schweblin, or Brian Evenson, her elegantly terse style lures you in and never fails to shock. She writes the kind of stories I admire most. Ones you carry around with you long after reading."
—Brian Wood, author of *Joytime Killbox*

"Wrapped up in fantasy or dreams, these men, women, and children are often confused over what is and isn't real, the reader seeing before they do how their anxious yearning will go unfulfilled."
—Laura Adamczyk, *The A.V. Club*

"Be forewarned: it might make you reconsider your interest in your neighbors, because it could lead to obsession and madness—or something odder and less reassuring than a tidy end, of which there are few in this wonderfully unsettling book of 10 masterful short stories."
—John Yau, *Hyperallergic*

"Joining a growing cohort of notable Korean imports, Ha's dazzling, vaguely intertwined collection of 10 stories is poised for Western acclaim."
—*Booklist*, starred review

"This impressive collection reveals Ha's close attention to the eccentricities of life, and is sure to earn her a legion of new admirers."
—*Publishers Weekly*, starred review

"If you're looking for a book that will make you gasp out loud, you've found it."
—*Kirkus Reviews*

"Ha's ability to find startling traits in seemingly unremarkable characters makes each story a small treasure."
—Cindy Pauldine, *Shelf Awareness*

"Her characters are trying their best to get by, and I found them deeply sympathetic, but they often face obstacles they just do not know how to confront. The stories are beautiful, inventive, gorgeously-written, and often heart-wrenching."
—Rebecca Hussey, *Book Riot*

"These aren't bedtime stories. Indeed, reading them before bed might not be a good idea at all."
—Peter Gordon, *Asian Review of Books*

"Like *The Vegetarian*—another surreal and haunting text by a Korean woman—*Flowers of Mold* unsettles and unnerves, effortlessly. . . . *Flowers of Mold* offers readers an alternative perspective on city life, relationships, and ambition; and while it may be dark and unrelenting, it is also hauntingly lyrical."
—Rachel Cordasco, *World Literature Today*

"As horror and art continue to steal and mix with each other, I'm sure we'll find more—on both sides of the aisle—that continue to push the envelope. *Flowers of Mold* pushes that envelope with its impressive style and stifling isolation, creating something that's as strange as it is incisive."
—Carson Winter, *Signal Horizon*

"In these stories, readers will find tales of alienation and unruly behavior that will likely jar them as much as any narrative of sinister creatures and haunted spaces."
—Tobias Carroll, Words Without Borders

"Here is, undoubtedly, one of the best translated short story collections of 2019."
—Will Harris, *Books and Bao*

"I'm raving about this book. . . . It is brilliant, modern, and surprising."
—Charles Montgomery

"In Ha Seong-nan's gripping and courageous *Flowers of Mold*, the author triple-underlines those distasteful aspects of our lives that we'd rather ignore: the putridity of leaky trash; the greasy, lingering smell of fried chicken; children's crackers crushed underfoot; the solid clunk of an alarm clock to the jaw. . . . Ha is a master of the short story and hooks the reader without revealing or resolving too much too cleanly."
—Samantha Kirby, *Arkansas International*

ALSO BY HA SEONG-NAN IN ENGLISH TRANSLATION

Flowers of Mold

Bluebeard's First Wife

WAFERS

HA SEONG-NAN

Translated from the Korean by Janet Hong

Curated by Janet Hong for the 2024 Translator Triptych

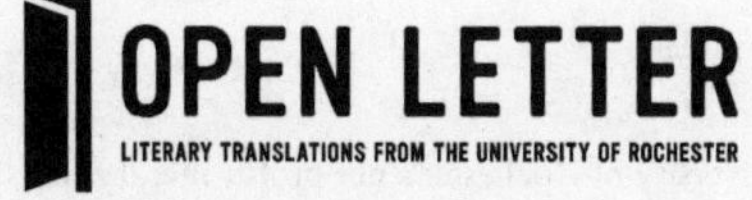

Original Korean edition published by Munhakdongne Publishing Group
English translation rights arranged with Munhakdongne Publishing Group, Paju.

First edition, 2024

Library of Congress Cataloging-in-Publication Data: Available.
ISBN (pb): 978-1-948830-98-0 | ISBN (ebook): 978-1-960385-03-1

The translation of this work is supported by the Literature Translation Institute of Korea.

This project is supported in part by an award from the National Endowment for the Arts and the New York State Council on the Arts with the support of the Governor of New York and the New York State Legislature.

Printed on acid-free paper in Canada.

Cover design by Eric Wilder

Open Letter is the University of Rochester's nonprofit, literary translation press:
www.openletterbooks.org

Contents

WAFERS

Autobiography

Since I hadn't been back since I left over twenty years ago, I thought I'd have a hard time finding the place she described on the phone. She said she was sorry for telling me to come all the way, but she needed to watch the store, so she couldn't step out, not even for a moment. She then snickered for a while, finally asking, "Could you have imagined me like this?" Her voice had become raspy, perhaps due to age or an unhealthy lifestyle. I wondered what had managed to tame her, recalling the wild thing she'd been.

Her face came to mind. Squirting spit through the gap in her front teeth, she would challenge boys a head taller than herself. She was as skinny as a metal chopstick, yet the fastest in our gang. She was the representative sprinter for her high school until her sophomore year, but by the time I met her, she'd dropped out and was hanging around beauty and sewing schools. That was well over two decades ago. They say time is scary, but reality is even scarier. Being part of that crowd offered no help when it came to making a living. She mentioned that nearly everyone from the group had married, started families, and secured jobs.

The streets were lined with revamped government offices and what looked like every single bank in Korea. Amid fast-food restaurants sandwiched between skyscrapers, I was relieved to have given myself extra time in case I got lost. Following her directions, I navigated my car through the hectic traffic toward the residential area. I expected winding, dingy alleys hardly wide enough to accommodate a single car, but to my surprise, I found a neat network of paved roads leading to various building entrances. The once tightly packed houses that barely allowed in sunlight and wind had been replaced by towering apartment complexes and low-rises.

The industrial road, which continued all the way to the outskirts of the city, seemed to have opened recently as there wasn't much traffic. Running parallel on the opposite side, a steel fence displaying the name of a construction company stretched endlessly. The road then transitioned to an unpaved lane, its surface marked by truck-tire tracks that converged at the entrance of the construction site. Each time I jolted over potholes and rocks, my head bumped against the roof of the car. Dust coated every window of my car.

Suddenly, the unpaved road ended, giving way to an uphill path that glistened in the sunlight, like a stream frosted over with ice. It was exactly as I remembered it. The few houses that once stood at the bottom of the hill were now gone, replaced by deep pits that looked as if created by an excavator.

From the other side of the hill, a whistle sounded. A little while later, the forehead of a boy appeared, and soon after, his whole body came into view. Having pedaled all the way up the hill, his body was drenched in sweat. Now that he'd reached the peak, he only needed to coast, resting his feet on the pedals. As his bike picked up speed, the seat bounced wildly on its springs, and he began to shout. "Move! Get out of the way! It's not my fault if you get hurt!" His bike bell was long gone.

My third novel, *Children of the Wind*, starts this way, with a boy shouting as he rushes down a hill. Some twenty years ago, that boy and I were both seventeen. The momentum from his descent carries him all the way down to where the apartment complexes now stand. When the bike begins to slow, he stands and pedals furiously. With each push of the pedal, the bicycle tilts dangerously to the left and right. As soon as he rounds a corner, a steep path appears, eventually leading to Revival Church, located in the basement of a store. He has no plans to fix his brakes. All he cares about is getting to the church as quickly as possible. Slowing down isn't on his agenda.

Sometimes, readers send in postcards or letters posing questions like, "Is the boy on the bicycle perhaps your alter ego?" Even when I wrote about a housewife spiraling into madness from conspiracies, or about a company employee finding a bloody knife on his bed with no memory of the previous night, readers asked similar questions. "At what point does truth end and fiction begin in your work?" Still, those sorts of questions are fine. And then there are times when fans call early in the morning, saying, "I feel as if you've written my story."

As I drove uphill, the steepness made me feel as though I were reclining. Despite flooring the accelerator, the car wouldn't go any faster. In the winter, this hill had become a slippery slope covered in ice. I remembered the way people would make their way down, sticking out their backsides and carefully lifting their feet to avoid falling. If someone higher up lost their balance and slipped, they would set off a domino effect, knocking others down and sending them all sliding uncontrollably to the bottom. Another hazard to avoid was the residue of briquette ash, discarded from the houses at the base of the hill. The ash, after mixing with the snow, would linger in the air, even after the snow melted.

When I reached the top of the hill, the whole neighborhood lay sprawled out below, unchanged from the day I left. Dust from the construction site had flown up even here, blanketing roofs and window frames with a thick layer of grime. The drainage pumping station lay sprawled between the sky and rooftops. Now that the rainy season was over, various parts of the station were overgrown with weeds. During the rainy season, water from higher grounds flooded the station, roughly three times the size of a standard field. The soccer goalposts put in by the local government office were regularly submerged in water and became covered in thick red rust. The water remained pooled even after the rainy season, either flowing into a ditch or seeping into the ground, and the pumping station became a breeding ground for long-legged flies. After the water drained, a bad smell lingered in the air. On humid days, the stench stayed low to the ground, settling heavily in this large basin area. I'm not sure if my mother was right in saying that the land value here wouldn't increase until the pumping station was relocated. She sold our new two-story building, barely breaking even, and left this place without a backward glance.

As I looked around, one patch of grass was noticeably lusher than the rest. The grass was greener, denser. I was certain that was the spot. It was there that Blackie was buried. A faint scar on my right cheek began to itch.

The old pharmacy and the stores flanking it had disappeared, giving way to a large barbecue restaurant. As soon as I turned into the alley, a middle-aged waitress burst out of the restaurant and flagged me down, fervently gesturing with her tongs for me to park and come inside. Though not quite the time for dinner, the place bustled with customers. Real estate offices had sprouted where the minimart and snack bar once stood, their windows plastered with brochures. It seemed a redevelopment boom had finally hit this area as well.

I stopped before the building where my family had lived for a little over two years. The façade—made up of tiles the color of red bean—was cracked in places, and many tiles had fallen off completely. Twenty years later, the ground floor still harbored a hardware store. Dangling from the overhang, just as I remembered, were multicolored plastic brooms with synthetic bristles, dustpans, and rubber hoses, all thickly coated with dust. Judging by the dark interior and closed door, the owner had stepped out for a bit. Even the shelves hanging on the walls had hardly changed from what I remembered, loaded with boxes holding small steel parts.

This very hardware store had appeared in my latest novel. The store wasn't entirely without customers, but it must have been difficult to earn a living selling a few bulbs or cans of paint. Rent was always late, and I was the one my mother sent every month to collect it. Even after entering the gloomy, cluttered store, it took some time before I could bring myself to call out to the owner. The owner was a young woman barely seven years older than me. Though she said she cleaned, the inside was like a giant trash bin. Yet, astonishingly, no matter what you asked for, she could easily locate it in that heap of garbage. After waiting in the dark for a while, surrounded by shovels, hammers, and saws glimmering faintly, I'd hear her soft voice, no louder than a whisper, drifting from the back room attached to the store.

"I'm sorry. The baby just fell asleep, so I can't come out right now. Please tell your mother that I'll have the rent ready the day after tomorrow at the very latest."

But of course, it was always a lie—both the sleeping baby and the promised rent payment.

The fact that the neighborhood hadn't changed at all felt surreal, like a movie set. I drove slowly through the alley, to avoid passing the book rental shop, as well as to pick out any changes. It wasn't difficult to locate the shop with the somewhat long name, Stories that Grandma Tells, but I couldn't remember what had been there twenty years ago. There must have been a salon or a rice shop with a solid cash flow. Whatever it had been, she was now running a bookshop where our gang had once cracked open a safe.

I pushed open the door to the bookshop. Except for the entrance, the four walls of the shop were lined with bookshelves, and one wall featured several specially designed bookcases that were stacked on top of each other. I had never dreamed that someone from the gang might read my work. They hadn't even read comic books back then, considering them a waste of time. Yet, one of them now managed a book rental shop, and I wrote novels.

As I opened and closed the door, an electronic chime rang out. The wall of bookcases in front of me trembled and slid to the side, folding back like a fan to reveal a living space. Beyond the small room, I glimpsed a kitchen, complete with a sink. A small, fleshy foot appeared over the threshold, searching the floor for a slipper. It was Chopstick. She had put on weight, so her cold, jagged edges seemed to have dulled a little. She had a physique that revealed no curves, no matter how much weight she'd gained, and she now resembled a thicker wooden chopstick. She dragged her slippers noisily toward me and then peered up at my face for a long time before punching me in the chest, just as she had twenty years ago. The difference this time was that her punches didn't push me back anymore.

Yunmi poured two packets of instant coffee mix into a cup and pushed it toward me, bursting into laughter. Her voice was gravelly, as if she were chewing rice mixed with dirt.

"I'm not sure this instant coffee would be to your liking, you being a fancy writer and all."

Though she spoke informally to me as she always had, I felt awkward responding in the same way, so I just nodded. After watching me bring the cup to my lips, she let out a little snort.

"Remember Kijin? He was the first one to spot you in the paper. I think about nine years ago?"

If it was nine years ago, that would have been the year my debut novel was first published.

"As soon as he mentioned seeing you in the paper, you won't believe how everyone reacted. 'So he finally landed himself in deep shit, didn't he, enough to make the news? What was it? Robbery? Fraud?' That's what they said!"

Yunmi cackled, hitting the table so hard that the coffee sloshed out of the cup. Quickly, she wiped the spilled coffee with her hand and rubbed it on her pants.

"Those idiots. They can't think beyond their own pea brains. It's fucking embarrassing . . . Anyway, you turned out to be most successful person from Stepping Stones."

Yunmi murmured, seemingly more to herself than to me, as her gaze drifted toward the door—the shop's only window. However, the glass in the door was covered by new book posters, blocking any view of the outside. She sighed, and a vivid image of the seventeen-year-old Yunmi flashed across my mind—petite, skinny, sporting a short haircut, which had made her look like a small boy. The sound of her quick, light steps, echoing in the night streets, seemed to linger in my ears. While I sat there sipping my coffee, several middle and high school students came in to return or borrow books. Yunmi scanned the barcodes and organized the books with practiced ease. I noticed that one entire row on a bookshelf was filled with copies of *Children of the Wind.*

"I guess writers are different. When I was reading your book, my legs got all restless and I felt this urge to run. I've told them a million times, but I always knew you were different. But still, how did you manage to remember everything from twenty years ago? You didn't get anything wrong. Did you keep a journal back then?"

A journal? The things we did at seventeen and eighteen weren't exactly what you would chronicle in a journal like typical teenagers. We were shadows, wandering the streets at night. Sure, we kept journals for school, but everything we wrote down was a lie, except for the weather. Perhaps that was when I started writing fiction.

Yunmi said the gang was getting together at our old stomping ground, but my mind kept drifting to Revival Church. The building where the church used to meet had been torn down a long time ago. Standing at the top of the hill, we gazed down at the construction site shrouded in darkness. She mentioned a large discount mart and sports center were going to be built there. Though we stood with our backs to the drainage pumping station, the wind kept carrying the stench toward us.

"We figured you'd wiped this place from your memory after you left," Yunmi said. She sniffed the air, and then changed the topic abruptly. "You know, this hill won't be here much longer. If you decide to visit again, you'll get lost for sure."

We walked down with our hands shoved in our back pockets, as if we'd gone back in time. Twenty years ago, I'd hurtled down this hill in a truck, wedged between a wardrobe and boxes full of odds and ends, convinced there was no reason to come back here again.

The stairs in our two-story house were excessively steep, and no matter how much we twisted the taps, the water trickled out ever so slowly, hinting at a possible blockage in the underground pipes. We had to collect water in the bathtub overnight to have enough for the next day. By morning, sediment resembling iron filings would have settled at the bottom of the tub. The water carried the foul odor from the pumping station. My mother would carefully scoop up some of the water for cooking, but even the rice and vegetables ended up smelling like rotten fish. When we finally moved to a new house in a different neighborhood, our family marveled at the water "exploding" endlessly from the taps, to borrow my mother's expression. As we washed our faces until our shirts were soaked, my mother kept remarking how different this neighborhood was from our old one. Apart from a two-week period when I suffered from diarrhea due to the unfamiliar fresh water and couldn't sleep because of the new environment, I quickly reverted to an ordinary high school senior. Even though I would sometimes wake in the middle of the night, memories of the stench and my old gang gradually faded. While our adventures at the pumping station occasionally surfaced in my dreams, they always disappeared with the morning light.

Without looking back, Yunmi asked, "Hey, you know one of the kids in the novel, the girl Minseo—it's her, right? Even if you changed everyone's names, you portrayed them exactly the same, so it's easy to tell who's who. Well, only we would know, I guess."

She didn't wait for me to answer. She became cheerful suddenly, clapping her hands and raising her voice. "Hey, to celebrate seeing each other after twenty years, should we raid a vending machine or something?"

Just like in the old days, we ran down the hill, shouting. Yunmi had gained a lot of weight over the years. Her hips jiggled as she ran ahead. I had a gut feeling that it hadn't been Yunmi who'd been calling and hanging up without a word for the past six months. Then who was it? I would find out tonight when I met with everyone.

Once a month, the gang gathered at a large pub located in the basement of a building in a busy district. Decorated with empty beer bottles and car license plates, the spacious pub had wooden crates full of ice scattered here and there, each brimming with a variety of imported beers. Seated around a crate of ice, they waved at Yunmi when we walked in. Though the pub was clean, a unique basement smell lingered in the air.

"Is that you, Jinseong?" I said. "Jinseong, right?"

"Yeah, that's me, dickhead, though I'm Haeseong in your book, aren't I?"

As I greeted the group and confirmed their names, they responded by mentioning the new names I'd give them in my novel. Some had arrived early, evident from all the empty bottles. It seemed most of them had stayed in this place that they had vowed to escape as soon as they grew up. Far from leaving, they'd brought other people here and started families.

"Man, it's been ages, but it feels like we just met up last week, doesn't it?" Kijin shouted, raising his beer bottle.

As he continued to drink and offer toasts, his aloof demeanor melted away. His habit of spraying spittle when he talked was still the same. He mentioned he was in the business of renting out heavy machinery.

Suddenly, Jaebeom, seated across the table, blurted, "Here's to us—the Children of Darkness!"

Yunmi kicked him in the shin with her plump foot.

"Ouch!" Jaebeom exclaimed, clutching his shin.

"It's *Children of the Wind*, you idiot, not *Children of Darkness*! How many times do I have to drill that into your thick skull?"

Jinseong, already slurring his words, knocked over a beer bottle by accident. The liquid spilled into his lap, but he was unfazed. "Who the hell cares if it's *Children of the Wind* or *Children of Darkness*? Same difference, since it's all about us anyway."

"You dumbasses. How is that about us? Is your name mentioned in the book? How about you, Jaebeom? I've told you a million times, it's a story, not real life."

Yunmi smacked everyone's heads within reach, causing Minho to drop his beer bottle, which shattered when it hit the floor. Minho had always gone around with a fringe of long bangs that hid his eyes. Even now, I couldn't quite see his eyes because of his hair. Despite his pale skin, which gave him a fragile appearance, everyone knew he was the most vicious among us. Blowing his bangs aside, he finally looked up.

"Even if it's just a story, spilling our secrets like that wasn't right. Yunmi told me to read it, so I did, but you know how it made me feel? Like a fucking worm under a blazing sun. It made me feel like shit. Why didn't you just use our real names and places while you were at it, huh?"

Back when we were seventeen and eighteen, we got up to stuff most kids our age couldn't even dream of. Booze and cigarettes were just the tip of the iceberg. We ventured into far more forbidden territories. After getting into university on my second attempt, I got bored with alcohol, cigarettes, and girls. Time trudged forward, yet nothing ever seemed as remarkable or worthy of a book as those wild days.

"It's fine for us dudes, but her?" Jaebeom chimed in, his eyes bloodshot as he gestured toward Yunmi. "She's not even married yet."

Yunmi spat on the floor and narrowed her eyes. She flicked a pack of cigarettes in her hand to get a cigarette to pop out. She stuck it between her lips and lit up.

"Mind your own business, loser. If you're so worried about me getting married, why didn't any of you ever propose, huh? None of you gave a shit about me. You were all hung up on that bitch Sujeong. Don't worry, people are way too busy to remember things from back then. No one's going to link Mikyeong from the book to me. I'm not that person anymore. The problem is you guys. Look at you, flipping out and making a scene . . . Those people over there have been gawking at us for a while now."

At the mention of Sujeong, everyone fell silent. Soon, a waiter came by to sweep up the mess. The table became more and more cluttered with empty bottles. Before long, everyone fell back into old habits, cussing and hitting each other, like we'd been transported back twenty years.

On my way back from the bathroom, someone grabbed me by the scruff of my neck. It was Minho. He dragged me back into the bathroom and locked the door behind us. Before I knew it, his fist connected with my face. A metallic taste filled my mouth as my lip split open. His hands felt just as rough and callused as I remembered.

"Hey asshole, do you even have a conscience? Didn't you feel any shame as you were writing about us? Pricks like you deserve a beating."

He punched me again, this time hitting my side. Before I knew it, I crashed to the filthy bathroom floor.

"So you think you're better than us because you left? Do you even know what Sujeong's life is like these days? You should've had the decency to take responsibility, man. You treated her like garbage and now you're airing her dirty laundry?"

Minho was no different from the occasional readers who asked what was true and what was fiction.

"Man, get it together," I said. "It's fiction, all right? Just a story, not real life!"

"You educated folks have a way with words, don't you? After you left, Sujeong came to me crying and said you two had gotten involved. She thought you really cared."

I was stunned. I had never been alone with Sujeong. Clearly, she wasn't to be trusted.

"Then how'd you know about that mole, huh? How'd you know if it's all fiction?"

I burst out laughing. Minho punched me again. It hurt so much that tears came to my eyes, but I couldn't contain my laughter.

It was only much later that I learned that Minseo, or rather Sujeong, had another nickname: Moley. When we were living in the two-story house, Sujeong and her family moved in next door. There was a fence separating our houses, but from my room on the second floor, I could see into their yard and rooms. At the height of summer, we would leave all our windows open. Since the houses were so tightly packed together, any loud noise would easily carry across several of them. It was then, from overhearing conversations through their open windows, that I found out her nickname was Moley. With a nickname like that, I figured she had a large mole somewhere on her body. Naturally, as a healthy eighteen-year-old boy, I was curious about where that mole might be.

I must have dozed off while studying, because around two in the morning I was awakened by the sound of splashing water. It was coming from Sujeong's house. I crept toward my window. Below, in the darkness, the faintly glowing shape of a woman became visible. The figure scooped up water with a bowl from a rubber tub, pouring it liberally over herself. The sight jolted me awake. Sitting with her back to me, she bent over to apply soap to a terry cloth and lathered her entire body. Her skin was soon covered in soap suds. She scooped up water to rinse herself. Slowly, she stood up, propping one foot on the edge of the rubber container. She then took a bowl of water, pouring it slowly over her head, allowing the water to cascade from her hair down to the intimate area between her legs. Her naked body was smooth and unblemished. It was the first time I had ever thought a woman's skin could be sweet. Right then, something fell from me. It fell out the window and landed near her feet. It was the pen that had been tucked behind my ear. Showing no signs of surprise, she slowly picked up the pen. She then looked up. The security light illuminated the contours of her face. It was Sujeong.

Some time later, I saw her at church, but she didn't mention anything about the incident. There were no moles on her smooth arms and legs, nor on her neck and chest, which sometimes showed when she bowed her head. So naturally, I assumed she had a mole in a more secret spot.

Having touched the dirty floor, my pants were soaked from the knee down. I turned on the tap to try to wash them, and wiped my swollen lips. The side of my ribs where Minho had hit me began to throb. I could see his face in the mirror. Sweat made his hair stick to his forehead.

"God, you still pack a punch. But how do you know about the mole? You mean she really has a mole down there, like what I wrote in the book?"

Minho wiped the corners of his eyes with his broad palms. According to Yunmi, Minho was married and had a seven-year-old boy and four-year-old girl. He and his wife sold cheap jewelry wholesale at the market.

"Jeez, I don't know. Who knows who's telling the truth? I guess I've always been jealous of you. You were better than me at everything. And when you got the girl I liked, I couldn't help being jealous. I did everything she asked for, but it got to be too much. And even that incident—I didn't want that. But she made me do it. I thought she would come to me then. I assumed you knew everything, since it's in your book. We thought Sujeong told you. I don't even go near the pumping station these days. I dragged everyone into this mess, all because of her. But when the smell's really bad . . ." Minho covered his face with his hands and sank down to the floor.

"Forget about that stupid dog," I said. "It wasn't just Sujeong. We all wanted to do it. Seriously, you're crying about that now?"

At the pumping station, the black dog lies buried where the grass grows lush. The grass there was greener, nourished by nutrient-rich fertilizer. We dragged Blackie to the station tower and hung it there. Thick, sticky saliva drooled from its mouth. Our eyes were wild with excitement. Every time we swung the bat, a dull thud echoed as it hit the dog's flesh. It took a while before its body hung limp from the tower. Sujeong stood watching from a distance, arms crossed. We hurled down our bats and collapsed on the ground, feeling as if all our energy had drained away. Yunmi glanced at Sujeong and spat, but her spit didn't go far. Yunmi panted, as if out of breath.

"Stuck-up bitch, standing there like she's some queen. She's just going to watch, is that it?"

We walked the late-night streets, just as we had over twenty years ago, but perhaps because we were older, we moved differently. We didn't move like shadows anymore. We kept bumping into signs and colliding with drunks coming from the opposite direction.

Jinseong still walks with a limp. It was Blackie who had caused Jinseong's limp. The foreman at the noodle factory had let the black dog roam the yard at night. As far as we knew, the factory was supposed to have the most cash on hand. But we couldn't even get near the safe, because we were chased off by the famished guard dog. A four-legged animal was faster than two-legged ones. Yunmi was the first to go over the factory's steel fence. Kiyeok and Jaebeom followed right behind. Minho ran ahead toward the fence. I was the last one. Suddenly, Blackie lunged at me, aiming for my neck. I figured it'd be better if it caught my arm rather than my shoulder. We knew that once a dog bites, it never lets go. The moment I stuck out my arm toward Blackie, it yelped and hit the ground. In Jinseong's hand was a bat. The dog changed targets instantly and growled at Jinseong, baring its teeth.

"When I count to three, we run, got it?" Jinseong whispered. "One, two, three—"

We started sprinting toward the others who were waiting anxiously on the other side of the fence. We ran at full speed, launching ourselves toward the fence. Just as I was leaping over it, I felt something sharp scrape my cheek. But I barely felt the pain. The second I landed on the other side of the fence, Jinseong's shriek pierced the air. Blackie's teeth were buried in his heel. I grabbed a rock, hitting the dog repeatedly, but with each blow, it bit down harder. Finally, Blackie released its grip only after it had torn a chunk of flesh from Jinseong's heel.

As we walked past the construction site, my gaze swept over where the church used to stand. The kids, who didn't have a single comfortable room at home, gathered at Revival Church every weekend. That church, which rented out the basement of a commercial building, always smelled of mold. Sitting on damp cushions, we took turns reading Bible verses and praying.

It was Sujeong who suggested we name our group Stepping Stones. I couldn't help but laugh at the name, but everyone looked serious. We raided vending machines, broke into the school store, even stole cars for midnight joyrides before abandoning them by the Han River. For these kinds of delinquents to name themselves Stepping Stones—it was ridiculous. In that group, I was the only one attending a regular high school. Most of them went to night school because of poor grades or family circumstances, and two, including Yunmi, had dropped out altogether. In short, we were all troublemakers. After slowly scanning our faces, Sujeong said softly, "I wish we can all become stepping stones for each other, silently doing our part and carrying on." After saying this, she bowed her head and looked down at the vinyl floor. I was sitting behind her and glanced at the reflection of her face in the mirror across from us. Her forehead was smooth and round. The kids began to stand up, but I couldn't believe what I saw next. Sujeong continued to sit primly with her eyes cast down and mouth closed when suddenly a corner of her mouth curled up, as if mocking everyone there. She slowly raised her head and watched the children go up the church stairs with a look of disgust. Then, our eyes met in the mirror. She didn't turn around, but stared straight at me in the mirror, and gave a little wink.

The lights in the hardware store were off. I strained to hear as I passed by, but no sound came from inside. Yunmi stuck close to me.

"The place changed owners a long time ago. Maybe about two years after you guys moved? The woman left with her child."

The boy who used to ride a tricycle without pants would now be in his twenties. The face of the woman surfaced in my mind. Despite spending the whole day in the dark store, her face had been covered with sunspots. Only later did I discover that those weren't sunspots at all, but bruises.

Sometimes, her husband made a tidy sum from the construction site, but he seemed to spend it on something else. The store barely survived on the petty cash the woman earned by selling odds and ends. By the time we moved, more than half of the deposit she had paid had been offset by the overdue rent. Her husband, a man with dark skin and a pointed jaw, always carried a large canvas bag. The bottom of the bag sagged, hinting at the heavy weight of the tools inside. With each step, the pliers, wrenches, hammers, and nails clinked and clanked against each other.

At dawn, he would stagger into the small room attached to the shop, dead drunk. From my room, I could haer and guess what was happening downstairs. Unspeakable profanities followed, then the child erupted into tears, abruptly woken. Between the child's cries, heavy thuds, blows landing on flesh. Muffled cries broke through, sounding like dry heaves, likely because she was covering her mouth with her hand.

When I went to buy a new bulb after an old one burned out, her face was mottled with bruises. She checked the bulb in a test socket, and after confirming it worked, she handed it to me. She looked even paler than before, as if she was being bled dry. As I handed over the coins, I blurted, "Why do you live like this? Run away! Before he bleeds you dry—run away. Just go!"

The woman looked blankly at my face. Her eyes were like a light bulb with a broken filament. She wouldn't be able to run away as long as her husband was still alive. She seemed tamed to that kind of life. I slammed the door shut and stepped outside. I heard her sobbing from inside.

Yunmi jabbed me in the ribs. The gang was smoking, standing a bit away from the hardware store.

"Who told you? It was Sujeong, wasn't it? To be honest, I was really surprised. I didn't think you'd spill everything. That's why they got so drunk at the pub earlier. It's because of the hardware store man. They never go near the pumping station now. Maybe you forgot and wrote a novel about it, but we can't forget, not even in fifty, a hundred years."

"What are you talking about? First Minho and now you, too? We buried the dog that chewed off Jinseong's heel, didn't we? Did something go wrong? Why are they freaking out over a stupid dog?"

Yunmi pressed her index finger to her lips and pulled me toward the construction site.

"You're the one talking nonsense! In your book, what we bury at the pumping station isn't a dog, but the hardware store guy."

She was right. In my novel, we bury the man at the pumping station, not the dog, though I've kept everything else the same as when we buried the dog. When the boy sees the man lying on the side of the road, he's already unconscious. It looks like someone has hit him on the back of his head. Blood is clumped around his hair, and the bag he always carried is lying next to him. If he'd taken the man straight to the hospital then, he might have survived. But just as the boy tries to pull the man up by his armpits, he changes his mind. He recalls the man's wife who receives beatings from him every day. Whenever the man happens to earn money, he never gives her any of it. The boy leaves the man lying on the street until dawn. While digging up the mud at the pumping station, the boy mutters, "No one will notice. There's always a bad smell coming from here anyway. No one would even think that something strange is buried here."

"So w-w-what are you saying?" I said, stuttering. "Are you saying something similar to what I wrote actually happened?"

I recalled Minho, sobbing in the bathroom of the pub. I watched him suck forcefully on a cigarette, like someone who desperately needed air.

"I didn't know why, but they told me not to come that day. I only found out much later. They said by the time they got there after getting Minho's call, the man was already dead. They had planned to just threaten him and rob him, but then—"

"Are you saying Sujeong was behind the whole thing?"

"She knew exactly when the man was getting paid. And just like when we buried the black dog, they said she was totally unfazed. She just stood there with her arms folded. She didn't even flinch."

The houses were packed so closely together, with no clear divisions between them, that words spoken from one window carried straight into another. The windows of Sujeong's room and the hardware store window were practically side by side. Sujeong could hear the woman sobbing as she endured beatings every morning. She also knew exactly when the man received his pay. After all, she had told Minho that the man would squander it all on gambling. Sujeong was also the one who had stomped on the man's body with both feet.

My head started pounding from the stench of the pumping station. Jaebeom stepped into the station first, holding a shovel we'd stolen from the hardware store. As his foot sank into the mud, he cursed just like he used to.

"Fuck me."

"Where the hell was it?" Kijin snapped.

The overgrown weeds scratched at our ankles.

"Shouldn't you know? You dug the hole," Kiyeok said.

Kijin coughed, spitting out phlegm. "It's been twenty years, damn it. Plus, who would've thought we'd be back here digging it up?"

We fanned out around the station and started digging. We dug clumsily, just as we had then.

"Why the hell did he have to open his big mouth so we're here doing this shit? Does he think he's special because he's a writer?"

"Why is he denying it?"

"Fuck *Children of Darkness*."

"Hey dumbass, it's *Children of the Wind*, not *Children of Darkness*."

We prodded the soggy ground with the tips of our shovels. A swarm of mosquitoes rushed in, smelling our flesh. A shovel struck something solid, and instantly we huddled around the spot. We unearthed a large bag, soaked through with mud and considerably heavier. Kijin unzipped it, dumping its contents. Lumps of metal fell out, along with mud. Minho recoiled, groaning. The handles had rotted away or gotten lost, but the metal remained unchanged, even after two decades. It was the bag the hardware store man had always carried around.

"Hey, keep digging in that spot," Jaebeom hissed.

Kijin flung down the shovel. "Hey, don't you remember? We put the bag in first. It's been over twenty years. Everything would have decomposed by now, or the rain would have swept it into the sewer. There's nothing left."

"I'm not so sure . . ." Minho stammered.

"You shut up. Who landed us in this shit in the first place? All because you fell for that bitch—"

"Damn it, everyone just shut up. Do you really want to get caught?"

They swore, clanging their shovels against each other's. The awful smell had now latched onto my pants. It would burrow into my skin and cling to me for some time. Readers sometimes asked what was real in my work and what was fiction. I'd exposed too much of my personal life in *Children of the Wind.* I raised my head to look for Yunmi, but dropped my shovel in shock. There was Sujeong, standing on the embankment, arms crossed. It seemed she had been watching us this whole time. She'd disappeared before finishing high school, and now no one knew where she was. Yet, something else nagged at me more than finding the man's remains. Someone had been calling me for the past six months, hanging up when I picked up without saying a word. It had to be her.

It seemed that one day, Sujeong would show up unexpectedly, intent on showing me her mole in that secret spot.

1984

In 1984, a lot happened. Cherry trees, which had been moved to Gwacheon Zoo from Changgyeong Palace, were relocated along Yunjung-ro Road in Yeouido. Around the time their blossoms faded, Pope John Paul II visited Korea. Nearly a million people gathered in Yeouido Square. In a photo taken from a helicopter, the white veils on the heads of all the people looked like drifting cherry blossom petals. After the crowd left, not a single gum wrapper remained, briefly making headlines. That summer, South Korea won six gold medals in the Los Angeles Olympics, landing in tenth place for the total number of medals won.

At least for me, the 1984 envisioned by George Orwell—where an unknown dictator rules over a class society and the "Thought Police" monitors everyone's actions through telescreens—didn't feel all that different from reality. At nineteen, I always carried five résumés in my backpack. Several times a day, the unsettling noise of patrol helicopters buzzed overhead, and soldiers marched through my dreams.

What captivated people that year was Israeli-British psychic Uri Geller's spoon-bending act. As if compensating for all the terrible incidents that occurred in Korea in the previous year, people eagerly embraced Uri Geller's performance. Families gathered around the television, spoons in hand. After that day, I felt the urge to bend a spoon whenever I saw one.

The spoons in Uri Geller's hand practically folded over in half. All he'd done was rub them with his fingertips—there had been no chants or grunts. A long, narrow table was set up in a TV studio. On it lay dozens of spoons, and Uri Geller bent each one effortlessly as he moved from one end of the table to the other. The host kept exclaiming, "This is not a trick! I can't believe my eyes!" Metal softened at Uri Geller's touch. Spoons bent, twisted, and even snapped.

The broadcast quickly became the most watched on television. Countless people witnessed Uri Geller's paranormal abilities. But there were always skeptics who wanted to expose him. One man from the audience rushed onto the stage and tried to bend a spoon with brute force but failed. He seemed shocked that the spoon was more rigid than he'd expected. The audience laughed. Uri Geller didn't stop there. He said he would transmit his paranormal powers to viewers, enabling them to bend spoons themselves. The interpreter relayed this message haltingly, as if reading from a script. "Even those far away can do it. All you need to do is watch me."

While my younger sisters scrambled to find spoons and vied for the best spot in front of the TV, I absentmindedly leafed through my general knowledge prep book that was as thick as a cookbook. The Formica kitchen table smelled of sour dishcloths. "Identify the work that is not by Dostoevsky: *The Brothers Karamazov, War and Peace, Crime and Punishment, Demons*." I found the question confusing, but my attention was on the television. "Why spoons?" I wondered. There seemed to be more interesting things to bend.

Whenever I thought about spoons, my grandmother came to mind. She used to say, "If you've got the strength to lift a spoon to eat, you can do anything." She never stopped working. For her, resting meant shelling beans or trimming vegetables. Even while watching her favorite soap operas, she'd sweep the floor with her hand, collecting stray hairs and dust. "The day I can't work is the day I'll put down my spoon," she'd say. True to her word, she ceased both work and eating three days before she passed. My mother, who'd resented my grandmother's non-stop working, became just like her after losing contact with my father and also never stopped working.

After dinner, my mother picked up another suit jacket to mend. This was her job: hand-stitching suit sleeves and hems that couldn't be sewn with a sewing machine. There was always an XXL-sized black suit jacket sprawled in front of her like a looming shadow. Bits of thread floated in the air and landed in our soup bowls. Not wanting to dirty their fingers by fishing them out, my sisters simply sipped their soup. Sometimes, threads stuck to our socks and traveled with us. In school, I'd find a black thread on a sock while changing into indoor shoes. Removing it, I felt like a bee that had carried pollen from far away. But by third grade, I didn't have the luxury to entertain such romantic notions. No matter how many times I removed them, loose threads always clung to me like tags, reminding me of my reality.

Mother stopped in the middle of a herringbone stitch, jerking her head up as if she'd pricked her finger. She scanned our faces, making sure all five of us were there before resuming her work. The spectacle of bending spoons with psychic powers held no allure for her. "Why ruin a perfectly good spoon?" she said, not bothering to glance at the TV.

Large companies required candidates to pass English and general knowledge tests for entry-level jobs. With sixty questions to answer in sixty minutes, there was no time to hesitate. You had to answer the question immediately upon reading it. Hiring for corporations, banks, and securities firms targeting vocational high school grads usually concluded before summer vacation. Students lucky enough to secure jobs began their training in October, reporting to their companies instead of school. After three months, they received their official assignments. Those who didn't make the cut returned to school to finish out the year. The recruitment criteria were specific: be in the top 30% of your class; hold at least a level-two certificate in typing, accounting, or shorthand; look presentable; and be at least 155 centimeters tall. I met none of these requirements, so I doubted anyone would even glance at my resume. Scraping a dried bean sprout off the table with my pencil, I mused that maybe life was just a Formica table littered with the dregs of meals, and employment was simply a matter of finding your spoon and clinging to it for dear life.

The whole street seemed to be holding its breath. Even the men who had been drinking under the parasol at the corner mini-mart since late afternoon had vanished. My sisters sat as rigid as statues, as if any movement might make them miss Uri Geller's psychokinetic feat. We were each three years apart, with me being the oldest and the youngest twelve years my junior. Though seven, she looked no more than five, her shoulder blades protruding pitifully, like the vestigial wings of flightless birds. Could she hold her own in the future? Just then, a thread from a suit floated slowly through the air like a drifting spore.

The face of a middle-aged man with a pointed jaw filled the TV screen. His eyes stared out with intense focus. His voice was smooth as silk.

The interpreter's words trailed behind, as if trying to keep pace. "Now, concentrate. Just focus on the tip of the spoon," Uri Geller urged, more orator than psychic. I felt a wave of post-dinner drowsiness wash over me. I wanted to lie in a small boat and drift down a river. As the room quieted, my tension dissolved, and I felt as weightless as a floating thread. The fluorescent lights dimmed to black and a distorted voice elongated through what seemed like a voice modulator. "Youuu caaan doooo iiiit. Bennnd the spoooon."

I reached out and grasped one of the spoons scattered across the table. My face, reflected upside-down in the hollow of the spoon, trembled as if submerged in bean sprout soup, suggesting that no matter how hard I tried, my greatest efforts would only amount to a spoonful. I opened my mouth wide, and my blurred face resembled the figure from Edvard Munch's *The Scream*.

Suddenly, my palm burned. Startled, I shook my hand. The spoon bounced off the table and across the room. My palm had turned white from the force of my grip. My second oldest sister slowly picked up the spoon. The youngest stared, speechless, while the third complained that Uri Geller's psychic powers had been unfairly distributed. Only then did I realize that the spoon was bent, its shape resembling a musical note. Mother clucked her tongue. "If only you'd concentrate this hard on studying or working . . ."

Phone calls flooded the TV station from every corner of the country. The host, in an astonished voice, announced they were deluged with calls from people who had bent spoons. My sisters touched the warped spoon and peered at me. The eldest inspected it, skeptical, even tapping it to make sure I wasn't tricking them. The whole thing had happened so fast that, even though I was the one who bent the spoon, I felt nothing. According to Uri Geller, I was just a conduit, a transformer on an electrical pole, merely bridging the energy he'd generated to various homes.

That night, I dreamt of my grandmother. We were in the middle of a fall sports festival. Flags fluttered in the wind and the air smelled of cotton candy. Children cheered. My petite grandmother was running in a relay, wearing her favorite white rubber shoes. She was so fast that her legs were a blur, kicking up clouds of dust. I was the next runner. As I jogged forward, I reached back to take the baton, but the hand-off was clumsy. Our hands nearly touched, but not quite. Just then, runners from other teams surged past us. Finally snatching the baton from my grandmother, I burst forward. When I looked down, I realized that what I was holding wasn't a baton, but a spoon.

The next morning, I headed to school with the bulky general knowledge prep book under my arm, since it was too large to fit in my backpack. I took the subway to Jongno 5-ga station, then transferred to a bus that would take me the rest of the way. On both the subway and the bus, all the conversations were about Uri Geller.

"You know H, right?"

I eavesdropped on some girls nearby, thinking perhaps this H had also performed a supernatural feat.

"H's cousin S actually bent a spoon!"

I caught snippets, but it seemed no one had actually bent a spoon themselves. That day, people who brushed past me fell into two categories: those who had watched Uri Geller and those who had not.

The bus dropped off the students of H Girls High School first, followed by those from B Boys High School two stops later. Only the students destined for the final stop, our school, remained on the bus, each cradling the same general knowledge tome under our arms. This book was the first thing we acquired when we enrolled, a compendium of everything we were expected to know, from politics and economics to the arts. Over time, the book swelled in size, the pages straining against the cover even when shut. Despite memorizing its contents for three years, I still mixed up Dostoevsky and Tolstoy, and kept forgetting the difference between fresco and tempera. Perhaps that's why the book never grew dull for me.

Arriving at school, I noticed students loitering in the hallway. This was unusual during morning self-study when the halls were typically empty. I wondered whether Uri Geller was the cause. I swung open my classroom door and was on the verge of announcing, "I bent a spoon yesterday!" when I spotted my deskmate, S, sniffling. Students were huddled around a list tacked to the chalkboard. Standing on my toes, I squinted at the paper. It was a roster of Group G students eligible to take the first round of examinations. My name was missing.

By October, our class had dwindled to half its original size. Those who remained gathered in the auditorium to learn the art of office makeup from a cosmetics industry professional or to listen to lectures by successful alumni. One alumnus, who had risen to section chief at a bank, confessed to ripping pages out of her general knowledge book and eating them during times when she struggled with memorization. A collective gasp echoed through the auditorium. Once a week, we even used fake bills to count money quickly and accurately. Job postings became increasingly scarce. Although we still had classes, most days were dedicated to self-directed study. Job openings at small- to mid-sized firms trickled in, maybe once or twice a week. You could spot students slipping out early for job interviews from a spot by the window. As the term wore on, fewer students attended the auditorium lectures. We had to secure jobs before winter break. After winter break would be graduation, and after graduation, we'd become disconnected from the school's job placement program, leaving us without any leads. We clung ever more desperately to our general knowledge books.

Just when the job market seemed to be at its driest, a memo from the courthouse arrived, announcing openings for typists. Jobless students swarmed. As we flooded the subway cars, an elderly man, jarred awake from his nap, asked if we were on a field trip.

A line of students stretched endlessly from the subway station to the courthouse. It was as though every young unemployed soul in Seoul had shown up. Résumés filled three large cardboard boxes. The queue snaked out the courthouse, spilling onto the Deoksugung Stonewall Walkway. Even the officials looked slightly flustered by the massive turnout, frequently checking their watches, and eyeing the unending procession of candidates. Among us were women who appeared to be at least ten years older. A friend glanced at them and hissed, "Seriously? Don't they feel bad taking opportunities meant for us?" There were so many applicants it was impossible to administer the test all at once. We were divided into groups based on our application numbers.

The examination took place inside a small indoor gymnasium. The middle of the gym floor was marked with basketball court lines. The smell of sweat and warmth lingered in the air, as if a game had ended a few hours before. Organizers had attempted to align the desks along the basketball court end lines, but somewhere along the way, the arrangement veered off course. The last row ended up in such disarray it was difficult to make out any semblance of order. Where had my row started to go wrong? As I eyed the rows of desks, people jostled me from behind, nudging me forward. There seemed to be at least five hundred of us. Even if I were to fail, I wanted to know my odds. The girl who had alerted all of us to the job opening was sitting in the very last row. My question about the total number of applicants rippled through the crowd before eventually looping back to me: "xx applicants." The chance of success seemed as unpredictable as the elastic on an old pair of underwear.

On my desk were a typewriter, a sixteen-page exam booklet, and a manuscript. Once the applicants settled into their seats and loaded their typewriters with paper, a man in a black suit bellowed, "Begin!" Suddenly, the gym echoed with the sound of clacking, punctuated by the noise of typewriter carriages returning to their starting position. My right pinky kept slipping between the keys, just as it had when I first learned to type. It would lodge there and swell up, appearing as though I had a thimble on. The manuscript for the typing exam was an excerpt from Lee Hyoseok's "When the Buckwheat Flowers Bloom"—a text that struck me as completely out of place in a legal setting.

The clatter of typing ricocheted off the ceiling and walls of the gymnasium. The first word everyone mastered when learning to type was "어머니"—Mother. The three consonants and three vowels that made up the word all sat on the middle row of the keyboard, serving as the ideal introduction to the "home" position. I'd once typed the word repeatedly, filling an entire sheet with it. When I continued to hammer out "어머니," I felt as though I were hollowing out the essence of the word from its shell. By the time I reached the final line, only the husks of alien-looking letters seemed to remain. The sound of typing, to me, was always cheerful. Whether I was happy, sad, or angry, the typewriter was constant. The tempo of everyone's typing began to escalate. As if the typewriter and I were the only things that existed in the universe, I couldn't hear myself breathe. As I hit the carriage return key, I glanced at the next desk. A girl with a short bob was biting her lower lip as she typed, as if holding back tears. Her two hands hitting the keys appeared desperate. Long, short, short. She seemed as though she were using Morse code to send an SOS.

"Stop!" shouted the proctor. His voice was drowned out by the noise and failed to reach the back rows. He dashed between the desks, shouting, "Stop!" until the typing finally stilled. Even before our papers could be collected, the next group of examinees filtered into the gym and took their seats. Those coming in and leaving collided in the narrow hallway. "No one's here for just a job," a voice muttered behind me. "They're hoping to snag a prosecutor while working in the courthouse."

On the subway ride home, my tension drained away, and I dozed off, my head lolling this way and that. I woke to a tap on my shoulder. When I pried my eyes open, I found no one there. However, a scrap of paper lay on top of my backpack in my lap. It was the size of a postcard and appeared to be cut from a shirt box. Tiny handwriting filled the paper, letters all slanting to the right. A boy around my age shuffled through the car, handing out similar notes to the passengers sitting across from me. His hands and clothes were stained with grease, as though he'd just changed the oil in a car and wiped his hands on his clothes. He'd thrown on layers of clothing without any consideration to their order—a tank top over a long-sleeved shirt, and then a pair of overalls on top of that. He moved down the car, placing a piece of paper on each person's lap as he passed. Reaching the end, he straightened and grasped a hand strap. As the subway swayed, so did he. In rhythm with the train's motion, he launched into his speech: "Ladies and gentlemen on this train," he began. His story went something like this: Sorry for bothering you, but I have four younger siblings at home. My father passed away some time ago, and my mother used to make ends meet by selling things on the street, but now she's bedridden after a car accident one early morning, so times are tough. I wish I could work a manual job to make money, but as you can see, I've got a bad arm from childhood polio. I would be grateful for any help, no matter how small, and I will do my best to carry on.

The boy had memorized the note word for word. As if he'd written it by sounding out the letters, the note was full of spelling mistakes. An elderly lady sitting next to me clucked her tongue. "Good grief! She sure popped out a lot into a cruel world." He slowly moved through the car again, collecting his notes. His movements were stiff and awkward because of his arm. Though he had circled the whole car, only a few hundred-won coins jingled in his plastic cup. Just then, the train came to a stop, and he got off. I glanced out the window and saw him pour his few coins into a torn plastic bag before slowly crossing over to the opposite platform.

On the way home, I ran into my mother, who was carrying a bundle of suits on her head. The weight seemed to make her clench her jaw. She smiled at me, her mouth clamped shut like a nutcracker doll. This was the first time she had gone to the warehouse to bring work home. A van usually came to pick up the finished suits and drop off the new ones. But lately, assignments had become scarce, and she was afraid she might end up with nothing if she waited for the van.

"So, I went to the warehouse myself before it ended up going to someone else. I rushed there as soon as I heard the van arrived, but I got only ten suits."

Mother walked quickly as though another woman might snatch the bundle away from her, but her legs couldn't keep up. She had to stop repeatedly to catch her breath, as though she were carrying the men who'd wear the suits. A motorcycle loaded with crates of milk sped past us. Dodging it, she nearly lost her balance. The bundle wobbled and slid down her forehead, and her head lurched forward. I ran to her, but couldn't reach her in time. With a grunt, she managed to reposition the bundle back on her head. I wanted to yell at her, the way she used to yell at my grandmother, and tell her enough was enough.

Back home, everything was in chaos, with my second and third sisters playing marbles. The eldest sat in a corner, solving questions from a workbook. College entrance exams were just around the corner. A pot of leftover instant noodles, with only the broth remaining, sat lidless on the doorsill, and the youngest, her mouth grubby, had fallen asleep without a blanket. The eldest rushed over to help Mother lower her bundle onto the floor. It hit the ground with a thud. The room felt even more cramped with the bundle amid the scattered books, pencils, and pot. I looked at the room from the entrance. It was undeniable—five children were too many. Families were no longer having so many children. The words of the elderly woman on the train came back to me. Like a bird, my mother had popped out too many eggs in a too-small nest. Had my parents hoped to take on this cruel world with sheer numbers? As I watched my mother spread the suits out on the floor, I couldn't bring myself to mention my typing test for the court job. False hopes had no place here.

I went up to the rooftop. Lights from windows both small and big stretched far into the distance. I felt I could jump from one roof to another and lose my way back. Someone had done laundry this evening. Clothes hung on lines, dripping water. Cigarette butts were soaking in a puddle. The teeth marks on the filters reminded me of my father's cigarettes.

I draped an arm over the clothesline and thought about the boy who'd been begging on the subway. I swayed my body from side to side. His note full of spelling mistakes came to mind. Perhaps because his story felt so close to mine, his words were easy to remember. "Ladies and gentlemen on this train . . ." The swaying seemed to produce that kind of speech. To my own ears, I sounded exactly like him.

T was a stranger, although we had attended the same school for three years. We must have crossed paths at the snack shop, bus stop, or restroom, but her face was totally unfamiliar to me. T had all the details for our job interview. I simply followed her lead. T said she had passed the second round of exams for Group G, but failed the final interview for reasons she didn't know. We took the subway to the City Hall station and walked toward the company building. We passed the courthouse where four police officers in plain clothes stood stamping their feet even though it wasn't cold. No one from our school had landed the courthouse typing job. Neither did they question the selection process. Maybe nobody expected to get it, since there had been so many applicants.

T and I walked side by side. Beneath the plastic tarp of a food stall, we noticed two pairs of legs—one in knee-high black boots, the other in summer flip-flops. T, who'd known about the interview in advance, was dressed neatly in a red coat, blouse, and skirt. I had found out only an hour earlier and wore my usual jeans and gray jacket. T wasn't very talkative. Whenever people brushed past us, T moved aside. Oddly, she gave off no scent. I should have at least caught a whiff of shampoo from her hair, which reached past her shoulders, but the breeze carried no scent at all.

The hallway was so quiet the bubbling of the steam heater was audible. The dark burgundy carpet absorbed the sound of our footsteps, and identical doors lined the hall. The office we were looking for was at the very end. The secretary led us to a conference room.

The CEO was a young man in his early thirties, impeccably dressed in a well-pressed white shirt. Two other men, around his age, joined us soon after.

"Two ladies and three men?" said the skinnier one who had just arrived. "One more lady and we could have ourselves a triple date."

When no one responded, he shrugged his shoulders. The bulkier man rifled loudly through the documents we had submitted through the secretary—résumés, student records, and transcripts.

"Clearly, studying wasn't a priority," he said, not bothering to look up.

I knew he was talking about me, even though he hadn't said my name. Suddenly, the memory of my mother's heavy bundle sinking down over her forehead flashed across my mind.

"Ah, but you managed As in gym?" he said, finally lifting his eyes to glance at me, or rather at my physique. "What are your hobbies? No, not you. You."

I slowly closed my mouth. In a small voice, T answered that she enjoyed listening to music. While the two men took turns asking questions, the CEO remained silent, simply observing us. The office was decorated with attention to detail. Even the carpet was a different color from the one in the hallway. I liked the walnut-colored blinds on the window. As I glanced at the small frames hanging on the wall, my eyes met those of the CEO. Suddenly, I remembered my dream of running while clutching a spoon my grandmother had handed to me. T was barely managing to answer the questions the men were firing at her. The skinny man had a knack for asking tricky ones. Every time she stumbled for words, she let out an "ah." After all, today was T's day. I felt relieved I'd at least get to experience an interview before graduating.

A strange voice hummed inside me. *Bennnd the spooon, youuu caaan dooo iiit. Bennnd the spooon . . .* Following my gaze, the CEO glanced to the side, and then behind him. Finding nothing, he looked at me with an expression that seemed to say, "What's up with this girl?" He soon appeared baffled, and then contemplative, as if lost in thought, wrinkles forming between his brows. His eyes roamed over the desk in search of something. Then, as though unable to find what he was looking for, he crossed his arms and cleared his throat before finally turning away.

"All right, we'll be in touch," the skinny man said, cheerfully rubbing his hands together. The CEO and the two other men didn't seem to think that general knowledge was all that important. As I left the office, I realized I'd never had the chance to apply what I'd memorized over the past three years. I felt empty. It was only after taking the elevator down that it struck me—I had no idea what the company actually did. "Trading company," T whispered. It had been the only term from our conversation that could be found in our general knowledge prep book.

We retraced our steps to the subway station. The same black boots and flip-flops remained below the plastic tarp of the food stall. The toes in the flip-flops looked frostbitten, like taro root. We passed the courthouse. The four officers were still stamping their feet. The street was eerily identical to an hour ago, as if the last hour had been sucked into a black hole. Surely, someone was erasing and rewriting an hour of history that had gone wrong. It was Orwell's December of 1984.

When I got home, the trading company had called. They hadn't mentioned when they'd let us know, but judging by the timing, they must have made their decision about ten minutes after we left the office. I stared at the message my third sister had taken down. *Your hired. Report to werk next Monday.* I gazed at the words for a long time. As if picking a fight, I asked my sister if they had mentioned my name on the phone. She exploded in anger, insulted that I was doubting her ability to take a message.

"How can I trust your message? You're ten and you still can't spell."

I'd finally landed a job, but it felt incomplete, like spending hours getting ready only to realize you'd forgotten to brush your teeth. I couldn't understand why T hadn't been chosen. A sense of unease followed me all day, as if I'd snatched away what was meant for someone else. I didn't know what to say to T if I bumped into her.

At our graduation ceremony, I tried to look for T, but strangely, all I could recall was the red coat she'd worn. I couldn't remember her face.

The man who'd drop off and pick up the garments in his van had stolen all the women's wages and fled. Mother sat in the middle of a pile of black suits and wept like a child.

"I thought you getting a job would solve our problems, but turns out it's like pouring water into a leaky bucket."

There was a stack of ten oversized suit jackets that hadn't been collected. They were so large they seemed tailored for giants, so we couldn't even give them away. My youngest sister said she would eat and exercise enough to fit into them someday, and made Mother laugh.

We headed to an underground shopping arcade nearby to buy shoes, a purse, and a two-piece suit. Crammed with small booths, the place was bustling with people, and sellers appeared to be having a late lunch or early dinner. They called out to customers, even grabbing their arms to pull them inside. "Step right in! Could really use the business. It's been a slow day!"

A pair of high heels displayed outside a booth caught my eye. Enamel heels with tight jeans were the latest trend, especially among college girls. The shoes sparkled under the fluorescent lighting. Without hesitation, I picked a pair of red ones. They pinched a little at the toes, but the shop owner said my feet were probably a bit swollen, as it was normal for them to swell in the evening. I also picked a small purse, just big enough for a wallet and handkerchief. Mom spent quite a while haggling over the price with the owner.

The faux diamonds on the chest of the black velvet two-piece looked like planets in a dark universe. When I stepped out of the dressing room in my new outfit, Mother's eyes widened.

"She just got hired at a trading company."

"Oh, how wonderful!" the owner replied.

After some back-and-forth on the price—asking for a 10,000 won discount here, adding 5,000 won there—we finally left with the suit in a shopping bag. That's when we spotted the same suit in another store. My mother rushed inside to ask for their price. It was much cheaper than what we had paid. Not one to let it go, she marched back to the first store. Before she could even complain about the price difference, the owner pointed to a "No Returns" sign hanging in her shop. Her sweetness and flattering had vanished. She no longer seemed like the same woman. Mother sank into a chair, demanding a price match. When the owner remained unfazed, Mother raised her voice. People passing by glanced at us. The owner refused to negotiate. The argument quickly escalated, with profanities flying from both sides. In a fit of rage, my mother flung the shopping bag onto the ground. The bag burst open, and my new black suit spilled onto the sidewalk.

The owner stormed off to the second shop, noisily dragging her slippers along. She rolled up her sleeves, accusing the other owner of deliberating undercutting her prices, leading her customers to demand refunds. The second shopkeeper was nonchalant. "What's all this fuss about?"

Mother, who hailed from Chungcheong Province, was not amused. The first owner stomped her feet. She practically foamed at the mouth, saying that the second shop owner was ruining the market with her absurdly low prices, and that she should be reported to the business association and be forced to shut down.

The second shopkeeper placed her hands on her hips unhurriedly. "Go ahead, report me! You think I'm scared of you?"

The first owner lunged at the second, grabbing a fistful of her hair. The two women tumbled on the shop floor. A crowd formed. My mother and I retreated. All we could do was watch the fight and then return home with our torn shopping bag. There was always someone stronger and faster.

Back at home, I tried on my red heels and paraded around the room. They only added a few centimeters to my height, but everything in the room looked different. My sisters giggled each time I nearly toppled over.

I layered a gray trench coat over the velvet two-piece, put on my red heels, and clutched my small purse. The subway was so packed that I could hardly breathe. A hand brushed against my rear. When I turned, the men behind me all wore the same innocent expression.

Despite only taking the subway, a wave of fatigue washed over me. The backs of my heels were on fire and my toes cramped so badly that each step was torture. People passed me one by one. The heel of my new shoe got caught in a crack in the sidewalk. I had to stop and wrest it free with my hands. There were now scratches on my new heels. As I passed the courthouse, the police officers whistled at me.

I thought I heard laughter. I looked around, but all I saw were office workers rushing to their jobs. Every so often, I had an eerie feeling as if my every move was being monitored. How on earth did college girls walk around in these heels? My ankle twisted unexpectedly. For a second, the world tilted, like a crooked frame on a wall. Nineteen eighty-four was drawing to a close.

I worked at my first job for twelve years. Diligence seemed to be in my DNA. In that span, my youngest sister, that skinny seven-year-old, grew to be the age I'd been in 1984. Back then, I'd believed I was mature, but seeing my sister at that age made me realize how hopeless I'd been. For all my brash audacity, I must have been a bumbling fool in the eyes of adults. If there's one thing twelve years in the workforce taught me, it's this: grades, certifications, being taller than 155 centimeters—none of it truly matters. We prepare too much for getting a job. That's what I said to the students who gathered in the auditorium. But neither the teachers nor the students seemed to agree with me.

As it turned out, the two men who'd sat in on my interview were the CEO's brothers-in-law. When the CEO and his wife divorced, they reverted to being old school friends.

"I never mentioned this before, but . . ." the CEO mused one day, years into our working relationship.

Reflecting on the day of my interview, he said a spoon had spontaneously come to mind, floating upward, pinning itself against the night sky to twinkle like the Star of Zion. To my grandmother and to many, a spoon represented faith. I've often wondered why T, with her better grades and looks, had been overlooked. The CEO revealed that after the interview, my face, framed by the red coat, had been etched in his memory, whereas T's face was a blur. I didn't correct him. I couldn't bring myself to say I hadn't been the one in the red coat. He suddenly slapped his knee.

"Ah, who was that now . . ."

After working together for so many years, I knew what he was trying to say.

"You mean Uri Geller?" I said. "That's right, he came to Korea in 1984."

Much was made of Uri Geller's debunking. When he appeared on the Johnny Carson show in America, Geller refused to bend any spoons provided by the studio except his own. He claimed he "wasn't in the mood" for spoon-bending that day, and some say he even fled the studio in tears. Eventually, it was revealed that Geller's psychic abilities were a sham, exposed by someone who'd been obsessed with debunking him.

When I think back to those days, the trivia I'd diligently memorized comes to mind. This training becomes apparent when watching TV quiz shows. Answers spring from my lips, honed by years of practice in answering questions immediately upon reading them. These displays never fail to amaze my nieces and nephews.

Recently, reports of sightings of my father have increased. An uncle spotted a man resembling him, passed out in a drunken stupor near a homeless shelter at Seoul Station. Another relative reported seeing an elderly man, a spitting image of my father, reading the newspaper in a teahouse near Pagoda Park. As she pondered on her way home, she became convinced the man had been my father. One thing became clear: my father seems to be drawing near.

Every so often, a voice inside me tells me to bend a spoon. Anyone who's tried before knows spoons are sturdier than they appear. Two of my sisters have since gotten married and produced five children between them. These kids have no idea who Uri Geller is. Whenever I encounter young people who have never heard of him, I can't help feeling old.

In 1984, in Korea alone, many people claimed to have bent spoons. The TV host had declared it so. I sometimes wonder: where have all those spoon-benders gone? When such thoughts cross my mind, I can't shake the feeling that someone, somewhere, is watching my every move. Of course, when I look around, nobody is there. Still, I glance at the sky, the streetlights, or the manhole covers—anywhere a telescreen might lurk—and offer a smile, saying, "Kimchi!"

Daydreams of a River

The new workshop at the factory was built on what was once the paddock of the old ranch. At the end of the paddock, two animal sheds stood in a boomerang shape. Instead of being torn down, these plastered, concrete structures were now used to store saw blades, oil drums for machinery, and imported wood. It was easy to guess the number of blocks that went into building each shed. Some rattled loose, and others near the roof had been intentionally left out to serve as ventilation windows. Throughout the village were these types of bare-bones sheds, assembled like LEGO houses.

A tour bus and several cars with Seoul license plates traveled along the unpaved road to the factory. Red dust, as if bricks had been ground to powder, wafted up from the lane. Rolling hills spread beyond the pasture. Here and there, short trees grew sparsely. Someone sitting at the front of the bus showed off their farming knowledge, saying it was an ideal location for a ranch, adding that if a cow happened to escape, you'd be able to spot it at once.

The red dust clung to the dress shoes of the Seoul staff, even to the bottoms of their carefully pressed trousers. The director and factory manager stood side by side at the factory entrance to hang up the sign. Since the young CEO from the main office was on an overseas business trip, he couldn't attend the sign-hanging ceremony. The wooden placard on which the factory name was inscribed in large cursive letters still reeked of varnish. The office staff stood in a circle with the factory workers and clapped. The director was so short his head barely came up to the shoulders of the tall, skinny factory manager. The problem was the difference in their arm lengths. It wasn't easy to put the two men at opposite ends of the sign in a single camera frame. If the focus was on the director, everything above the factory manager's forehead was cut off, as well as the first letter of the sign. But if the focus was on the manager, the director's stomach would be cut off. In the end, symmetry was barely achieved with the director holding the bottom of the sign and the factory manager holding the top.

The manager didn't shake hands with the people from the main office, despite meeting them for the first time. He walked hurriedly, hands jammed inside his pant pockets and his torso leading the way before his feet. His unusual gait made him conspicuous. A saw blade had taken off two segments of his left middle finger, as well as his right ring finger and pinky, back when he'd learned his trade at the sawmill. The director, however, was a vigorous man in his early forties. He always had a hard-sided leather briefcase in his hand. Several employees complained of having had their knees or thighs stabbed by a corner of his heavy briefcase while passing him in the hallway. All year round, he carried his suit jacket squeezed under his armpit, giving off the tired air of a traveler who had just stepped off a plane. Even when going between the CEO's office and his own, or coming back from the bathroom, he took short, hurried strides, as if late for a meeting.

There were too many people at the ceremony to fit them all in one picture. About a third of the seventy or so staff members ended up with the backs of their heads being photographed, and out of those whose faces were captured, five or six had their eyes closed. A few who hadn't realized the ceremony was beginning were caught running belatedly toward the entrance. The hands of those applauding enthusiastically were blurred, as if they'd been rubbed out with an eraser, or clasped together as if in prayer. Caught also on the bottom-right corner of the photo was a dark smudge. A black dog had come out of nowhere. There were many strays in that area. But it was the woman, not the dog, who ruined the photo.

The woman stood three people over from the director, alongside the other female office staff. As though conscious of the camera, her gaze wasn't directed at the director or factory manager hanging up the sign, but at some indistinct point beyond the picture's frame. And those eyes glowed red. Much later, in a book titled *The Basics of Photography*, she learned what causes the red-eye effect. In short, she had been looking directly at the camera when the flash went off. And while she'd been gazing at Y, Y had been gazing back at her through the viewfinder. Y isn't in the picture. He'd been holding the camera, pressing the shutter button some five meters away.

It had been Hanil Trading's most prosperous year. Every six months, the company issued a recruitment ad in a trade newsletter. On the day of the sign-hanging ceremony, the entire staff from both the main office and the factory had attended, except for the CEO. During this period, Hanil Trading had the most employees in its history since its founding. Among the staff lined up on the factory manager's side stood a man with a white Yankees cap set crookedly on his head, his long legs splayed like the pegs of a clothespin. The man, A, was a year younger than the woman. He didn't look at all interested in the ceremony. His face was partly obscured by the shadow of his cap brim, and the camera had caught only his profile. He was the last young man left in that village. Everyone at the factory came from there, except the manager. Two middle-aged women prepared lunch for the workers, cleaned, and handled various tasks at the factory. Four men held Class 1 commercial driver's licenses, and nine operated the machinery at the workshop.

More than fifty workers from the main office trailed the factory manager like a herd of cows, ambling around the two sheds, workshop, and office. At sunset, the rancher would have opened the paddock gate and led the cows scattered around the ranch back to the sheds. The sheds had probably been arranged in a boomerang shape to prevent the cows from going astray.

The workshop was as spacious as a hangar, with a wide opening in one wall that was outfitted with double doors to let in large trucks. The director and a few female staff members applauded in front of machines equipped with large circular saws. A plank of wood was placed on a machine workbench for a demonstration. The deep reddish-brown heartwood suggested it was cherry wood. When the manager switched on the machine, the conveyor belt started moving and the stainless-steel saw spun into action. They had to shout to be heard over the noise. The plank edged toward the blade. The noise grew louder. The wood slipped back a little, resisting the saw, but the blade spun faster, its edge a whirl of circles. The woman felt dizzy.

"Cherry wood's dense, tough to slice through! Plus, this is a cross-grain piece—it's a beast to plane. Even the old-timers watch their hands around this stuff." The manager barked in a near shout, as if angry. "But nothing beats this wood!"

The blade bit into the wood, sending dark sawdust flying out from both sides. Her nostrils tingled. But the director was more interested in business than the wood's type or traits. "I hope you're not planning to get rid of all this sawdust. You can still use it, can't you? Maybe mix it with a kind of glue and make things like particle board?"

The manager laughed silently, revealing his yellow teeth. "Sure, it's good for plenty of things, but for making particle board? I wouldn't bother. They'd end up too flimsy and weak, real poor quality. Using that sawdust for heating in the winter—now that's the best."

Meanwhile, the wood was cut in two and came to stop at the end of the workbench. Nevertheless, her ears continued to ring, even after the machine stopped and silence fell over the workshop.

The two concrete columns seemed to have been put up hastily for the ceremony, since there was no gate, much less a chain-link fence. Elderly folks from the village flocked into the yard, trailed by stray dogs. Most of these seniors were related to the factory workers. Straw mats were spread out between the sheds and workshop, and tables of varying shapes and sizes were set up. The middle-aged local women who'd been mobilized for the ceremony bustled about, carrying foil-lined plates of boiled pork and layered rice cakes with red beans, their plastic sandals slapping loudly. The elders grew tipsy off just a few shots of liquor. A few stood up and started swaying side to side, despite the lack of music. Whenever they lifted their legs, their white socks peeked out, stained with reddish dirt. The elders sitting down also had faces ruddy with drink. An old man poured liquor for another old man, who was actually his nephew, and this nephew, observing all formalities, received the drink with both hands and turned aside to swallow it. Dogs circled the tables, eyeing the people, while the elders displayed their few remaining yellow teeth or danced with their eyes closed, as if listening to distant strains of music, sometimes flying into a rage at the dogs trying to snatch a morsel. They'd stomp their feet or hurl a rubber shoe at them. The dogs arched their backs like bows, their raised tails rigid like poker sticks. When a woman flung a piece of pork their way, they pounced for the dirt-covered scrap, shoving their noses in the dirt and planting their paws to hold their ground. A cloud of red dust rose. But the black dog, with its long legs and pointy snout, managed to get the meat each time. An old man pointed at it. "See that? Smart as a whip, that one. Comes from our dog and that one over there."

The old man beside him tossed back his shot and shook his head. "How can your dog be the daddy? He isn't even the right breed."

"Look at those eyes," the first man said, not backing down. "They're our dog's all right. Saw your mutt leap my fence, clear as day, to get to mine."

"You can't tell the difference between a piss pot and a hat without your specs on."

"Who's fussin' over the daddy here?" a third chimed in. "They're just dogs for crying out loud. Worry about your own selves."

An old man slapped his knee. Nearby, another stuck his foot out for a playful jab in the man's side. Yet another elder lifted his cloudy eyes, glancing around and snickering. Laughter sneaked past his crooked teeth.

The boiled pork smelled bad. Those with strong stomachs put some garlic on top, bundled the whole thing in lettuce, and crammed it into their mouths. Even before swallowing, they would open their mouths, still full of food, to knock back shots of soju. The office staff and factory workers sat with a low Formica table between them, each group as guarded as if at a labor-management negotiation. Assistant Manager Lee from the office got to his feet, rattling an empty soju bottle with the handle of a metal spoon wedged in the neck. He tucked the end of his tie into his shirt pocket. A flush had spread down to his neck from the rounds of drink served up by the factory crew. A worker, having exchanged a few words with him, called out, "Looking sharp there!" Laughter erupted around them. Startled by the commotion, a scruffy dog that had been lingering by the tables started barking at no one in particular.

In the group photo of over seventy people, Assistant Manager Lee stood out. He wore a navy-blue double-breasted suit with gray pinstripes and gold buttons embossed with an anchor. If he'd had a pipe in his mouth, he would have passed for a sailor. His suit drew comments from all over the yard. Someone gave a long whistle. He waited for the laughter to die down before shaking the soju bottle once more. Meanwhile, the factory manager and director murmured in hushed tones, heads close together. Urged by Mr. Lee, Miss Kim from the trade department stood up. She was nicknamed "Kitty" for her big eyes and tiny mouth. "Sing! Sing!" the men hollered, loosened up by drink. Flushing a deep red, she introduced herself briefly and sat down to the men's cheers.

The woman kept tasting dirt in her food. Across from her, a yellow dog with loose skin and eyes crusted with sleep was watching her. It seemed the dog had recently had puppies. The woman tossed her a piece of meat, but it was snatched away by the swift black dog. Instead of lunging for the food, Goldie cowered and shrank back, her ten sagging teats swinging in different directions with each movement. Holding out another piece of meat, she coaxed Goldie closer, and the animal licked the woman's hand for a long time before gently taking the morsel. Her teeth seemed weak. Bits of meat escaped from between them. When she finished, Goldie sat behind a young man in a Yankees cap pulled low over his face, who was nursing his drink in silence. It was A. Across the table, some of the older men scolded A for not removing his cap before his elders. A woman passing by with more meat and drink intervened. "Let him be, everyone's got their reasons." One of the men glared at her with bloodshot eyes. Since A's face was hidden by his cap, the woman couldn't see his reaction.

The water tap was tucked away behind the sheds. As the woman made her way there, Goldie padded along behind. With each step, the dog's baggy flesh bumped and jostled against itself, causing ripples to break out on her skin. She looked uncomfortable, as if she were wearing a coat several sizes too big. If the woman were to pull down a zipper somewhere on that hide, a small puppy just might spring out. The tap was attached to a long rubber hose, which was filled with sand and a tiny maple leaf. She turned on the tap and waited. The water that emerged from the end of the hose was so cold her hands nearly went numb. The back of the sheds was cluttered with a pile of discarded items: a hodgepodge of bricks, Styrofoam and silt, pots, rubber tubs, and even a deflated, child-sized inner tube. When she turned around, Goldie had vanished. She clicked her tongue, but the dog didn't appear.

It was dark inside the shed, even in the middle of the day. North American walnut logs were stacked on one side. Y and the woman had started working at the company the previous year. They braved the winter at the Incheon port, where forklifts wove ceaselessly between enormous shipping containers. The cold chafed her skin red beneath her pants. Each week, new shipments of lumber arrived from North America. Logs as long as twenty meters and as wide as an arm's span formed mountains on the loading docks. Atop these piles, she could see the Incheon pier—ships anchored, laden with containers, against a backdrop of incessant activity of cranes, trailers, and longshoremen. Their job was to check the number and type of logs against the invoice. Y hopped from log to log. The woman did the same, feeling the pier draw near each time her body was airborne. The soles of her shoes wore down quickly. That winter, she went through three pairs of shoes. Despite wearing gloves and boots, her hands and feet became numb. When the cold became unbearable during log inspections, they'd leave the docks and jaywalk to the food stall across the street, instead of walking all the way to the overpass. Y held her hand. His hand was lukewarm. As she sipped a cup of hot oden soup, her skin itched as it began to thaw. She wanted to see Y from those days, but he wasn't in any pictures.

The shed smelled of animal excrement and tree sap. Under the dark ceiling, sockets missing lightbulbs dangled from cords of varying length. You could see the village across the street through the brick-sized windows. When night fell, the cows locked up inside the sheds would have seen the flickering lights of passing cars through these openings. Many of these sheds stood at the base of mountains, clearly no longer in use. Suddenly, a tongue licked the back of her hand. It was Goldie. Deeper inside the shed, perched on the stack of walnut logs, was A. How long had he been there? He was smoking.

"Don't get the wrong idea. I wasn't following you. You see those old farts out there? They'd jump down my throat if I lit up in front of them." He flicked the cigarette butt from his fingers, sending it arcing through the air and out the window.

"There was an outbreak here. White spots appeared on the cows' brains, like the holes in a sponge. All the dairy cows died. We dug pits for them and even had to borrow excavators to move the carcasses. Excavators came around here for two weeks. The spots where they're buried are soft. We filled the pits and tamped down the dirt, but as the cows rot, the pits keep sinking."

He got down from the logs. He was much taller than she'd thought. Goldie and her swinging flesh went to him. He heaved a deep sigh. She caught a whiff of liquor on his breath.

"By next February, I'll be on a boat. A tuna reefer. Once you set out, it might be two years before you touch land again."

He walked toward the shed entrance with Goldie trailing behind. Before he stepped out, he turned to look at her, sighing as though drunk. And then without further explanation, he said he was the type to see a thing through if he put his mind to it.

The old men caused a commotion trying to find their shoes among over twenty pairs of white rubber shoes scattered across the yard. Even when they flopped down on their behinds, drunk, they snickered like schoolboys splashing in a creek. Since every one of them was dressed in a white hanbok, it was difficult to tell them apart. They looked different one moment, yet in the next, they seemed like the same person. "Aigo, Father!" Daughters-in-law, who were elderly themselves, came running, wiping their wet hands on their baggy trousers, kicking up red dust. The factory manager accepted every drink that his staff poured him. Drunk, he kept urging more liquor on the director, who sat across from him. Liquor sloshed out from the shot glass he held with his four fingers. The finger that had its tip severed was stubby, with new skin having grown on top of it. The director stubbornly turned down every drink, using a meeting the following day as his excuse. Though he hadn't had a single drink, he looked exhausted, as though he'd just gotten off a long-distance flight. A fine layer of red dust clung to his hair, which was slicked back with pomade. Every time, the factory manager slurred, "Ah jeez, not a single drink?"

The director's car was the first to leave the factory. Those returning to Seoul by bus scrambled to the entrance where the bus was parked. The yard offered a clear view of the people climbing aboard. Drunk men staggered to the side of the road and urinated for a long time. Their suit trousers were wrinkled and their shirt collars grubby. Darkness was moving in from the direction of the bus. The strays roamed the yard and thrust their noses into the ground, sniffing for meat. The rest of the city people split off into different cars. The woman and Y were supposed to catch a ride with Assistant Manager Lee, but Y was still snapping photos of the factory. Loosened up with drink, the factory manager had taken his hands out of his pockets and now went so far as to wave at the camera. In less than a year, he would lose two more of the remaining four fingers on his left hand. The circular saw had been cutting through cherry wood when it hit grain running in a different direction and jerked up. In the blink of an eye, two fingers were severed, spraying blood like sawdust. The accident threw the main office into chaos. Upon hearing about the accident, the CEO, who was twenty years younger, called the factory manager a "fucking idiot." He made numerous calls to check if the manager had violated any safety regulations by failing to use a protective device. He also asked Mr. Lee to secretly investigate if the manager had been drinking on the job.

The woman called out to Y, who was taking his time. As she was getting in Mr. Lee's car, she glanced toward the sheds and workshop, but A was nowhere in sight. The village women were clearing away the mats on one side of the yard, while stray dogs scavenged for scraps of food. The factory workers would probably keep drinking well into the night. The young man in the Yankees cap wasn't by the entrance either. As the bus pulled farther away from the factory, she continued to scan the area for A, like a farmer on the lookout for a cow that had escaped. Wondering if he was hiding, she peered at the trees, then laughed to herself. Being so tall, A couldn't possibly conceal himself behind such small trees. She'd wanted to wish him good luck at sea. She'd even clicked her tongue for Goldie, but there was no sign of the dog either.

Darkness fell quickly. Animal sheds flickered in the dark. There wasn't a single streetlight along the road. They had to go slowly, since the headlights lit only a short distance ahead. Mr. Lee's tongue kept darting out to moisten his parched lips. The road wound treacherously, and at each sharp curve, Mr. Lee pumped the brakes. Y slumped in the backseat, head drooping as he dozed. Though they were unable to catch up to the bus that had left much earlier, they should have been able to see the taillights of the other cars. At first, they assumed they couldn't see the cars ahead because of the winding road, but after driving for twenty minutes, they realized they must have veered off course. They were the only ones on the empty road. It was pitch black everywhere, with no houses in sight. They would have to press on until they came to a signpost. Mr. Lee started driving a little faster. Just as they were going around a bend, a white object darted out from the opposite side of the road. Mr. Lee slammed on the brakes, but the object hit the bumper and flew into the dark rush field. The car hurtled forward for another five meters before stopping. Mr. Lee peered at the road behind them through the rearview mirror, but the faint glow of the taillights revealed nothing. Roused by the impact, Y blinked groggily and glanced about with puffy eyes.

Mr. Lee made a face. "Shit." He rolled down his window and spat outside.

Leaving the engine running, he climbed out of the car. Through the rearview mirror, she saw him move farther away. He was soon swallowed up by darkness.

Y yawned and said it was most likely nothing. "Probably a badger or a squirrel."

She'd caught only a flash, but it had seemed much bigger than that. The object in the headlights had been white.

Mr. Lee returned about ten minutes later. Instead of getting in the driver's seat, he stood outside and smoked. When he climbed in, the smell of liquor and cigarettes filled the car. "It was a dog," he said.

The village had an unusual number of strays, but her gut feeling told her that it hadn't been a dog. Back at the factory, the old men had been wearing white. They flashed across her mind, then vanished. Mr. Lee scrubbed his face with both hands. "I don't know. It's too dark to see anything."

The bottom of the hill, about three meters below, was as black as a well. It was impossible to search every spot with a flashlight.

"Mr. Lee, are you sure it went that way?" Y called out from the dark. "I don't think that's where it was."

The dark was disorienting, making it difficult to tell where they'd hit it. After crashing into the bumper, it had hurtled off the road. Mr.

Lee raised the flashlight above his head, sweeping its beam across the field. The light punched holes in the darkness, which spread out like a vast carpet. Dense clumps of rush grass. Dry bushes. Deserted animal sheds. The flashlight passed over the field once more when suddenly, in the beam, she noticed the grass quivering. "Over there! It's alive!"

She was moving before she finished speaking. The slope wasn't steep, but the soil was so dry she slipped. "Don't move the flashlight!" she shouted without looking back. "Yes, right there! Keep it on that spot!"

The dry season had turned the rushes brittle, and they tangled around her legs. She heard Y following close behind her. The ground was firm underfoot, but without warning, it would give way to spongy depressions. She recalled A's story about the many pits scattered around the village that were graves for the diseased cows. According to him, they were now just sunken patches of earth, with the carcasses decaying beneath. Perhaps he'd made the whole thing up to scare a city girl. She walked toward the spot revealed by the flashlight. On a patch of flattened rushes where broken stalks trembled, a dog lay panting. She brought her face close, thinking it was Goldie, but it wasn't her. The tongue that lolled from its gasping mouth looked unnaturally long.

"So it was a dog?" Y said, catching his breath. Then he shouted toward Mr. Lee. "You're right! It's a dog!"

It was still warm. When she touched it, its breathing grew quieter. She buried her fingers in its ruff and stroked the fur. It must have been hit in the stomach. Each time her hand went near that area, the dog silently bared its teeth. The rushes were sticky. Beside her, she felt something mushy. The entrails had spilled out and lay splayed on the trampled rush.

"Let's go," Y said, turning around.

That second, the dog's eyes that had rolled back flashed toward Y. The dog surged up and clamped down on the woman's wrist with the last of its strength. Its fangs pierced her flesh, causing her arm to go numb. Lifting her arm also raised the dog's head, making her limb feel unbearably heavy, as if it might snap off. Once it had latched onto her wrist, it refused to let go. She saw its eyes then. Rolled back to show mostly whites, its eyes were filled with tears. Its saliva seeped into her veins.

She would recall those eyes about ten years later when she found herself biting down on someone's arm. The man struck her repeatedly in the face with her own purse, the buckle whacking her in the eye. She tried to get a good look at his face, but she couldn't, because one of her eyes had swollen shut. Even as she was dragged along the side street, she bit down harder and refused to let go.

The dog's fangs seemed to have pierced through her muscle to the bone. She couldn't help thinking that if it continued to hang on, her hand may have to be amputated. The memory of the factory manager's stubby fingers flitted through her mind. She shook her arm frantically, but the fangs sank deeper into her flesh. Y, alerted by her scream, hurried back, leaping through the rushes. The dog's saliva seeped into her bloodstream, and she had the thought that she might become half dog. Like a dog, she stared into the darkness. It seemed she could hear, even see, the rustling of a small insect within the rushes. Y kicked the dog, also kicking her arm in the process. The dog would not unlatch from her. Y felt around the grass. Then there was a large rock in his hand.

The woman was dragged deeper into the side street by a man whose face she couldn't see. She lost a heel along the way. Her stockings ripped, and her skin scraped along the cracked sidewalk and started to bleed. The narrow street leading to her house was always deserted. Even though low-rises flanked the street and every detached home was filled with people, she was always the only one there. The security light had burned out a long time ago, but no one replaced the bulb.

When she'd sensed someone behind her, it was already too late. The man had been hiding behind the stairs of a low-rise, approaching her silently from behind. A rough hand clamped over her nose and mouth. His other hand grabbed at her purse that was slung over her shoulder. She couldn't breathe. She tried to twist away, but his hand only tightened. His palm reeked, damp with sweat. She had no choice but to bite down so that she could breathe. "Ahh!" He jumped back, clutching his hand. She could have fled in the opposite direction right then, but she lunged and bit him again. Her teeth didn't sink easily into his muscular arm. She bit down with all her strength. His flesh gave way. His muscles seemed to crumble between her teeth. He jumped in pain. His blood trickled between her teeth and down her throat. It tasted briny. The man whacked her face with her purse. The buckle struck her in the eye. Yet, she clung on. He pummeled her, crushing her nose. She felt something hot gush down her face. The crunch of several top teeth breaking reverberated in her head. Oddly, her mind flashed to the eyes of the dog that had bitten her wrist and refused to let go. She felt no pain. He dragged her along the street while bashing her head against a building wall. Once, twice, then everything turned white. She wanted to open her mouth, but she couldn't. She believed her dog nature had finally emerged.

"Once a dog bites, it never lets go," said H, whom she would run into years later. He rolled up his pant leg to reveal a pink keloid scar, glossier than the rest of his skin. A dog bite wound. He scratched at the scar. "If I got this hurt, can you imagine what happened to the dog?"

The man whose face she hadn't been able to see flung her to the ground at the end of the street and hurled the purse at her face. "You fucking bitch!" Still enraged, he stomped on her stomach and thighs with his boots before spitting on her.

"Why didn't you just let him take your purse?"

Everyone who came to the hospital said the same thing. They shook their heads as they gazed down at the woman in bed, her eye swollen shut, nose fractured, three teeth missing, and body covered in bruises. Some asked if there had been valuables in her purse. But no, she'd only had a single ten-thousand-won bill that day. No one could make sense of it. Any time a visitor said something, her mother, who had been caring for her, muttered, "Stupid, stupid girl," and heaved a big sigh. The woman looked down at her feet that were sticking out from under the sheet. Her skinned heels were oozing blood and a toenail had fallen off.

Y frowned as soon as he came to the hospital. He was wearing snug leather pants that looked uncomfortable and boots that came up to below his knees. After glancing several times at her battered face, he sat at the foot of her bed. "You look like a different person."

She gave him a small smile. "Don't worry. The swelling and bruising will go away. The doctor straightened my nose, and as for my teeth, I can get implants."

"See?" Y said, slowly shaking his head. "You don't understand."

Until then, the woman had no idea that he'd joined a motorcycle club. She came home a day earlier than her discharge date. That night, Y didn't come home. When he returned late the following morning, he neither washed up nor ate, instead going straight to bed. She smelled the winter wind she'd smelled on him at the Incheon port, as though he'd been roaming about all night. "You've changed too much. You're not the same shy girl who couldn't even look at a boy."

Her bruises healed and she got dental implants, but Y's complaints continued. When she asked him why he was always out, he said he was bored. Eventually, he stopped coming home in the morning.

The headquarters of High Speed, the motorcycle club, were located in an auto body shop just outside Seoul. A sign reading "We remove dents!" stood out front, and the ground in front of the garage was stained with grease and motor oil. The shop owner was around Y's age. He said that by day he repaired vehicles with the help of his two employees, and by night and on holidays, he rode his motorcycle. Y wasn't there. Even the club members couldn't get a hold of him. Notification of rides—date, time, and location—was sent via email to the members, who would meet and ride together if they were available. The owner mentioned their current favorite was the new road by Munhak Stadium. In a corner of the body shop, a bulletin board was dedicated to High Speed members. "I need to talk to you. Please come home." She pinned her note where it would be most noticeable.

Y didn't return. The woman's uterus, once as small as an apple, had swollen to the size of a melon. Blue veins spiderwebbed over her breasts, and she felt her groin pull whenever she rose to her feet or sat down. During the ultrasound exam, the obstetrician let slip, "What a handsome fella!" It was a boy. Inside her, the baby grew hair and developed fingernails and toenails. They said that around this time, fingerprints started to form. As soon as a stethoscope was placed on her belly, the baby's heartbeat echoed in the examination room.

The body shop owner recognized her. He said he'd seen Y on the road near the airport about two weeks ago. On the bulletin board was a message from Y: "Please let me go. Stop clinging to me. I'm so sick of it." It was his last message to her. While staring at the note, she thought about what he'd said about being bored. According to the body shop owner, Y had recently gotten a new bike. She headed for the road he'd mentioned. The new road by Munhak Stadium connected to the Yeongdong Expressway. The taxi driver stopped several times, asking for the exact location she meant near the stadium. She also went looking for Y around the Jayu Motorway, but there weren't any spots for the taxi to stop. Motorcycles sped along the night road, many crossing the median line. The cab chased after them, but they were too fast. It was difficult to find Y's motorcycle amid the others. Most of the club members stored their bikes at the body shop. The owner had pointed at one in the corner. "That there is Y's new girlfriend."

Y's new girlfriend was a 1,450cc model, made of light titanium. If Y had gone around with a woman riding behind him, perhaps one with long hair, she would have been able to spot him easily. She stuck a new message on the bulletin. "I'm so bored. Come back." More than a week passed, but Y didn't call.

The clinic that had been recommended to her on the phone was small and shabby. There seemed to be few women of childbearing age in the town where it was located, for the clinic's only patients were pregnant women who'd traveled from far away and a few bargirls. When she'd called, the nurse hadn't bothered to ask any basic questions, such as how far along she was. But she added there would be a cost for the disposal of the specimen in addition to the surgery. She didn't tell her mother, who would only say she was a stupid girl. The operating room, with missing tiles and holes in the floor, resembled an old bathhouse. Perhaps her feet had swollen, because she felt better once she'd removed her shoes and climbed onto the operating table. Metal containers filled with bandages sat by the head of the bed. She placed her feet in the stirrups and lay down on the table. There was black mold growing in a corner of the cement ceiling. Everything felt surreal, as if it were someone else's life. The stirrups were cold against her skin. As her belly tightened, something squirmed inside. She chose to imagine it was just a melon. How could she have carried such a big thing around? The clatter of stainless steel came from the consultation room, as if the staff were handling metal tools. She whispered to herself: "It's okay. You tried your best."

The factory was quite far from Seoul. She was able to get the job because all the young local women had moved to the city. The boss made it clear there was no maternity leave available, blaming the worsening recession. Power saws roared non-stop from nine in the morning till nine at night. Initially, she struggled to hear the person on the other end of the line, but she adapted to the noise soon enough. Naturally, her voice grew louder, too. When she would lie in bed at night, she'd still hear the buzz of the saws. Sometimes when she called home, her elderly mother complained about her loud voice and said she was about to go deaf. The factory was always full of itinerant workers. The boss didn't care about their backgrounds, but she didn't like interacting with them. Afraid she'd encounter the man she'd bitten, she developed the habit of scrutinizing the arms of the new laborers. Even if no one else knew, the biter and the bitten would surely recognize each other.

A trailer loaded with North American oak arrived. The laborers who'd been scattered around the sawmill swarmed toward the trailer. A red pennant flag was attached to the end of the longest log on the flatbed. The center of the oak was light pink or dark brown. Compared to cherry wood, oak was easier to cut and nail down. The driver's door opened and a giant sack of a man hopped down. His hair was disheveled, as if he'd had the windows rolled down.

"Ah jeez, you were bitten by a dog?" he said, noticing the scar on her wrist. He suddenly pulled up the hem of his pants and thrust his knee at her. "Look, a dog bit me, too. They don't let go once they get a hold of something," he said with a wince. "If my scar's this big, imagine what happened to the dog! I made sure it would never chew meat again."

The logs on the flatbed matched up with the invoice. As she inspected the flatbed, the man rambled on, jiggling his leg.

"Excuse me, but do I know you? I feel like we've met before."

She started heading back to the office but he blocked her way.

"I'm sure I've seen you before . . . Are you sure you don't remember me?"

His face was unfamiliar. He walked back to his trailer, slapping his gloves against his leg. The flatbed tilted up, and logs tumbled onto the ground. The noise of the saws from the workshop was deafening. The driver came running, his belly bouncing. Suddenly, Hanil Trading's sign-hanging ceremony flashed through her mind. But it was the man who recognized her first.

"Hanil Trading, right?"

She recalled the Yankees baseball cap. "A?"

He looked let down. "You don't recognize me? You asked me how I'd been bitten by a dog. You were shivering, so I lent you my pullover."

It was H. Yet, his face remained unfamiliar.

"It was a green waterproof pullover . . ."

In the group photo, she's wearing a green pullover. Her eyes are red, for she'd been looking directly at the camera. So fixated on her red eyes, she must have overlooked the fact that she'd borrowed the pullover. She'd believed A was the only young factory worker there that day. He had set out on a reefer ship that February, just as he'd told her. About a year later, the company received word: A had vanished without a trace from an island in the South Pacific archipelago while his boat was anchored at port.

When the wooden sign was unwrapped from the newspaper, it smelled of fresh varnish. Some parts of the sign were sticky since the varnish hadn't completely dried. People around the yard started to gather. The director raised the sign with a sly expression. Exactly ten years later, he suffered a heart attack. He always had the air of a weary traveler who had just stepped off a plane. The CEO was eventually conned by the assistant manager who'd looked like a sailor. Assistant Manager Lee had conspired with a friend at the American branch to embezzle imported lumber. A year after the sign-hanging ceremony, Hanil Trading began to decline. The seventy-plus employees dispersed, and the name of the company disappeared from the trade newsletter. The factory's sign, carved from walnut wood, had probably been used as firewood for some house a long time ago.

While studying photography, she learned that the red-eye effect typically occurs when the pupils are dilated. Why were my pupils dilated? Was it really me that Y had been watching through the viewfinder twenty years ago? Other female employees from the company had been standing next to her, including Miss Kim, who resembled a cat and was very popular with the men. The woman's gaze had been directed at some point beyond the frame. Was I really looking at Y? She couldn't even remember borrowing H's pullover.

Y might not have been the one she was watching. He takes a few steps back with the camera in his hands, raises it to his eye, hesitates, then backs up some more. Now he's standing about five meters away from the group. The pasture stretches out behind him. As more than seventy people scuffle about, red dust rises to their knees. Above the pasture is the deep autumn sky. The workshop was built on what was once the paddock. The workshop door opens and a cow ambles out. Soon other cows come out of the paddock. They head toward the sheds. The woman blinks, and the cows vanish, their mooing lingering in the air. There is no pasture, no workshop. What she's looking at is herself in twenty years. Her pupils are dilated. That's when Y presses the shutter.

Assistant Manager Lee, dressed in a suit with gold buttons, backs up the car and parks in front of the factory entrance. The woman is looking for A to say goodbye, but she can't find him, nor can she find Goldie who had followed him around. Y looks as young as he had at the Incheon pier when he leapt between the logs from North America. Several cars carrying the office staff leave the factory, and a cloud of red dust rises around the tires. She and Y cannot fathom how much they will change in twenty years. Her wrist is still smooth, unmarked by the dog's bite. Nothing has happened yet. At this point, her belief—that biting and being bitten is part of life—hasn't yet taken root.

In the pictures that Y has taken, a young H is wearing a green pullover—the same one she'd borrowed and is wearing in the group photo.

To her, H's face is still that of a stranger. He leans forward, listening to what the factory manager is saying. When Y raises his camera, the factory manager waves with his seven fingers. A part of the shed wall is visible. The white brim of a hat peeks out from the shed. Below, what seems to be Goldie's tail is showing. A is hiding, watching the woman leave. She cannot recall H's face for the life of her. It's as if a man from the distant future has leapt into the past. Neither can she recall the keloid scar he claimed to have shown her. She calls out to Y, who is taking his sweet time. Her forehead is round and smooth. She was at her most beautiful then.

House of Wafers

The house was perched precariously on a hill rutted with sloppy holes the excavator had made. It was clear that instead of striking the roof of the next-door neighbor's house, the excavator bucket had missed its target, lodging in the slab fence of the woman's house. A panel of the wall was knocked down, as if it had been intentionally removed. Displayed for all to see were the rusted metal steps of a squat-toilet outhouse that had its door flung wide open, and a water tap from which weeds sprouted through the cracks, drawing the gazes of those walking by.

Three in the afternoon. Construction workers with farmer's tans sat on the collapsed wall panel and ate their buns. Behind them stood houses with roofs blown off and gaping holes in the walls, stripped down to their frames. The woman stood under the harsh sun, staring at the ruins. The side street was lined with ten cookie-cutter houses facing each another, all with identical features, from the number of rooms and arrangement of windows to the doorknockers shaped like lion heads. But the side street, along with the row of houses facing her house, was transformed into two lanes, now part of a four-lane road. When the road opened, a redevelopment boom hit this quiet street that had remained unchanged for the past thirty years. The woman's house, located at the very end of the street, suddenly found itself sitting alone, surrounded by cars that sped by twenty-four hours a day.

Construction waste was mixed with furniture and belongings left behind during the move. Steel rebar covered in cement jutted out from a pile of bricks, twisted like crowbars. Only a doll's blonde head protruded from a windowless frame and a heap of broken glass. The kind of doll that closes its eyes when laid down, it was lying with one eye wide open, as though something heavy had pressed down on the other. The wallpaper, featuring hundreds of Minnie Mouses holding balloons, was covered with the scrawls of a child learning to write, similar to the babbling of a toddler. *Momi Mami Mumi Muma* . . . There wasn't a single correct word, but the woman could tell immediately what the child had tried to write. That kind of understanding had never existed between H and her.

The house next door was completely crushed, as if it had been stomped on. As pressure was applied from above, the interior was forced out through the exterior walls. The tiled kitchen, once the envy of other housewives, had been pushed out all the way to the main gate. The volume of waste from the demolition of a single house was much greater than the size of the house when it stood intact. Waste the size of royal tombs was heaped up throughout the ruined lots.

The woman had returned home. Considering she had been away for ten years, she didn't have much luggage. She could have brought back even less, but just in case, she'd brought several bottles of maple syrup, the local specialty. While carrying back the souvenirs, she had moments when she felt the place she'd lived for ten years was only a tourist spot she'd visited on vacation. Just like the girls from that place, she wanted to step through the front gate and shout, "I'm home!"

There was no room for her to set her foot on the narrow sidewalk, due to the garbage piled onto it and the trucks parked to remove it. The small wheels of her suitcase got stuck in the cracks of the broken pavement. Each time this happened, she had to yank up the suitcase by the handle, and several times the suitcase wheels bashed into her ankle. People bumped into her as they passed. There wasn't a single familiar face. In the past, the news that she'd come home would have reached the street before she did. Would her homecoming have felt more real then, since the news would have been repeated all over the street? Because she had imagined dragging her suitcase home so often, the fact that she was back felt like a dream.

When she saw the excavator with its bucket, she recalled what her father used to say. "New wine needs to go in new wineskins." The old excavator must have mixed concrete at some point in the past. There was dried concrete all over the bucket.

Several men, who had crammed their mouths full of bread, continued to stare at her. One man finished his bun and whistled. "Hey Miss, how about a date?"

"'Miss'? She's a total ajumma," a voice said, sounding as though his mouth was still full.

The first man cocked his head. "You can't tell by just looking at her face."

The second man lowered his voice to a whisper. "Maybe not, but you can tell if you look at her ass. There's no bounce. You know, like a monkey's tail . . ."

Even strangers could tell. What has my shovel been digging for the past ten years? While sitting in the cramped seat of the airplane for the past thirteen hours, deep creases had formed on her silk blouse and skirt. At the Incheon airport bathroom, she found a hole in her stockings, likely snagged on the seam of her shoe, but she couldn't be bothered to change. In the past, it would have been unthinkable, yet now she hardly cared. That, more than anything, was truly frightening. She turned and made eye contact with a young man eating his bun, sitting apart from the crowd. Military trousers covered his long legs. Even his arms hanging down between his legs were long, and his dark hands were so big that the 200ml carton of milk he was holding looked tiny. He almost choked on his bread and tears came to his eyes. Feeling thirsty all of a sudden, she felt an urge to pound him on his back.

There was no way to tell the original color of the front gate that was now covered in green rust. The window grills and mailbox had corroded so much they looked as though they would crumble on contact. Her father used to repaint the gate and grills every two or three years. Bubbles of paint would form on the lion head doorknockers and drip down the grills, hardening like candle wax. The gate's columns, which her sisters claimed looked like chocolate, had lost their tiles, revealing the mortar underneath. She was about to ring the doorbell when she remembered it had stopped working a decade ago, having shorted out during a heavy downpour. She pushed open the gate and tried to close it behind her, but it didn't latch properly and creaked open again.

The yard was crammed with an empty doghouse, rusted bicycles, refrigerators whose doors wouldn't stay shut due to old rubber gaskets, fans with broken blades, and a sunken sofa with worn upholstery. Inside an empty aquarium was a single bathroom slipper, and two more aquariums like it behind the outhouse. While making her way to the front door, her feet kept bumping into various knickknacks, such as plastic flowerpots, washbasins, and medicinal pots.

All the doors were open, but her mother was nowhere to be seen. Different types of shoes were strewn across the entrance, covered by a thick layer of cement dust. The front door didn't fit properly into its frame and couldn't fully close. She peered into the living room without removing her shoes. She took in the wall where big and small clocks hung. Even the living room was full of scavenged junk.

Her mother strode into the yard, not through the front gate, but through the hole in the wall fence. In her hand was an old electric rice cooker. She was wearing the same sweater she'd worn in a picture from two years ago, except now it fit tightly, as she had gained weight.

"Mama!" she blurted childishly, similar to the scrawls she'd seen on the wallpaper down the street.

Her mother's sagging eyes twitched. "Huh? Who's this?"

Her mother had put up thick plastic sheeting on all the windows facing the construction site. Yet, by afternoon, dust seeped in through the cracks and settled into a white film on the floor. Sweeping caused the dust to scatter in the air. Thanks to the plastic sheeting, they didn't have to deal with drafts last winter, but the walls and ceiling were completely covered with black mold from the condensation formed due to the temperature difference between the inside and outside of the house.

Two weeks ago, the woman had sent a letter saying she was coming home. She described the past ten years of her life, ending the letter with her flight number and arrival time. But the letter never arrived. She hadn't experienced any issues with the mail in the past when she'd sent home hats or woolen mufflers that elderly women in the west liked to wear. So where could her letter have gone? Did the post office think all the houses on this street had been demolished?

Wearing her reading glasses, her mother held the bottle of maple syrup at arm's length and read out the roman characters she recognized. "What's the big idea, bursting in here without any warning? Your store holding up fine without you?" Whenever she was flustered, her mother, who, as a nine-year-old, had fled to a foreign city because of the war, would slip into the dialect of that place. While her mother lined up the maple syrup bottles on the floor, mulling over who should get one, the woman tried to remember what she'd written in the letter. *Dear Mom.* She couldn't recall the next sentence or anything else she'd written. Her memory kept skipping to the end where she mentioned her flight number and arrival time.

When her eyes opened and she looked at the time, it was exactly midnight, which meant it was six in the morning back where she'd come from. She tossed and turned, trying to fall back asleep, but her mind only became clearer, as if she'd washed her face. She lay awake, waiting for dawn. Through the small window overlooking the yard, she watched the headlights of cars speed by. Her mother always fell asleep with the television on. If someone turned it off, she somehow knew and mumbled with her eyes closed, "Leave it on. It's just getting good." Who knows how she came to possess it, but she pushed around a shopping cart from a big supermarket to collect all her junk. In the living room alone were four grandfather clocks. On some mornings, she had to listen to the chiming of each clock, which all struck at different times, lasting over ten minutes. An image of her grandfather in his later years became superimposed on her mother. For some reason, her grandfather had been obsessed with umbrellas. Whenever he'd bring old umbrellas home, her mother would glare at him. So many broken, useless umbrellas became new in his hands. It was a time when there was always a spare umbrella to take on a rainy day, even if he'd left his on the bus or subway. What will I obsess over one day? H once said that what she felt for him was not love, but obsession.

Her mother, who'd also gotten up at dawn, was crouched over the kitchen drain on the tiled floor, relieving herself. The urine hit the floor in a steady stream, continuing for a long time. Her mother had given birth to three daughters over the span of ten years. The sound of her mother relieving herself with gusto, as if letting go of all her tension, made her feel as if she could finally breathe. Never once had she been able to relieve herself so freely. She'd been the same with H, and with the man she'd briefly dated before H, flushing the toilet to mask the sound of her peeing, or letting out a trickle, little at a time.

About thirty years ago, when the neighborhood was developed as a model housing complex, the houses on this street were featured on Daehan News, a clip shown in theaters before movie screenings. Narrated with that distinct, announcer-voice accent, the newsreel began by describing the "new women" who were liberated from the traditional kitchens where they had to squat or hunch over to work, instead showing the women from this street in white frilly aprons, chopping and washing dishes at the Western-style counters that came up to their waists. For a while, the women flocked from one theater to another, eager to catch a glimpse of themselves on the big screen.

She could put up with everything else, but it was torture to cook, wash, and brush her teeth in a kitchen that reeked of urine. After her father died, the house deteriorated rapidly. The other houses on their street replaced their squat toilets with indoor flush toilets. The sisters, however, had to put on their shoes in the middle of the night and walk across the yard to use the bathroom. When their rain gutter rusted and fell off, the water flowed directly into the eaves of the house next door. Only after several complaints from the neighbor did her mother replace the gutter. They were also the last house on the street to replace the briquette furnace with an oil boiler. She went to the outdoor tap and twisted it open. Muddy red water gushed out, along with small, black bugs. The pipes seemed to have been damaged during the demolition. But even if clean water were to flow, she couldn't exactly wash her face in the middle of the yard, totally exposed, with no wall to hide behind.

Her mother's sudden weight gain led to knee problems, making stairs particularly painful. She'd clean the house every two weeks, finishing up by dusting the second floor, but this stretched to once a month, and then once every other month, and after a certain point, she stopped going upstairs altogether. The first thing the woman did when she came home was to clean the second floor. The window didn't open easily, as if the sill had its teeth clenched and was refusing to let go. Though plastic sheeting covered the window, there was a thick layer of dust on the floor. Dust had accumulated even on the empty hanger hooked on a nail in the wall, as well as inside the vase on top of the dresser. She left footprints wherever she went. Certain spots on the floor were more worn than others. When the dust was swept away, she could finally see the floorboards. The nail heads sticking out from the wood were rusted. Just a few nails hammered into the edge of the floorboards were done properly. The rest were bent or driven in only halfway. The sisters had naturally avoided these areas.

Their father had promised a piano for the girls' room, but he wasn't able to keep that promise. One Sunday, a desk for the girls was delivered. As they were moving it upstairs, their father's foot plunged through the second-story floor. The woman, who had been watching from the bottom of the stairs, saw the chandelier swing wildly before a crack appeared in the center of the ceiling. Wood shavings rained down, and their father's foot sprang through, as if he were executing a front kick. "What the hell is this?" her mother exclaimed, running out from the kitchen. His leg was dangling from the ceiling, the rest of his body out of sight. The sisters rushed upstairs to find their father, who had never imagined his foot could go through the floor, blinking in bewildered astonishment.

The incident left their father with an injury to his right scrotum, causing him to limp for some time. He hobbled about town, seeking the builder who had sold them the house. It was then that the street's residents realized all twenty houses had been shoddily constructed. The men joined forces. They discovered that the identical layout and features—every aspect was exactly the same, inside and out, down to the color of the kitchen tiles—were not for aesthetic unity but to lower costs. The builder had even cut corners with the cement by mixing in sand, and rumors circulated that he'd also bribed city officials for permits. The builder evaded capture, causing the women to lament their men's inability to catch this one man. But the men understood they were up against multiple individuals, not just one person.

Her father held a board over the hole, unleashing a torrent of curses against the builder while nailing it in place. The nails he hammered along the edge of the board pierced the floor and protruded through the ceiling below. After a while, maybe he felt he had vented enough, for he stopped trying to track down the builder. The builder's name would resurface with each new problem, but in time, the residents' complaints stopped, too, as if they had all made a pact to forget.

The sisters, being young and slight, continued to scamper upstairs, but their father never again spoke of putting a piano in their room. The girls were haunted by nightmares of the house collapsing. In their dreams, the second floor gave way, and they plunged into the master bedroom where their parents slept. Despite the second floor being less than two meters above the first, they dreamt of falling endlessly into a dark chasm. Their screams echoing, trapped, like cries within a well. Sometimes they imagined themselves pinned beneath a collapsed roof, as wooden planks and beams crashed down around them. Mice droppings and scurrying rodents rained on their faces, and as they struggled to stand, roof tiles cascaded down. While the girls had these nightmares, they shot up in height and experienced their first menstruation. Though unbidden, they walked on their toes, heels raised, as if affected with equinus.

"Remember, we've got the upper hand here," muttered her mother, as she stood holding the ladder. The lightbulbs, untouched for over a decade, were sticky with dust. They kept sticking to her hands. All five bulbs hadn't burnt out at once; one had gone out, then another, until the last one gave out, probably about two or three years after the woman got married, according to her mother. After stumbling into the dark living room late one night, her mother had bumped her shin against a corner of the table. She'd also broken a vase while feeling around on top of the display cabinet. Unable to reach the chandelier, she thought a step ladder would be handy, and happened to find a discarded one on the street. That had been the beginning. From that day onward, her mother began to bring home the things that people threw out. She'd even purchased lightbulbs at the hardware store and set up the ladder under the chandelier, but lacked the courage to lug her heavy body onto the ladder. She'd nervously raise her foot to the rung, only to lower it back down. One day, while roaming the neighborhood, she wondered if anyone was discarding a tall man and laughed at her own joke. As time passed, she decided to stop thinking about the living room. It was her way of coping. She put the second floor out of her mind as well, remembering it only once or twice a year, if one of her daughters or relatives happened to visit. Her world became confined to just the master bedroom and kitchen.

Beside the chandelier was the mark left from when her father's foot had gone through the ceiling. Every time she saw that patched-up hole, she recalled his youthful face. One summer day during a downpour, a driver failed to notice her father crossing the street. All he could offer was that he hadn't seen her father, who'd been completely drenched. After that, the woman saw a man who resembled her father in the middle of Myeongdong and followed him for more than a block. She even saw him standing on the bus home, gripping the handle. In three years, she would be the age her father was when he died.

The man who'd snatched up the remaining houses on the street planned to open a large barbeque restaurant. He had eyed the woman's house as well, but her mother was not easily persuaded. "No way. Does he think I'm stupid? I'd never sell for that lousy amount!" She'd learned from her husband's death that life doesn't always go according to plan, yet she remained defiant, vowing to hold out for a better offer. Their mother had no money for repairs, the sisters lived far away, and the house was too big. She would have to find a buyer before the demolition crew left. During her ten years of marriage, the woman had also believed she held the upper hand. When she screwed the new bulb into the socket, light filled the room. Her shadow sprawled across the living room floor. She arched her back, like a cat alarmed by its own shadow.

The local bus departed from the bus stop in front of the subway station, weaved through all the side streets in the neighborhood, and then returned to the first stop. The woman like this route. Even if someone unfamiliar with the area missed their stop, they could avoid the hassle of changing buses, for if they waited a little longer, the bus would pass by the same spot again. The only drawback was that, after having been away for ten years, everything had changed, and she couldn't get her bearings. High-rise apartment complexes filled the neighborhood, leaving her to wonder where these large vacant lots had been in the first place. Every time the bus stopped in front of a new building, she strained to recall what had been there before. She couldn't remember. Whenever she found buildings that remained unchanged, she couldn't help giving a little cheer. The cram school she'd attended for three months when she'd studied to retake the college entrance exam was the same, though everything around it had changed so much that the school seemed to have relocated to this spot. The bus stopped so frequently it couldn't build any speed. There were designated stops, but if a passenger called out to the driver, the driver let them off.

She didn't mind the sunlight shining through the bus window. In this rainy region, the park bustled with people trying to enjoy the sunshine whenever the sun came out. They took off their jackets and tanned their skin without a second thought. Sitting in the sun, she became drowsy. A month had passed, but she was still jetlagged. She thought she'd dozed off for just a second, but the student standing next to her tapped her shoulder. When she looked up at the girl, she gestured toward the bus driver with her chin.

"Excuse me, Ma'am!"

She looked around, and again a voice came from the driver's seat, "Yes, you! The lady looking around right now."

The female students on the bus burst into laughter, and every gaze swept toward her. The driver's eyes reflected in the large rearview mirror were staring at her. But from where she was sitting, all she could see was the back of his head. "Aren't you going to get off?" he scolded. Only then did she look out the window. The bus was passing the demolition area.

An excavator, positioned askew on a pile of rubble, began to move. Each time it shoveled up waste, a cloud of gray dust rose into the air. While the monotonous task of scooping trash and dumping it into the truck's bin continued, a young man dragged a long hose and sprayed water over the dust. Wherever the water hit, the dust settled, and the smell of damp plaster wafted through the air.

The heavy downpour washed away the yard. All night in her sleep, she heard feet stomping on the roof tiles, shattering them. When she woke in the morning, the floor was soaked with water that had seeped through the ceiling boards. Her mother's urgent voice rang out from the yard.

The clay pots that had bordered the yard were broken, the pieces mixed with the red dirt. Her mother went to the lot next door and lay down in front of the excavator. The driver climbed down and stuck a cigarette in his mouth. "What the hell? I don't think this old lady gets it."

"That's right! I don't get it!" her mother shouted. "And why can't you understand you need to stop this minute? You ruined my property!"

While the driver kicked at the ground, another worker tried to reason with her. "Lady, think of it this way. If you've got a box filled with dirt and you dig some out, the box doesn't just vanish, does it?"

"You kidding me? You think the ground's like a box? It's made up of the dirt you're digging!"

The worker turned and spat. The delays caused by the old woman were frustrating to the laborers with quotas to meet. Her thinking had become very simple since her husband's death. Once she believed she was right, there was no convincing her otherwise. Spotting a tall man in a beige jacket walking by, she called him over, as if she knew him. "Oh, good. Come here for a sec." He looked at the heap of dirt she pointed to, then down at her. His eyes darted to the excavator driver's face before returning to hers. Believing she'd found an ally, her voice grew louder and she began to cry. All the woman could see was the back of his head, with its neat haircut. After a few words from him, her mother stood up from in front of the excavator.

When the man introduced himself as S, she remembered his father's face. Like a mnemonic device, a nameplate bearing the name of S's father flashed across her mind. Years ago, the children on that street would memorize the nameplates of every house, reciting them as if they were their friends' names. There were twenty fathers on that street, all living in nearly identical houses, with the same number of rooms, the same location of the bathroom, and the same door-knockers. These men were of the same generation, bound together by an understanding that, at their age, they should have a mortgage and house of a certain size. Apart from a civil servant, elementary school teacher, seafood merchant, locksmith, and one whose job was unknown, the rest were factory workers. They worked hard, but as if there were an unspoken rule that their house was both the starting point and final destination of their lives, no one ever left that street unless they died.

The man whose job was a mystery—if she remembered correctly—was S's father. A couple of times a week, S's father stepped out of the house wearing a suit, only to return at night, drunk, pounding on someone else's front gate. If no one answered, he would kick it and curse. Normally, he was a quiet, timid man, who hardly looked anyone in the face.

Once, S's father opened the unlocked door of her mother's house and stumbled into the master bedroom. When he lifted the blanket and climbed into bed next to her sleeping parents, her mother woke in terror. That night, young S came to take his father home. Up until then, he had been shorter than the woman. S's father, still drunk, smacked his son for disturbing his sleep. A red handprint appeared on his pale neck and the back of his shaven head. S, his cheeks flushed with embarrassment, said nothing, slung his father's arm over his narrow shoulders, and staggered out.

Her mother pushed a cup of ginger tea toward S and asked him again if what he'd told her earlier was true.

"Like I said," S said, reaching for the tea, "there's something called a cadastral map. It's all there."

"How do you know this?" she blurted without thinking. This had been H's habit, needing confirmation before believing anything.

S glanced at her. "Because we've gone through this already. If there was no such thing as a cadastral, anyone could draw a line with his foot and say the land's theirs."

He added that the buyer was offering a reasonable price and that selling might be wise. Her mother agreed with a meek nod. Though it wasn't the season for ginger tea, S drank every last drop before getting to his feet. He was now much taller than her, the top of her head barely reaching his shoulders.

S had returned home as well, taking a job as the driver of a local bus that shuttled between the subway station and nearby apartment complexes. One day she was returning from the city after meeting a friend and pressed the buzzer to get off at the next stop. To her surprise, the driver sailed past it, causing a stir among the passengers. He spoke loudly, without looking back. "Excuse me, Ma'am. Why don't you come sit right up here?" That's when she realized the driver was S.

S said he had happened to glance at her house during his route one day. The kitchen door had opened right then, and she had stepped into the yard to toss out a basin of steaming water. That was how he'd discovered she had returned to town. Once, her sister had run into S in a park in Europe. After spending half the day with him, her sister had described him as quiet. Now, he'd come home and had been driving a bus for nearly five months, after seeing a recruitment ad for drivers on a bus window. He often looked toward her house from the bus stop but hadn't seen her again until he'd looked in the rearview mirror and discovered her dozing on his bus. Concerned she'd miss her stop, he'd woken her by calling out to her.

Dozens of times a day, S's route took him past spots that had shaped his life. A left-turn sign marked where his house once stood. His parents had moved to the country after their house was demolished. When she asked if he was originally from Seoul, he laughed, explaining that no one from their street was. Back then, Seoul had been crowded with job seekers from all over the country. S was born in a small town near the Nakdong River, where he'd lived until the age of four. There, after the dam was built, fog would roll in knee-high.

As passengers climbed on and off, S pointed out landmarks, like the large shopping mall that had replaced the wedding hall. She remembered the hall's ridiculous exterior with its strange dome that resembled a mosque, and its list of names as it changed hands repeatedly. S had married a college classmate there. "They tried to make the place look elegant, but it ended up being a total mishmash of gothic-style décor."

She noticed he had dropped formalities at some point, but she didn't mind.

S's wedding had been in January, a year after hers. Due to the heavy snow, the bus transporting the bride's guests and family didn't arrive on time. Luckily, it was the off-season and there were no other weddings scheduled that day. The bride, who'd been waiting anxiously in the bridal room, went in and out of the wedding hall, and the bottom of her dress became stained with wet snow. When her guests finally arrived, there was a bustle as the groom's guests, who had gone to eat, were summoned back for the ceremony. Eleven years later, also in January, S separated from his wife. The timing struck the woman as unusual—both the January wedding and the January divorce.

At the subway station, another driver took the wheel from S, though it didn't seem like S's shift was over. S explained that he'd seen her earlier in the day and had asked his colleague for a favor. He took her to a food stall with a red tarp, where the owner was busy preparing for the evening. Apologetically, the owner said nothing was ready yet, but brought over some sliced cucumber as an appetizer, which S ate as he gulped down soju.

She and her sisters had left home one by one around the time the second-story floor began to creak under their weight. The woman had married rather suddenly, drawing caution from a relative who had come to Seoul for the wedding. Her mother silenced the criticism, declaring that if people were too careful, they would never marry at all. Everyone kept their mouths shut after that, as if they agreed. But they'd been right. H hated the way she walked on the balls of her feet, her heels raised. He said it scared him, how she would silently draw near and stand behind him like a ghost. Even when he was alone, he kept turning around to check that she wasn't behind him. Although H's house and store were built of solid wood, she never managed to correct her habit of walking on her toes. Despite walking carefully, as if she were treading on thin ice, her marriage lasted only ten years. She and S finally rose to their feet after draining three bottles of soju. The stall was now packed with tipsy customers.

The ruins of houses were bathed in moonlight. There were no security lights, but the passing cars provided enough light to see. S reached for her hand, which was rigidly by her side, and held it tightly as they walked toward her house. His hand was hot and damp. She saw her house at the end of the street. As if her mother had fallen asleep with the television on again, a faint light flickered from the master bedroom window. She could feel his pulse. She tripped on a pile of lumber, but S's firm hand caught her by the shoulder.

S pulled her into an empty house. From the outside, the frame had seemed intact, but once she stepped through the doorway, she saw the wall ahead was missing. The ruins of other demolished houses spread before her. In the flickering light of passing cars, his face appeared and vanished, twisted in a strange way. She suddenly saw his face as a boy's, with the schoolboy buzz cut. "Oh, it's you," she said, touching his cheek. They had ridden the same bus to school. She remembered seeing him standing inside a crowded bus just as it was about to pull away. As people were pushed toward the back, S stumbled, and his face became crushed against the bus window. Clutched in his hand was a small English vocabulary booklet. The more he struggled to free himself, the more his nose was squashed, and his cheek and left eye became distorted. She saw tears in his eyes as his face remained pressed against the glass.

Now his tense face made him look as if his face were pressed against the bus window again. She couldn't help but laugh. S's hand, which had been moving toward her chest, suddenly stopped. Oddly enough, though she could clearly see him as a boy, she had no recollection of him as an adult. S's face drew closer. She tasted soju, cucumber, and red chili pepper paste on his tongue—a mix of sweet and bitter, mingled with the unique flavor of his saliva. Once, they had been too embarrassed to look each other in the eye. She realized this was only the second time they were meeting alone. Doubts crept in, making her wonder if he might think less of her, but she squeezed her eyes shut.

Later, like her mother, she squatted over the kitchen drain to urinate. The forceful, hot stream splashed onto her slippered feet and dampened her groin. In the morning, she woke to find her entire back covered in bruises.

She admired his ex-wife's taste. There were items she had left behind in his officetel. S said the sky-blue bed sheets and pillowcases were a purchase from a trip to Europe. The woman also liked the large plates gilded with brown leaves. When she stayed over, she often used the pillow his ex-wife had once used, a pillow stained with the previous woman's saliva. The ex-wife had left behind many things she'd painstakingly picked out, taking only a white puppy named Milk. She'd packed carelessly, taking some of his remote controls and accessories by mistake, rendering his devices useless.

When she agreed to accompany S to his hometown, the woman sensed that her world was expanding. She'd never imagined she would visit this place near the Nakdong River known for its apple orchards. When she left the house, wheeling her luggage behind her, her mother didn't say a word. Even though she had her issues, she knew when to turn a blind eye.

As soon as the woman stepped into S's officetel, a white puppy barked loudly at her. By the window stood a woman with her back turned. She knew right away that it was the ex-wife.

The front gate was open, but she didn't see her mother or her shopping cart. An international letter was sitting in the broken mailbox. H's face flashed across her mind, but it soon disappeared. He would have sent an email if he'd needed to get a hold of her. Thinking it was one of her sisters, she pulled the letter out of the mailbox, but it was the one she'd mailed to her mother a few months earlier. The envelope bore a stamp indicating it had been returned to the post office due to an unconfirmed address. She sat in the second-story living room and tore open the envelope. The two pages inside had gotten wet and then dried, causing them to stick together. The ink had bled, and she could barely make out the writing. The two pages summed up her ten years of marriage, but when she strained to remember that time, nothing came to mind. All she could recall was ten years ago, a time before she got married, when her bottom had been firm and perky, like a monkey's tail.

The woman lay down, staring up at the ceiling. S had rushed out into the hallway without putting on his shoes and grabbed her wrist. He explained his ex-wife had stopped by simply to return the remote control for the air conditioner. Something like powder drifted onto the woman's face. Dust drifted slowly in the air, like dandelion spores in the breeze.

S and his ex-wife would continue to meet. She would come to his officetel to deliver missing items, and on some days, he would go to her place. Otherwise, the two had too many things that would become useless. The dust wasn't coming from the construction site. It seemed the house itself was turning to dust. Just as the shoreline gradually recedes because people carry the sand away on their feet, the house might, over time, erode away to nothing.

Her shoulder blades ached. As she turned to lie on her side, part of the ceiling came crashing down, narrowly missing her nose. Before she could fully grasp what would have happened if she had remained on her back, the walls began to tilt. The wooden planks that had been attached to the ceiling clattered down, signaling the house's final surrender. The moment she attempted to sit up, the opposite wall caved in and collapsed on her. The floor, unable to bear the weight, broke apart, and she plummeted down to the first floor. What she saw last were the clocks, each displaying a different time. Her vision faded to black, and in the distant darkness, she heard roof tiles shatter as they hit the ground.

When she regained consciousness, she found herself still trapped beneath the rubble. Above her, footsteps moved briskly across the ruins. Something had struck her eye, and though she tried to open both eyes, one kept closing. She recalled the blonde doll she had seen on a heap of rubble the day she returned home. The heavy bucket of the forklift, meant for the neighbor's roof, had instead veered off and knocked down their fence, causing a shift in the foundation of their house. Over time, this misalignment put increasing strain on the foundation. The recent heavy rainfall had battered their yard, worsening the issue. Had the contractor not performed such shoddy construction thirty years ago, the house might have withstood the added pressure. She thought about the doors that refused to stay shut and the windows set at incorrect angles. The sloping ceiling should have been a clear warning sign.

Her mother believed she had accompanied S to his hometown. Perhaps S had waited for her, then ended up going alone. Since the house was scheduled for demolition soon, there wouldn't be a rush to clear the rubble. If S hadn't left, if he had decided not to go because she didn't show, he would drive the bus by this place at 5:40 in the morning. She tried to move her legs, but they were pinned down by something heavy, and she couldn't budge.

She passed out again. Thirty years ago, she and her sisters had stood at the front gate, gazing up at the roof of their new home. Before that, they had been forced to sleep in the cramped space under the television set, as there was no other space to stretch out. They gaped in awe at the two-story house, which looked like a house made of cookies, as if it had sprung straight out of a fairy tale. Craning her neck to see the top, the second sister shouted, "Look at the red roof! There's a chimney! Finally, Santa Claus can come to our house!" Their young mother wept, moved by the sight of the varnished wooden stairs and the grand chandelier that required five lightbulbs.

The girls scrambled up to the second floor, which had two small rooms, a living room, and a staircase leading directly down to the yard, allowing the entire floor to be rented out. The floor, stylish and modern like the one downstairs, featured veneer floorboards that accentuated the woodgrain. Under the clear varnish, the grain flowed like a stream. Their mother, who'd followed them upstairs, set her foot on the floor.

"Oh my, ten people could easily lie down here."

Having experienced war at the age of nine and been forced to flee to a new land, her mother had a habit of assessing a room by estimating how many people could sleep there. As she moved to the center of the living room, the floorboards creaked under her weight, like the crunching of flaky cookies. Her mother walked gingerly, as if on thin ice. Crunch, crunch, crunch. The sisters giggled. Their mother carefully tested every inch of the living room, searching for the spot where the creaking was loudest.

"This house is like a cookie house!" her second sister cried. "As if the floor's made of wafers! Listen, it sounds like you're biting into a wafer cookie."

The girls moved around on tiptoe, shouting in unison, "Be careful!"

up the veranda to shout at Uncle [illegible]. They [illegible]
[illegible] and [illegible] come [illegible]. They [illegible]
more [illegible] and the [illegible]
ladder [illegible] the [illegible].

The [illegible] up to the second floor, which had [illegible]
[illegible] leading directly down to the yard,
allowing the [illegible] the [illegible] and [illegible]
[illegible] downstairs [illegible]
[illegible] than [illegible]
Her mother, who [illegible] four on the floor.
"[illegible] people [illegible] down [illegible]."

[illegible] and [illegible]
[illegible] and her mother had a habit of [illegible]
[illegible] people could [illegible] the [illegible]
of the [illegible] room, the [illegible]
[illegible]. Her mother [illegible]
[illegible]. The sister [illegible]. Their mother [illegible]
[illegible] for the [illegible]
the [illegible].

"This house [illegible]," her second [illegible]. As
[illegible] sound [illegible] into a
[illegible].

"[illegible] in [illegible]," [illegible].

That's Life

A short, middle-aged woman with dark, tattooed eyebrows is standing in a studio. She should have memorized her lines by now, since she must have repeated them a dozen times, but she seems tongue-tied in front of the camera. She gulps, as if swallowing a peach pit, and finally begins to speak. The camera zooms in on a piece of paper she's holding. Like the other guests, she has drawn her own house in the center of the page and filled out the surroundings. As a result, the two-bedroom bungalow is taller than the hill behind the house and bigger than the church. She has even sketched a well from which she drew water countless times as a seven-year-old. In winter, her frostbitten hands had cracked and bled. As though she doesn't want to remember that time, she's made the well very small. She's also included an aspen tree whose thorns had stabbed her when she'd been carrying the bucket. The spearlike tip of a branch had penetrated deep into her thigh, and her mother had rubbed soybean paste on the wound. The salt from the sauce had seeped into the wound and burned. Though the wound healed, she says a scar resembling a bellybutton remains on her thigh. The memory of her younger sister teasing, "Sehee has two bellybuttons—one on her belly and one on her thigh," is still vivid in her mind. As she grew taller and bigger, the scar moved up toward her belly, a mark she knew her family would remember. The map looks like childish scribbles, as if drawn by the young girl she'd been when she left home years ago. Though her former home has crossed her mind numerous times, she'd never attempted to sketch it before. The name of that place has vanished from modern maps, gradually replaced by new names with Chinese characters. Now, these old names exist only in the conversations of the elderly.

He's a fan of the show *I Miss You*. He sits with his eyes fixed on the television screen, hands tucked between his legs and a blanket wrapped around him. The temperature plummeted overnight. The woman licks her lips a couple of times, as if her mouth is dry. The guests on the show have similar circumstances: poverty, a wandering father, the sudden death of a mother or perhaps a stepmother. Maybe because their stories are similar, the guests look somewhat alike.

The woman is in search of her father, brother, and three younger sisters. She vaguely recalls the name of the village, but has forgotten her father's name. The screen flickers and lines begin to crisscross. Even the sounds meld and hum, and a blurry silhouette wavers, paining his eyes. It seems he might miss the climax of the show—the emotional reunion of long-lost family members. The TV station deliberately stages the first meeting in the studio for dramatic effect. As if sharing people's personal details aren't enough, broadcasting their faces covered with snot and tears is deemed necessary. General Tom Thumb calls it a commercial tactic. He cites a village with a psychiatric hospital as an example, saying that when the villagers saw the isolation ward at the hospital, they felt their own problems were small, which made them have a more optimistic outlook on life. This isn't true at all. However, even General Tom can't deny the power of television. They were on air for only ten minutes, but those who saw the segment flocked to the circus. "It's General Tom Thumb!" the children cried when they spotted him. On holidays, the show sold out and additional showtimes were added, and they received bonuses on top of their regular pay. Still, General Tom grumbled, even while collecting so many tickets that his arms ached. He complains that appearing on a TV segment like "Life Like a Tumbleweed" only reinforces stereotypes about acrobats, and constantly spews stories he has collected over the years. No one in the Royal Family can outtalk him. But the man, his roommate, knows the truth. He knows that General Tom learned his Korean history through a TV documentary called *Our History Special* and that his knowledge about table setting came from a cooking show. In fact, a careful examination would reveal that his grandiose "view of history" has been lifted directly from commentators on various programs. To General Tom, the television was both his mother and father.

The girls are probably in the next container, blow-drying their hair and ironing their clothes. Living in shipping containers, they rely on electric blankets and portable heaters for warmth. More than half of the twelve containers house families and are each equipped with a refrigerator and television. Families with older children even have computers. This morning, the shuffle of the girls' slippers woke him. The girls start their day by going to the bathhouse. Once they return, they put on their makeup, style their hair, and iron their clothes. When the generator is overloaded, the television is the first to be affected. The clothes worn by the people on-screen blend together, forming a rainbow.

After thirty-seven years, the woman is reunited with her older brother. The dull-witted brother keeps using the honorific with his younger sister, while she treats him like a salesman who has come to her door. Neither sees the youthful face they remember in each other. Ultimately, the host steps in, blaming time for tearing the family apart. At this stage of the reunion, guests usually fall into one of two categories. Both sides work to piece together their memories like a jigsaw puzzle, and when a crucial memory clicks into place, they burst into tears belatedly. They hug each other and roll on the studio floor, gasping and looking as though they might faint. But if their memories don't match up, they move to another spot and search for clues until the end of the show. If all else fails, a genetic test serves as the final step.

The man keeps his baby picture in his wallet, not because he anticipates a reunion like this. Still, he feels lucky to have it. Sometimes, while riding the subway over the Han River bridge, he imagines worst-case scenarios. If the train crashes into the water, I need to hold my pocket closed to keep the picture safe. Then how would I swim to the surface? Should I learn to swim with just one arm? Once, when one of the container homes went up in flames due to an electrical fault, he wondered where else he could safely store the photo. But General Tom has no such worries. He stopped growing at the age of seven, and it was then that his mother left him at a zoo. The seven-year-old Tom found himself standing in front of the elephant cage until closing time. Training elephants later became one of his many jobs at the circus. He said it was no accident he let go of his mother's hand in front of the elephant cage rather than anywhere else. He claimed he could have found his way home if he really wanted to, yet never explained why he didn't try.

Water drips down the Styrofoam wall, evidence of a big temperature difference inside and outside the container. Overnight, the trickle soaked General Tom's cherished poster of a starlet. If he saw it, he'd curse and rage, but right now he sleeps wrapped in a blanket, smacking his dark lips as if sucking on sugar water. Though his real name is

Dongcheol, the circus family calls him General Tom. Or just Thumb, if they're in a hurry. Surprisingly, he puts up with it, saying curtly, "It's not like Dongcheol's my real name anyway." Everyone in the Royal Family uses stage names, either borrowing names of celebrities or cartoon characters, or adding their last names to their acts. Some members even change their last names altogether, like their ringmaster. Once, when the man confessed he wanted to go by the name Greyhound, General Tom looked at him sullenly and said, "Like the buses with toilets in the back?"

The television is working again, but *I Miss You* has ended. Shoes drag past their container. It seems the girls from the Chinese troupe are also going out. The circus was once home to over three hundred members, with many young people running away from home to learn acrobatics. The ringmaster had been one of them. But by the time the man joined, the troupe had dwindled to fifteen, consisting of retired acrobats, the ringmaster, the assistant ringmaster, a family of monkeys, and an elephant. The ringmaster informed him that two aerial acrobats had left without notice just that morning. Sometimes people came specifically to watch aerial acrobatics. "Wouldn't it be nice if you could fly?" the ringmaster mused with a humorless laugh. A young tightrope walker, returning after a year and a half away, dyed the members' hair red and blue, showcasing new hairstyling techniques she'd learned. Across the country, circus troupes were barely surviving, and many had disbanded. As a result, a few new members joined the Royal Family. One of them had been General Tom.

Starting around two years ago, a Chinese acrobatic troupe has made up forty percent of the Royal Family. Girls in their early to mid-teens left home to earn money, performing tricks using everyday objects like bowls and clay jars to demonstrate their physical flexibility. They deliberately chose to stay in the containers farthest from the ringmaster's, but he already seems to know what they're up to. The girls roam shopping malls or nightclubs until late at night. The ringmaster knows precisely when to tighten or loosen his grip on the members. Though he turns a blind eye for now, once the circus opens its doors, no one would be able to slack off. The girls' laughter grows distant. General Tom returned to the container at dawn, having stayed in the animal tent until then. Because of the sudden temperature drop, they had added two oil stoves, on top of the three heaters. Usually, he's the first to complain about the noise the girls make, but now he's asleep, sucking his lips.

The electric heating pad is scorched black on the side with the coils. The man's backside is hot, while his nose is cold. When he opened his eyes, he found himself hugging General Tom. On a day like this, it's okay for them to sleep in. The truck, which had left after the trailers carrying the shipping containers, is stuck in Gangwon Province due to heavy snowfall. The roads are frozen. Even if the truck arrives on time, driving the support pillars into the frozen ground would be impossible. They would have to wait anyway, at least until the ground thaws. This is why the ringmaster isn't overly concerned by the delay. He had remained calm and collected even when a typhoon swept through the circus tent. It seems the ringmaster is responsible for their "Life Like a Tumbleweed" label, which the young acrobats hate so much. According to the weather forecast, the temperature will rise in three days. By then, the ground should thaw, and the truck carrying the tent materials would have arrived.

Winter is a slow season for the circus. If they put on a show on weekdays, only around ten people attend, barely enough to cover the cost of oil for the heaters scattered around the tent. Even with few attendees, they must perform if there is an audience. The applause hardly reaches the stage, but the ringmaster expects nothing less than their best. It's one of the reasons the Royal Family circus has survived while other troupes are fast disappearing. The ringmaster is stubborn and holds extremely high standards, but he did reduce the number of performances in the off-season.

Finding a venue is becoming increasingly tricky. Pitching a tent requires at least 10,000 square feet of empty space. Plus, there are twelve shipping-container homes for the members. Though each is only about 70 square feet, they take up considerable space, since they cannot be stacked vertically on top of each other. Locations bustling with people are ideal. If they're near subway stations or terminals, even better. They used to tour only satellite cities where there were plenty of vacant lots due to redevelopment. Now, apartment construction is on the decline. When they do manage to find an empty lot and set up their tent, residents from nearby apartment complexes complain about the loud music blaring all day.

The girls are excited about the delays, claiming they're sick of the circus. Jina, a trapeze artist, has calluses on her hands. Despite a safety net, she says that when she's sitting on a swing fifteen meters in the air, her palms sweat as if it's her first time. Hanging upside down, with all eyes on her, she doubts whether she can perform the trick, though she's done it countless times. Even after doing a somersault in the air and successfully catching the second bar, her heart keeps racing, and it's only much later that she can hear the applause. Jina got measles once. She tried to find a job that would keep her on the ground, but returned to the circus before a year was up. She resumed her repertoire, but said she was tired of the circus. Jina is going out, all dolled up. In her broken Chinese, which she'd picked up in a short amount of time, she shouts toward the container where the Chinese girls are staying. She knows better than to tell them to hand out half-price vouchers on their way to the shopping mall.

It's the men's job to distribute vouchers in the city. General Tom hates being described as a tumbleweed, but it's probably because it strikes a nerve. The Royal Family moves from city to city, staying in each city for about a month. This time, luckily, they were able to find a vacant lot, but next year, this lot won't be available. There are fewer and fewer spaces to pitch tents. The ringmaster's dream is to have a permanent venue. However, if the Royal Family finds a permanent location, the man will have to leave the troupe.

The photograph is slowly fading. The color of the T-shirt he was wearing that day has completely faded. In the picture, a boy and a tall, burly man with a monkey perched on his left shoulder are standing together. The boy with a bowl cut looks about eight years old. He's scared of the man next to him. In fact, he hates him. However, since such emotions are too much for an eight-year-old to contain, his face is crumpled like a sheet of paper.

The man has a large, thick hand on the boy's scrawny shoulder. The boy can feel the strength in the grip. The act isn't a sign of affection, but silent pressure. In winter, the man would exercise in the middle of the inn courtyard, wearing only a tank top. On some days, he would stick his head under the water pump and let the freezing water soak his head. His dark, yellowish teeth were chipped and uneven, some broken in half. They'd fallen out or gotten damaged as he learned to chew metal nails. He usually kept his mouth closed, but when he drank, he would show his teeth and laugh. There were many days when he hardly brought in any money. Then they would sleep in his truck. He took his daily wages to the bar and stayed for days. Sometimes people would come to the truck to collect overdue room and board, asking the boy, "Hey, where's your dad?"

"He isn't my dad!" he'd snap.

Then they would rap him on the head and pinch his cheeks. "Did you fall out of the sky then? Or sprout from the ground?"

"He's not my dad!" he would shout, clenching his fists. "He's not my dad!"

What he said was true. The strongman wasn't the boy's father.

This city is neat and flat, like a model city inside a glass box. They say the area used to be a peach orchard. The only remaining evidence of this is the name of the large hall in front of the subway station. Countless peach trees were uprooted, and apartment complexes took their place. According to the strongman, the woman had come from a place where many peaches grew. What happened to all those peach trees? The man scans his surroundings.

"Hey, Book of John, maybe you should have become a mailman."

General Tom is sitting on the rear rack of the man's bicycle. His short legs dangle halfway down the wheels, and on his feet are children's shoes adorned with cartoon characters. He faces backward, as if he's riding Tinkerbell, the circus elephant. During performances when he falls off the elephant while attempting to climb on, the audience erupts in laughter. His face collides with the elephant, and he is flung from the stage, landing headfirst. While the elephant stands calmly in the center of the stage, he paces back and forth, devising ways to climb on. He drags a trampoline over, jumps, and tries to land on the elephant's back, but fails when the elephant steps aside. Some audience members laugh so hard they cry. Finally, he manages to mount the elephant, but ends up facing the wrong way. Oblivious, the elephant trots around the ring, causing General Tom to slide off, clutching its tail, as he's dragged here and there. "Tinkerbell and General Tom Thumb" is one the Royal Family's most popular acts.

On the bicycle, General Tom sits backward on the rack, back-to-back with the man. He claims it's for a better view, but the man knows it's to avoid the wind. Although he's wearing gloves, the man's hands are raw from the cold. The howling wind sounds like the whining of a saw, piercing his eyes, even through his hat and mask. The sight of the man with dwarfism sitting backward on the bicycle draws attention.

Not many people know an area as thoroughly as a mail carrier, but a mail carrier can't travel across the country as quickly as a circus performer. The man's book of maps, worn at the corners, is marked with red circles indicating where the Royal Family has pitched their tent. During their month-long stays in those towns, the man explored on his bicycle. If he learned that peaches used to grow in an area, he would go there. There were many empty houses. Whenever he saw thick planks nailed over the front door, his heart sank.

"Hey, Book of John, you're better off in the circus," General Tom says, about to recount a story he's heard. "These days, people don't even put nameplates on their doors. They don't want to give away their personal information. Just look at this forest of apartment buildings. If you can't find your folks, let them find you."

He had joined the Royal Family on his own. It's already been eight years. He vaguely remembers going to the circus as a boy, holding his mother's hand. Her pink hanbok rustled with each step she took. Most of the audience members are elderly. His parents could be among them. He pedals furiously, ringing his bell even though there are no pedestrians. The circus tent hasn't arrived yet, and the ground hasn't thawed, but the rent for the vacant lot continues to accrue. The half-price tickets declare "100% Satisfaction or Money·Back Guarantee!" in large, red letters. Though the tent is not up, the show has already begun. People rarely come without discount vouchers, so distributing as many as they can is crucial. The man and his partner, General Tom, work hard at this task.

The area used to be a peach orchard, but not a single tree remains. The man has drawn his old house countless times. It had been at the end of a narrow, dead-end street lined with identical houses. Each house had painted gates with two lion-shaped doorknockers. He even remembers his blue front gate and the door chime that sounded like the chirping of a bird. Drunk men would often stumble into his street at night, banging their heads against his gate. One of his jobs in the circus is to collect tickets. One glance at a face per ticket. His line was always a little longer.

He notes all the facilities in the city: a department store, a discount mart, a shopping mall with a theater and nightclub, a swimming pool named after a famous swimmer, eleven small parks, one large park, and a driving school. He has seen them while cycling around the city, a task made easier thanks to the extensive network of bicycle paths. He didn't see any alleys or side streets. The old narrow streets, just like peach trees, have vanished. General Tom reads aloud the signs on buildings and streets, observing the slowly receding landscape. "We price match!" "A summer vacation in the middle of winter." "Parents are liable for children's safety in water." Then, as if recalling something, he asks, "Hey, Book of John, you remember what those bastards looked like?" On their way back, they ride over the discount vouchers littering the street.

Although General Tom calls him Book of John, he's known as the Man with Ten Hands. The one who taught him to juggle is the burly man in the photo with the monkey. He would take the monkey and the boy to country fairs in his small truck. Finding a suitable spot, he'd draw a circle in the dirt with his shoe, creating their stage for the day. As soon as he put the monkey in a red dress and let it go, the children would come running. When the adults arrived, he'd chew metal nails and bend rebar with his neck. The monkey jumped and cackled amid the applause. As the show progressed, he started selling his medicine, which he kept in the back of his truck. The black liquid in small glass bottles was touted as a cure-all, to be ingested or applied to wounds. The boy put the bottles in a small plastic basket, distributed them to customers who raised their hands, and collected their money.

For the final act, the man boasted he would perform an incredible feat. He removed his shirt and tossed it aside, revealing a belly that sagged over his belt and bellybutton. Scars and pink keloids, resembling insects from afar, marred his stomach and shoulders. Young women recoiled in disgust, but the man grinned and thrust his belly at them.

"In a little while, that truck is going to run over my belly! Not a whale's belly, but this belly right here!"

Once his spiel was over, a young man who had suddenly appeared climbed into the truck and started the engine. The strongman placed a wooden board over his stomach and lay down before the front wheels. On the board were distinct, black tire marks, suggesting the truck had gone over it before. As the truck lurched forward, someone in the crowd screamed. Hands shot up here and there. The boy scurried around, distributing tonic bottles, but the truck never rolled over the man's belly. He repeatedly got up and lay down in front of the truck until the impatient crowd grew tired and eventually dispersed. Once everyone had left, the man paid the young driver a few coins.

If they managed to secure a room at the inn, the man would spend days drinking. He'd tie the boy's arm to his own with a rope while sleeping, preventing the boy from lying comfortably. The man's breath smelled of garlic, and his armpits reeked of sweat. The man always slept shirtless, and dozens of insects appeared to be squirming on his skin, making the boy scared they would crawl onto him. Curled up next to the snoring man, the boy longed to grow up quickly, to become as big as the man.

"You little shit, you don't know how lucky you are," the man had said while teaching him to juggle. A box of medicine bottles sat at the man's feet. "You see these scars? I had to start with knives." The man pulled out a bottle. "Listen up, I hate repeating myself. You're going to juggle these. But since you're just starting out, I'll give you two. One smack for every one you drop, got it?"

Bottles fell and shattered at the boy's feet, the dark liquid splattering his legs up to his knees. Since he had to stand before the crowd, the man hit him only in areas covered by clothing, like his thighs and back, leaving marks resembling insect trails. Before scabs could fall off on their own, wounds reopened and bled afresh. At night, he fell asleep, tied to the man's hand. Moans escaped his mouth whenever his flesh touched the floor. The blood made his clothes stick to his skin, so that every time he changed, wounds reopened. Exhausted from training and peddling medicine, he had trouble sleeping.

When people raised their hands, he approached them, juggling the medicine bottles to their applause. The man, sitting on the medicine box and wiping sweat from his face, threw knives at the boy. The boy caught them and juggled five knives, earning more applause. Now the man took over selling the medicine, but people often watched the show and left without buying anything. When it was time for the man to lie down in front of the truck, the boy sat behind the wheel. As he started the truck and jerked toward the man, screams erupted. Suddenly, the truck door opened and hands dragged the boy out. It was a young, rough-looking man, who reeked of alcohol. "Who else has seen this stunt before?" he shouted. "This is a scam! He's a con-artist! They were here last year and all he did was lie down and get up!"

The strongman leapt up from in front of the truck, thrusting his sagging belly at the intruder. "A scam? Don't you see this board? When I give the signal, the truck will drive over it!"

But the young man didn't back down. He climbed into the driver's seat and stepped on the gas. The truck lurched forward. "Why don't you lie down again? I'll drive over you this time."

"Who do you think you are, ruining someone's show like this?" the man shouted. "Who sent you? Who?"

The young man hopped down from the driver's seat and kicked the medicine box, shattering the bottles. The startled monkey cackled, dragging its metal cage along by a rope. The strongman punched the young man in the jaw, and in return, received a kick to the stomach.

Although his stomach should have been strong enough to withstand a truck, he fell over easily. The two rolled on the ground, stirring up clouds of dust. The spectators remained, watching the commotion, which subsided only when the police arrived and took them both away.

The boy stayed in the truck with the monkey, waiting for the man to return. He could have run away if he wanted to. He could have driven the truck down the street and gone far, far away. Although he didn't have a driver's license, he knew how to drive.

The woman had brought him to the strongman, saying, "He's got no manners. There's nothing better than a beating for a child who doesn't listen."

The man had grinned, nodding at her words, but his attention was fixed on her pale thighs. When his hand crept up her thigh, she slapped it away as if swatting at a fly. "Don't underestimate him because he's young. He already knows how to read."

Just like the faces of his parents, all that remained of this woman, whom he'd called older sister, was a silhouette of her face.

"Don't ever forget. When the knife in your heart grows dull, sharpen it. Don't forgive them. You understand, Book of John?" General Tom repeats himself, making sure his point is clear.

People toss the discount vouchers on the ground. The trail of discarded vouchers leads them back to their lot. "It looks like a helicopter scattered all these vouchers. This is good. People won't be able to ignore them when they're walking down the street. Besides, it's so cold everyone's staring at the ground anyway." General Tom chuckles, amused by his own thought. "Hey, Book of John, if the show's boring, do you actually give them their money back?"

The truck with the tent theater still hasn't arrived. The ringmaster stands in the middle of the lot, his hands clasped behind his back. The wind sweeps through, but even the dust seems frozen and doesn't stir. The ringmaster dreams of having a permanent venue one day, as well as a circus school. He has shared this dream during his television appearances, speaking of a "systematic circus education" his school would offer. But the troupe members aren't sure what that means. Currently, they do aerial acrobatics one day, juggle on a unicycle on another day, and do motorcycle stunts on yet another day. A central support pillar for the tent theater will be erected where the ringleader is standing, and a flag bearing the Royal Family's emblem will fly at the top of this pillar, visible above the tent.

General Tom and Minji have been bickering since morning. Minji, who stands at eye level with him, shows no signs of apologizing. Minji will be turning eight in the new year. Minji's mother, once a trapeze artist, transitioned to ground acts like riding the unicycle and spinning plates after giving birth to Minji and gaining weight. Minji's father is a tightrope walker. Growing up in the circus, Minji has naturally picked up some tricks. Sticking out her tongue in concentration, she can move forward or backward while balancing on a large ball, and when she follows her mother's large unicycle on stage with a small one of her own, she earns applause from the audience. She has never had formal training, having learned instead by watching the other acrobats, and she is never disciplined for mistakes or punished for laziness. General Tom muses that Minji has indeed received a "systematic circus education," likening it to kindergartens in France or England. In the spring, Minji is set to start elementary school, but the Royal Family moves locations every month. The upcoming performance will mark their 8002nd performance. Discussions about finding a permanent venue have been ongoing since the man joined the circus eight years ago. To send Minji to school, they need to find a permanent location by the end of the month. If Minji's parents have a lot on their mind, they tend to make mistakes during performances. It seems the ringleader has summoned them twice for a talk. Minji, viewing General Tom as her equal due to his height, is upset he won't play hide-and-go-seek with her. She used to speak to him with respect when she was younger, but now she talks to him as if they're the same age. Her mother, observing this, laughs instead of scolding her. This angers General Tom, who is two years older than Minji's mother. When she playfully pats his backside, he becomes furious. Swinging his short arms, he storms off into the animal tent.

The ringmaster imposes a curfew on some of the young men in the circus. He's expecting the truck carrying the tent to arrive in the afternoon. Setting up the tent is a two-day job. Although they rent most of the heavy equipment, there are many small jobs that demand attention. Once the tent is up, they must build the stage inside, laying down mats for seating. In the wintertime, they put down layers of Styrofoam as well to keep the chill away. They must also install facilities for aerial acrobatics at a height of fifteen meters. Electrical cords are strung between the containers, and laundry hangs frozen on clotheslines tangled up with cords, but once the theater goes up, it will hide the unsightly appearance of the containers. Female members attach sequins to the edges of their costumes to make them sparkle like fish scales.

All day long, General Tom guards the animal tent. He vigilantly monitors the heaters, since a drop in the interior temperature could spell disaster. It feels like early summer inside the tent. Sitting by the elephant cage with a serious look on his face, General Tom appears to be reflecting on that fateful day twenty-five years ago. A zookeeper had discovered him standing in front of the elephant cage after closing time, mistaking the unique-looking boy for a lost circus boy. "Which circus are you from?" That question had changed Dongcheol's life forever.

"You stupid idiot!" the strongman had yelled, kicking him in the stomach for not running away. He knocked him to the ground, saying his head was full of worms. Returning to the lot from the police station, he'd assumed the boy had taken the truck and fled. He took the boy to a meat stall at the market. He gulped down a bowl of rice wine, his Adam's apple bobbing violently as wine spilled from his mouth. He refilled the bowl and handed it to the boy, who found the taste rancid. "You little shit," he said, knuckling the boy on the head. "Makgeolli tastes better when you gulp it down." That night, he didn't tie the boy's wrist to his own.

They couldn't perform the truck show anymore. The man grumbled, saying that people had gotten too clever. The age of selling snake oil was over. He said even the nails tasted different, as if made with different ingredients. Not that he had any teeth left to chew them. He had a large target made at a carpenter's shop and painted concentric circles on it, each a different color. He stood the boy in the very center of the target. He flung a knife that stuck in the outermost ring. The boy spat on the ground, mimicking the man, and said, "I want half."

Only later did the man grasp what the boy meant. As he raised his hand to strike, the boy said quickly, "Let's be honest, even half is too little. If you miss, I'm the one who dies."

The man spewed profanities at him, but the boy was unfazed. Jumping up and down in anger, the man panted, "That's it. That's the most I can give you."

News of the "Human Target" act spread quickly. Each throw brought the knife closer to the boy. The crowd held its breath, while the boy clenched his teeth and squeezed his eyes shut. The knife landed right under his armpit or between his legs. When it flew past him and rattled in the board, he felt like he might wet himself. The man called it "the wail of the knife." During the day, even sober, the man's hands shook like those of a person with a tremor. For now, his aim was true, but no one knew when it would falter. The boy opened his eyes. He learned to keep his eyes on the knife, watching as the tip grew bigger. From a certain point, he began to anticipate the knife's path. When the man fell asleep, he would go outside and practice throwing the knife at the target set up in front of the truck. On the target were numerous knife marks outlining his body. The top of his head reached the two-point ring. He had grown. He was no longer a boy.

"You think you could do it blindfolded?" the ringmaster asked him.

Enrico Rastelli, the famous juggler, had juggled ten balls simultaneously—a record no one in the world has been able to break. The man learned to catch five balls with his eyes closed. "Do you think you could do it on a unicycle?" "You think you could do it while skipping rope?" The ringmaster's challenges kept coming, and the audience cheered.

One day, the ringmaster summoned him again. "You think you could do it blindfolded?" This was the same question the ringleader had asked when he first joined the Royal Family. "No, I'm talking about knife throwing. Using a human target. Thumb said you've got a gift for knife throwing."

He practiced by aiming at balloons filled with water. For half a year, he popped the balloons, but the ringmaster didn't rush him. When he finally stopped popping them, General Tom stood at the target. The stage was empty except for the ringmaster and the circus family who held their breath.

"Look here, be careful with my parts! I'm still a single man," General Tom said. The first knife flew past him. "Hey, hey, watch my mouth, too. I've got to eat. And my ears! I'd look weird if I lost my ears!"

Every time a knife flew by, General Tom shuddered. It was from this point that they became roommates.

The strongman was always drunk, even during the day. He laughed with his mouth hanging open and threw knives while drunk. Still, he managed to miss the man and hit the target, but it was all a trick. The man would watch the knife fly toward him, and then move his arms and legs imperceptivity, twisting his body out of the way. Little by little, the man assumed control. Instead of selling the cure-all medicine, they started selling soap, or stainless-steel cookware sets. Things were different from when he received spare change as his wage. The older man no longer swore at him, nor did he unbuckle his belt.

"Do you remember that woman?" he asked the older man. "The woman who brought me to you . . ."

He poured another glass for the older man, who spilled nearly half of it. "Who was she and where did she live? Do you remember the name of the town by any chance?"

"Ah, her!" the older man exclaimed. When he woke the next day, she had disappeared, along with everything in his wallet. Only the boy remained, sleeping in the corner of the room.

"She saw my strongman act at the market. What was it now? She said she came from a place with a lot of peaches. I asked her how her skin was so soft and she said it was because she ate so many peaches. She ate so many that she was sick and tired of them . . ."

The man had no reason to remain with the older man. The knife soared through the air and struck the target. The crowd clapped and whistled. The older man threw ten knives in total. The young man's hands were covered in cuts and scrapes, always inflamed from being frequently wet. His feet and legs bore similar scars. He planned to travel to all the places known for their peaches. The knife vibrated, flying toward his shoulder. This time, he didn't move out of the way. The blade grazed a bit of flesh. A murmur moved through the crowd. A girl screamed and fainted. The older man blinked his bleary eyes, staring at the target.

All his belongings fit in a small plastic bag. As he tied the laces of his running shoes, the older man blustered, reeking of liquor, "Don't tell me that was painful! That little scratch? You don't know how good you have it. Back then, I got stabbed and hurt every day. That was our life."

He picked up his bag and left the inn. The older man ran out barefoot and blocked his way. Showing his few remaining yellow teeth, he groveled pathetically. "How about this? We split everything fifty-fifty."

For some strange reason, he had no memory of eating peaches. In the summertime, vendors would come to the market with carts heaped with peaches, but he never bought any. The fuzz bothered him, making him itch all over. He slung the bag over his uninjured shoulder and walked toward the bus terminal. His legs shook for some strange reason. Behind him, the old man kept shouting, "Fine then! How about sixty-forty? Have a nice life then, you little fucker! Alright, alright, you win, let's make it seventy-thirty—"

He can't remember whether he was six or seven at the time, only that it was a Sunday. He sat in a long wooden pew, mumbling the reverend's words under his breath. The last part of the Bible verse he'd recited that day still echoes in his mind. It had even been set to music for the kids. John 3:16.

That day, the girl who worked as a maid at his house was to take him home after church. His mother dressed him in his best clothes on Sundays. He was wearing a black suit with a red bowtie. The girl told him to open his mouth wide and popped a large candy in it so that he couldn't complain. The candy was so big he couldn't even roll it around in his mouth. When he tried to speak, sticky candy juice dripped onto his suit. Instead of taking him home, she led him to a bus terminal. In the women's bathroom, she changed him into ordinary clothes that the local boys wore and purposely mussed his neatly parted hair with her fingers. His mouth was smeared with candy juice. She was holding a large bag filled with her clothes, which he hadn't noticed before. She lifted her sweater and untied the cloth diaper wrapped around her waist.

"Ah, I thought I was going to go crazy. I could barely breathe with that thing on."

"What are you hiding in there?" he asked, but she acted as if she couldn't hear him.

"That'll teach them. Let them have a taste of their own medicine."

She kept saying things he didn't understand. They boarded an express bus with a greyhound logo on the side. Sleep washed over him. She urged him to walk faster and gave him a noogie. They changed buses several times. When he finally woke, he found a monkey in a red dress in front of him.

The truck brought the tent, along with some snow that hadn't yet melted. The ground was still frozen, making the setup of the support pillars difficult. Although the circus rents most of the larger equipment, the men are responsible for driving the aluminum pillars into the ground and covering them with the tent's colorful canopy. When the ground thaws, spectators will drag in mud, dirtying the mats, so wooden planks will have to be laid down from the entrance of the tent all the way to the asphalt road. A truck enters the lot, honking its horn. The doors of the container homes open, and performers peer out. The girls run out to touch the snow on the truck. Setting up the tent will take two full days, but the show has already begun. Once the tent is up, loud music will blare all day long. Half-price vouchers have been scattered throughout the city.

When the show starts, he will stand before a target he won't be able to see. In the center of the target General Tom waits, the size of a seven-year-old. While he throws the ten knives, no other thoughts, not even of home or his mother, enter his head.

General Tom is rushing toward the truck. He wants to know what in the world has taken so long, how much snow there was to cause the truck to be two days late.

Shadow Child

The pamphlet had promised a view of rolling hills and tributaries of the Han River that sparkled like silk strands, but the only view from the window was of six colossal, spherical tanks atop giant tripods, each marked with the company logo. These tanks had remained in sight, from the moment they exited the highway all the way to the sanitarium. The year after the sanitarium was built, a conglomerate with several subsidiary companies had bought up the entire surrounding area, razed the hill where sanitarium patients liked to go for walks, and erected a factory. These tanks now blocked the view of the river, but to save on costs, the sanitarium had decided not to print new pamphlets.

As his wife opened the suitcase, she whispered to his mother that perhaps it was better this way. Inside the three suitcases were sweaters suitable for colder weather, though winter was still two seasons away. She began placing his underclothes in the drawers, commenting that the view outside was very similar to the one from his office window at the research institute. His mother let out a discreet sigh, making sure he couldn't hear her from where he stood by the window. "What good will come out of remembering?" she wondered out loud, only for the woman to slam shut the drawer, saying, "Mother, that kind of thinking only makes him worse. This is a good sign. Look, he's been staring at those tanks this whole time." But the man's gaze was fixed not on the tanks, but on the dozens of bicycles lined up against the factory wall.

Every time he opened his eyes, he could see one of the tanks at eye level from his position in bed. An iron ladder, shaped like the number "7," hung from the top of the tank near the inlet down to the bottom of the tripod. For the past two months, no one had come near the ladder. The inlet, resembling arrow keys, appeared completely sealed, and the circumference of the tank seemed as wide as the outstretched arms of roughly twenty adult men. The tank visible from his bed was marked with the conglomerate's logo—a large dove carrying an olive branch in its beak.

Even after waking, the man tossed and turned in bed, his mind occupied with what could be filling those enormous tanks. Some days, he imagined they contained crude oil, while on other days, he envisioned grain. Just as he couldn't guess the contents of those tanks, he had no idea what filled his own head.

The truck, which had lost control, leapt onto the sidewalk, and hit the man's shadow, cast long by the streetlight. Miraculously, the man was unharmed, not even the tips of his fingers were injured. When the driver slammed on the brakes, the truck flipped over and its tires spun in the air. The loosely secured crates in the cargo bed spilled out, including chicken coops made of wooden planks and thick wire. The frightened chickens squawked and flapped their wings, and soon white feathers drifted over the road. The only thing the man could remember was the chickens' squawking. He didn't even recognize his mother.

He raised his right arm toward the white plastered ceiling. The needle mark on his pale forearm still hadn't faded. Clenching and unclenching his hand, he examined the hollow of his palm, where the lines of life and fate intersected. Did he drop a clay pot he'd been holding? Or did a bird escape from his grasp? His right hand felt strangely empty, as if something had slipped away, but he couldn't identify what it was that his hand seemed to remember.

He was jolted awake by a noise that split into two before fading away. Silence again. it was always a little past six in the morning when he woke to the sounds of boisterous laughter, footsteps pounding the dirt, and the occasional chime of bicycle bells and rattling chains. There was commotion in the factory yard out back as the night shift workers left and the morning crew arrived. The head office was nearby, and workers, dressed in blue uniforms, rode their bicycles to and from the factory.

He heard the sound of plastic slippers moving slowly toward the lounge and bathroom. Thunder Boy's bed was empty, and he could hear his voice coming from the lounge. He must have taken a detour on his way to the bathroom.

"You see 'em? You see 'em, don't you?"

Judging by the gunfire noises Thunder Boy was making, he was recounting the tale of Operation White Horse during the Vietnam War. While sharing the same room, the man had become familiar with Thunder Boy's countless sagas. Sometimes Thunder Boy would act like a seventy-year-old, and at other times he'd bustle around all day with the vigor of a man in his twenties.

To act out the stories he told, Thunder Boy would roll on the floor of the common room or leap onto a chair, and as if he were a scout on a mission, casting suspicious glances at onlookers staring up at him.

He was deployed in Bacom, northwest of Cam Ranh, in March of 1970. In the subtropical climate, he prowled fully armed, wearing a bulletproof vest. Sweat from his helmet made it difficult to open his eyes. Right now, Thunder Boy was crossing a river that came up to his chest, searching for enemy hideouts. During these crossings, he spread his legs like stilts and walked awkwardly. Since he had to raise his arms above his shoulders to avoid getting his rifle wet, he struggled to maintain balance, made more difficult due to the rocks in the water, as well as the sudden drops in the riverbed. His gear, weighing over 30 kilograms, became even heavier when wet, hanging off his limbs. "If you're not careful," he'd warn, "forget catching the Vietcong! You'll just get swept away in the mud and become fish food."

Suddenly, Thunder Boy dropped to his stomach and began to crawl on the common room floor. He was creeping through a subtropical forest thick with banyan trees, kudzu vines, and betel nut trees, unnoticed by enemy troops. A young man with a shaved head who'd been watching burst into uncontrollable laughter, but Thunder Boy was unfazed. He was deadly serious as he mimed putting two canteens around his waist, tapping them with his palms to make sure they were secure. "In the Vietnam heat, you can't last even an hour without water." A helicopter appeared from the direction of the vending machine. Thunder Boy, red-faced with exertion, mouthed words, showing he couldn't hear anything else because of the noise. The man had heard the story many times before, but he still couldn't help laughing.

Outside, the bike storage area curved along the wall fence, filled with dozens of bicycles locked to stainless steel racks and leaning in different directions. The factory operated in three shifts, and the yard was only noisy during the ten-minute shift changes. Otherwise, sunlight bathed the yard, conjuring an image of young men playing jokgu, while young women chatted in small groups. Before he had a chance to wonder whether he or his wife was part of that scene, the image vanished. His wife called every other day. Though he should have gotten used to her voice by now, each time he asked, "Excuse me, but who's this?" There would be a moment of silence, followed by her sigh. He looked out at the tanks as she requested, but his gaze soon shifted to the bicycles.

The shift changes at the factory happened at 6 a.m., 2 p.m., and 10 p.m. About ten minutes before each shift, a group of bicycles would appear below the tank tripods. One or two bikes always led the way, weaving through the tripod posts in an S shape, followed by others. By the time the ones in front reached the storage area, noisy footsteps came from the opposite direction, signaling the end of the shift. Over a hundred factory workers would mingle, unlocking and locking up bicycles in an orderly fashion, mirroring the precision inside the workshop.

Some workers didn't start pedaling right away. They ran beside their bicycles, gripping the handle and then hopping on once they had gained momentum. Pedaling quickly while half standing, they appeared as if they might tip over, but caught up to the bikes that had left first. They wove between the tripod posts, gliding once they had built speed. The man observed them for a long time as they scattered, all dressed in identical uniforms. A colorful vinyl awning covered the storage area, but left the bike fenders exposed. The fenders glinted in the afternoon light. A bike with a red seat caught his eye.

Thunder Boy, who'd been visiting other rooms with a towel draped around his neck, hurried back when breakfast arrived. He'd come about two weeks after the man. His hair, once neat and short, now covered his ears. It was unlike him to pass by without making a comment, particularly when he saw the man picking out all the beans from his rice.

"Look here, son. Do you know why eight thousand farmers rebelled?"

Thunder Boy was about to recount the tale of the Gabo Peasant Rebellion of 1894. Plucking a missed bean from his mouth, the man humored him. "Because of poverty?"

Thunder Boy nodded several times, uncovering his own breakfast dishes. At the time of the rebellion, Thunder Boy would have been a vigorous twenty-one-year-old. The peasants, with white cloths wrapped around their heads and armed with bamboo spears and clubs, had stormed the government office. They seized weapons and raided the storehouse of grain collected through illegal means, redistributing it to the poor. Whether he was reliving those historical moments or simply enjoying the meal, Thunder Boy chewed the stir-fried zucchini thoughtfully.

The man had been fine with beans, until his mother, after seeing his lunch one day, mentioned how much he'd hated them.

"You made all kinds of excuses. They smell funny, they're stinky like fermented soybeans, they have a weird texture . . . Once I got so frustrated that I hit you in the forehead with a dirty spoon." She laughed. "A red bump appeared on your tiny forehead, and there was some rice stuck to it . . . Gosh, you were such a stubborn kid. You'd clamp your mouth shut, refusing to eat. I'd threaten and coax you, but nothing worked. In the end, I lost. I said you didn't have to eat them anymore. It was a battle all right, a real battle." Shaking her head, as if she didn't want to dwell on those times, she added, "That's when I knew. I knew you'd achieve whatever you set your mind to." His mother stopped eating the beans she'd picked out and closed her mouth.

The next day, lunch was rice and beans again. He caught a whiff when uncovering his rice and found the smell so off-putting that he had to cover it back up. From that moment on, he couldn't eat them anymore.

"You know how bad it got with the landlords in those days? They'd lend grain or money, but only if the farmers put up their land as collateral. And the interest rates? Sky-high. Miss a payment and the land was gone—just like that! Farmers lost everything and were forced to become tenant farmers. For a while, we had no choice but to drift from place to place." Thunder Boy kept muttering, as if to himself. "Ever hear of voluntary servitude? It's when you've got nothing left to sell, except yourself. So you go to a rich family and become a slave because you have no other choice . . ."

Thunder Boy had too many stories to tell. His earliest memories dated back to the days of Prince Yeonsan of Joseon. He boasted of how he has lived through five hundred years, witnessing and experiencing unbelievable things. According to him, the wife who came to visit him once every two weeks was his fifth wife.

The man stopped picking out the beans and blurted his name: Kim Minki. The name itself seemed to give off an unpleasant smell. Each time he looked up, he was greeted by the image of Noah's dove on the tank. His wife's advice to look out the window didn't seem to be helping. The inlets at the top of the tanks hadn't been opened since the man arrived at the sanatorium. They were red with rust. He suspected that the tanks might be as empty as the inside of his head.

The man stared at the bicycle with the red seat, secured to the third grid from the left of the rack. With every shift change, the bicycles switched places, but the one with the red seat had always remained in the same spot. The sight stirred an odd sensation in him, like a burn in his groin. A plastic booster seat, large enough for a three- or four-year-old, was attached between the seat and handlebar. He pictured the owner, perhaps on weekends, taking a child for a ride. Hundreds of workers bustled about during shift changes, but none touched the bike with the red seat. Where was its owner? The man wasn't interested in the tanks at all.

It was his cousins who informed him that he was a baseball fanatic. The identical twins, a year younger than the man, appeared at the door five minutes apart, mirroring the way they were born and catching the man off guard. Despite not having seen each other for a long time, they greeted him with a casual wave, indicating their closeness. The twins began bickering as soon as they came in and perched themselves on the cot next to his bed. The first to arrive scolded the other for making him wait at the entrance for nearly twenty minutes because he'd been on the phone. The other said being busy was a good thing. The man looked back and forth at the two identical men with curly hair. It was impossible to tell who was the older twin. They said he had been the only one among their relatives who could tell them apart. A relative had once asked how he managed this, but he'd never shared his secret. Now, however, the twins looked exactly the same to him. Even their voices were similar, and they both chose the same fiber drink from the assortment of beverages in the fridge.

The twins could clearly recall the first professional baseball game that was played at Dongdaemun Stadium. Dressed in a suit vest, the former Korean president had thrown the first ceremonial pitch, and the ball had flown straight through the strike zone. The roar of over thirty thousand spectators had filled the stadium. It had been a game between MBC and Samsung.

"Man, when it went into the tenth inning, my hands were sweating like crazy!"

"Yeah, that hit by Lee Jong-do was insane."

"Imagine how Lee Seon-hui felt when Lee Jong-do touched home plate . . . A grand slam to finish the game—"

Only when they were talking about baseball did the twins find themselves perfectly in sync. Suddenly, the older twin's face turned serious. "Hey, remember what else happened that day?" he said to the man. "We were freaking out because this guy was late. He had all the tickets. And we had to keep dodging these luggage bikes, because we were standing in the middle of the market. When that massive line of people in front of the stadium all went inside, I thought we were going to miss the game for sure. He's always been late to everything and he's still the same way."

The other twin laughed. "That happened? It was so long ago I can't remember."

If the man used to be able to tell them apart, it would have been because of their completely opposite personalities.

March 27, 1982. He was in the ninth grade, and the school year had just begun. He'd gone to Dongdaemun Stadium with the twins. He counted on his fingers, realizing more than twenty years had passed. His mother laughed, saying his habit of counting on his fingers hasn't changed. She recalled how he'd been unusually bad at math as a boy, even using his toes to do addition when he ran out of fingers. This had worried her as a young mother, but she'd also found it hilarious. Late March weather was unpredictable, and since he hadn't taken his jacket because it hadn't matched his outfit, he was probably chilly on his way home after the game.

The twins were like ten-year-old boys, joking and poking each other in the side and stomach. The man pictured Lee Jong-do hitting a home-run in the bottom of the tenth inning. He heard the roar of the crowd. A white ball flew toward him. People in the front seats leapt up, arms outstretched to catch it. The ball was headed straight for him. He jumped, ready to grab it, but the moment he thought he'd caught it, it had slipped through his fingers, causing chaos below as everyone scrambled to grab it. The man looked down at his empty hands. He seemed to remember the sensation of the baseball settling into his hands. This emptiness he felt in his right hand—was it from dropping the ball then?

"You guys remember? I almost caught Lee Jong-do's ball," he said, slapping his knee in disappointment.

The twins looked at each other, confused. "What are you talking about? The ball didn't even come near us. It flew out of the stadium, didn't it?" the older twin said, nudging his brother.

"I don't know," the younger twin muttered. "I couldn't even see where it went, because everyone was screaming and jumping around. Jeez, can you believe that was twenty years ago? We were fifteen."

Their eyes glazed over, as if traveling back in time. The older one smacked his lips. "Hey, was there even color TV back then?"

Instead of answering, the younger twin looked at the man. "Did they have color TV then?"

The older glanced at him, too, and then elbowed his brother in the side. The younger twin clamped his mouth shut.

They started to talk about the band Songolmae, and then moved on to the girl who'd lived across from them. A hardcore fan, she'd been the same age as them. The twins' voices grew louder. She'd liked the older twin, but the younger twin had talked to her once, pretending to be the older one. The younger twin didn't agree with this version of the story. He claimed that the girl had liked him, since he looked just like the older twin but had a better personality. The twins reminisced for over an hour, but their conversation was interrupted when Thunder Boy entered the room. The older twin turned at the sound and recognized the elderly man. The younger twin turned as well, and both cried at the same time, "It's Park Sungbae!" Thunder Boy, however, seemed dazed at the sight of the identical men.

The man from Room 204, who'd been rooting for a comeback by his favorite team, missed the dramatic grand slam scene and dozed off, his head resting on the sofa. The people here dozed off frequently. The man suddenly realized he was engrossed in the game. The baseball that cleared the fence sailed out of the relatively small ballpark. The winning team ran out of the dugout, shouting wildly, and rushed onto the mound. The end credits slowly scrolled up on the screen.

Thunder Boy was now demonstrating swordsmanship to a young man with a shaved head, using brooms as swords. He passionately described the various methods, like the Native Sword, the Golden Rooster Stands on One Leg, as well as the Wild Tiger Hides in the Forest. The young man nodded attentively. Thunder Boy leapt forward with his left foot, thrusting the sword above with both hands. He then moved his right foot back, dragging his left back as well and swinging the blade down between the opponent's thumb and index finger. The young man kept forgetting the sequence. They tried sparring next. Whenever the young man tried to strike at Thunder Boy's head, he easily sidestepped it. This time, Thunder Boy swung his sword from above his opponent's head down toward the side. As the young man raised his sword in defense, their blades clashed, creating flashes of light. Meanwhile, the man listened to the crashing of two broomsticks.

As the two continued to leap and dash around the small common room, several people who'd been watching television went back to their rooms. The young man struggled to remember the sparring sequence, though it consisted of only five stances. Thunder Boy, too, couldn't recall more than that. The young man swung the sword diagonally instead of striking down, and Thunder Boy, who'd stepped to the side to dodge the attack, was struck in the ribs. His face flushed red with pain and anger. The young man stood with the broom in his hand, looking unsure. Thunder Boy went to the young man to review the sequence again.

A middle-aged woman sat in an armchair next to the television, absorbed in her knitting. To avoid the dust stirred up by the brooms, she shifted to the sofa between the man and the patient from 204. She wore low-heeled shoes, with tips woven like dumplings. The ball of yarn rolled off her lap and came to a stop at the man's feet. She had dozed off. He reached out to pick it up, appreciating the rough texture of the yarn. The ball was a little bigger than his grasp, but it didn't feel quite right. The man touched various things around him, searching for what his hand remembered. A wallet proved too thin, and the doorknob felt too cold.

She woke from her nap. She shivered and resumed her knitting. After completing each row, she held the half-finished sweater against the man's back, only to find it too small. She grumbled as she tried to stretch it. In the end, she removed the needles and began to unravel the sweater. Her skirt soon overflowed with yarn. She muttered, while casting the yarn back onto the needle. He didn't realize she was talking to him until she raised her voice.

"You're the spitting image of your father . . ." she said, glancing at his face. "Even your torso is too long, just like his. This is supposed to be a standard size, but look how small it is."

It was a white sweater with cable patterns on both sides. "You better wear it, even if it's itchy. You can't just let it just sit in a drawer." When he didn't answer, she barked, "I've told you a million times, when an older person speaks to you, you've got to respond!"

"Yes, Ma'am!" he blurted without thinking.

She turned her head to look at him and frowned. "Are you mocking me?" She stood up abruptly, the ball of yarn falling to the floor. Her shoulders shook with anger. "So you're going to hit me like your dad now? You rude, wicked boy!" She raised her hand and slapped the man's cheek. He didn't even have a chance to speak. She clutched her knitting with both hands and stormed out, leaving a trail of unraveling yarn behind her. Though the woman was small, his cheek felt numb, and tears formed in his eyes. Thunder Boy, who seemed to have been struck in the ribs again, was also hopping up and down, rubbing his side.

His mother peeled the apple in one continuous strip, the peel dangling down, almost grazing her lap. Rain from the previous night had created puddles all over the yard, leaving the bike with the red seat soaked. Some workers who had brought their bicycles to work had to leave them behind due to the heavy rain. Others, donning raincoats, bravely pedaled off, but the rain blurred their vision and slowed them down. No one claimed the bicycle with the red seat. The man pictured himself on this bicycle, a young child in the plastic child seat. He could almost see the child's hair, soft like fuzz, fluttering in the wind, the delicate folds of skin on the back of the neck. He heard the child's giggles as they hit a rock and bounced slightly in the air. An absurd song popped into his mind then: "Daddy and me, we're just the same. Eyes, nose, and mouth, ding dong dang!"

"Mom, what kind of son was I?" he asked, standing by the window.

His mother paused while peeling the apple and looked up at him. She remembered the son he had been—a baseball fanatic who hated beans, a boy who offered kisses as birthday presents, a young man who landed a job at a research institute, just as she'd wished. But he might have taken money from her wallet or gotten into brawls at school and lied about the bruises, claiming they were from falls. He might have camped outside a girl's house, instead of pulling an all-nighter at the study hall as he claimed. He might have become an abusive husband from watching his father beat his mother. But all he could remember was the image of frightened chickens, their wings flapping wildly, sending white feathers adrift in the air.

"You were a good boy," his mother said, sighing deeply.

He hadn't recognized her, but this didn't surprise her. Even the doctor had expected him to recognize her, but he had failed to recall anything. He gazed down at his hands. "Mom, was I holding something? I keep feeling as if I've lost something. I just can't shake that feeling."

His mother remained silent. The knife in her hand slipped, and the peel broke, dropping to the floor.

The factory operated non-stop, its lights shining into the room even in the middle of the night. Thunder Boy fell asleep with his hand resting on his forehead. When asked why he slept this way, he said it was because he had too much on his mind. From the man's bed, he could see the back of Thunder Boy's head. Illuminated by the factory lights, the surgical scar running from the top of Thunder Boy's head to the nape of his neck stood out. They had started calling him Thunder Boy because his scar was shaped like a lightning bolt, and the nickname had stuck. His hair, cut short for the surgery, now covered his ears, but it didn't grow over the scar. Even with careful combing, the scar split his hair like a natural part. Thunder Boy had fallen asleep after spending much of the night packing and unpacking his luggage, preparing for his return home the next day. The man mimicked Thunder Boy's pose, placing his hand on his forehead as if deep in thought, but his hand felt heavy, like a rock.

He could tell the sound of heels in the hallway belonged to a visitor. They weren't the shuffling of plastic slippers worn by the patients. The footsteps stopped in front of the man's room. Without opening his eyes, he knew who it was. The steps approached his bed, and he caught a whiff of cosmetics. It was his wife.

She stood by the window and gazed out at the view. She leaned her arms on the windowsill with her backside jutting out, saying nothing for a long time. Her eyes appeared lifeless. She didn't look much different from the other women he had seen in the hospital halls. Her thin hair was dry and frizzy, and she rarely smiled. Had I been happy with her? Each time he saw his wife, a sense of guilt overwhelmed him. He didn't dare to embrace her, fearing he would feel nothing. She sighed, just like his mother had.

She pointed at something outside the window and let out a dry laugh. "Bikes . . ."

Had she figured out he'd been watching the bicycles all this time, rather than the tanks? After a lengthy silence, she finally spoke. "Do you remember when we went to Chuncheon?" She said it was about a year before they got married, on the day of the March 1st Movement. They had taken a ten-minute boat ride to an amusement park, a spot popular with young couples. As they approached the island, a bicycle rental shop caught their eye. They were told touring the entire island by bicycle would take less than an hour. It seemed every couple there had rented bikes.

"But for some reason, you hesitated. Until then, I never thought you couldn't ride a bike. At the institute, you were known for being good at every sport, like swimming and tennis." She had insisted on renting a bicycle. "When you said that riding a bike was the only thing you couldn't do, I thought you were joking."

He climbed onto the back of the bike behind her. His legs dragged on the ground. "You were heavier than I thought," his wife said, her laugh like the buzzing of a mosquito. "I really got a workout that day."

A woman pedaling with a large man seated behind her drew everyone's attention. People assumed they'd swapped places as a joke. The bicycle was unable to slow down on a steep slope and hurtled toward the river. He tried to stop it by putting his feet out, but it was no use. They plunged straight into the river.

"The water was freezing cold. I thought my heart was going to stop. I panicked when my feet wouldn't touch the bottom. The more I struggled, the more river water I swallowed."

The river was polluted, filled with weeds and litter discarded by tourists. The man managed to pull the woman to the riverbank. "If you hadn't been a good swimmer, I would have drowned that day. I never rode a bike again after that. You teased me, asking if you'd turned me off bikes forever because you were too heavy. But the truth is, I was scared of the water. Every time I even glanced at a bike, I felt like I was about to drown."

He walked toward his wife and took her hand. He felt as if he were pulling a beverage can from a cooler. Her hand twitched slightly in his before slipping away. She gave another sigh. "But I've been thinking about riding a bike again. I even picked one out already . . ." Her hand felt unfamiliar to him.

It wasn't Thunder Boy, but the wife who came to visit. She kept finding knickknacks in his drawers. Back at home, in the middle of the night, the sound of a baby shrieking from the apartment upstairs had continued for over half an hour. Concerned, they went upstairs and rang the doorbell, but no one answered. Thunder Boy then stepped out onto his balcony, intending to climb the gas pipe to the apartment above. He'd done something similar in the past and felt sure he could do it again. His wife tried to stop him, but he ignored her. After all, nothing bad had happened to him for the past five hundred years. He climbed onto the balcony railing and managed to grab hold of the gas pipe. However, as soon as he lifted his other foot off the railing, he discovered, to his shock, that he had no strength in his hands. He plummeted into the flowerbed below his third-floor apartment, hitting his head during the fall. It turned out that the baby's parents had slipped out while the baby was asleep.

Thunder Boy had been a famous actor, and most of what he remembered were the roles he'd played in movies. "Did you know?" Thunder Boy's wife asked the man, her face bare of makeup, as she wiped tears from her red, swollen eyes. After a car accident left him with a head injury, the only thing erased from his memory was the fact that he'd been a movie star. What remained were the characters he had portrayed. Although the latest surgery was successful, the doctors couldn't guarantee what would happen next. She sighed, noting that this time, his stay in the hospital would probably be longer. "I just hope that when he wakes up, things will be different. Maybe he'll stay out of trouble this time. Wouldn't it be nice if he believed he was playing the role of a patient? He wouldn't be so bored then. If he thought it was all part of an act, maybe the shots and exams wouldn't even hurt." She managed a small smile at the thought.

When he turned his head, he saw the empty bed. In his dream, Thunder Boy's head had been stitched together in several places. "Young master, you might as well call me a soccer ball now," he had joked with a laugh, stroking his patchwork head.

Someone had removed the red seat from the bicycle. He looked carefully at every single bike in the rack, but the red seat was nowhere to be found. Instead, he saw a bicycle with rusted springs where the seat once was. Since the red seat had still been there the previous evening, someone from the night shift must have taken it early in the morning after their shift ended. They wouldn't return to the factory until ten o'clock that night.

"Do you remember—" his father's cousin began. Relatives who came to visit tended to open with these words. Each time he heard them, he felt like a scarecrow, patched together with the memories of others. The cousin's hand, as brittle as a dried leaf, clasped his for a long time. He could feel the faint pulse of the old man, like groundwater flowing deep underground. His cousin spoke of his father's funeral, recalling how mature and dignified the man had been, even as a child. Meanwhile, a little boy who had come with the cousin was jumping on Thunder Boy's bed as if it were a trampoline. The cousin scolded the boy occasionally, but his warnings were ignored. With every jump, the bed springs creaked, and the child stuck his tongue out at the pigeons outside the window. In the hallway, the man's mother and wife whispered with the cousin's wife.

"It must have been when you were eighteen," the cousin reminisced. He called out toward the hallway, "He was eighteen, wasn't he? When he visited?" His mother confirmed this from the hallway. Turning back to the man, the cousin said, "You came with those twin cousins of yours, remember?" He called toward the hallway again, inquiring about the twins.

"They're doing just fine, no worries about making a living, that's for sure," his mother replied.

The cousin resumed his tale. They'd gone to the river with the cousin's children to go fishing. It had just rained, causing the water level to rise. They waded across the river to a deeper spot, the chilly water reddening their skin. They failed to catch a single fish. As they crossed back, the current turned their legs numb. The older ones led the way, followed by two younger girls holding hands. Suddenly, a strong surge swept one girl off her feet. In her panic, she clutched at the other girl, and both vanished into the water, the current too strong for the elementary-school girls. A boy on the bank screamed, "They're getting swept away!" but no one dared to dive in. Just then, the man plunged into the stream, grabbing the girls by the scruff of their necks and pulling them out of the water to safety. Drenched and terrified, the girls opened their mouths and began to cry.

"No, it was Jongki!" the cousin's wife interjected from the hallway. "It was Jongki who saved them, not Minki."

"Jongki?" echoed the cousin, confused.

"Yes, your brother's younger son."

The cousin chuckled awkwardly. "Oh, never mind then. Forget what I said. Just erase it from your memory."

The cousin, who smelled of Chinese medicine, told many stories, yet advised the man to pretend he hadn't heard them.

Later, the man accompanied the cousin's family to the taxi stand. The little boy kept lagging behind, lingering in front of a store. As he was opening a bag of chips, he spilled almost half in the lobby. When the taxi arrived, the adults got in, but the child ran off. The man had no choice but to chase the boy, finally catching him by the wrist. The boy's fist, full of crumbs, fit perfectly inside the man's larger hand. As the child climbed into the taxi, his hand slipped from the man's grip like water. Even after the taxi left, the man stood there, staring at his open hand, haunted by the memory of the child's fist.

All day, the man stared at his hand. His mother and wife whispered together in the hall. His mother kept saying no good would come from remembering, and his wife snapped back at her, asking if she wanted to ruin her only son. The man recalled the way the boy's hand had felt in his. If he'd been holding a child's hand, when had he let go? Neither his mother nor wife had ever mentioned a child. The truck had skidded on the wet road, striking the man's shadow. Chickens squawked in fright, and white feathers drifted in the air. The man shook his head to dispel the ominous thought. He decided not to say anything to his family. Though it was only the beginning of autumn, his wife had packed a suitcase full of winter clothing. It was clear that he would spend the winter there.

He walked toward the bike that was missing a seat. Scaling the factory wall wasn't difficult. The bicycle, neglected for months, had rusted, and the pedals were difficult to turn. Crooked letters, written in white paint on the frame, spelled: Shinyeom. Conviction. He traced the letters with his fingertips. The word had been his favorite since middle school. These markings seemed to confirm that the bike was indeed his. The rope that had secured the wheel to the rack had decayed, leaving only a thick wire behind. Dust covered the child's seat as well. When had he last gone home? Surely the child had not outgrown this seat. He cut the wire with a pocketknife, a sense of urgency building within him.

The red seat, four grids away, came off easily when he pulled it up. Whoever had taken it probably assumed that the bicycle with the red seat had no owner. He removed the red seat and reattached it to his own bike.

As soon as he lifted his feet off the ground, the bicycle began to wobble. He quickly put his foot out to steady it, then returned both feet to the pedals. However, before he could complete even two rotations of the wheels, he toppled over, scraping his cheek on the ground. Stinging pain followed, but he remounted the bike and pedaled once more. Five rotations led to twenty. As he lurched forward, he completely forgot about the white building in front of the tanks.

Workers from the graveyard shift appeared, their faces pale and their breath foul from having their mouths shut all night. They chatted and joked as they unlocked their bikes. From the direction of the tanks, the first shift's bicycles appeared, their bells chiming. One worker grumbled about his missing seat. Someone nearby joked, "Be careful you don't get poked in the ass."

The workers began to ride off, some racing each other. The man teetered forward, but eventually found his balance, trailing far behind the others. Gripping the handlebar, he attempted to catch up. The plastic seat rattled. The handlebar felt just right in his hands. Perhaps this handlebar was what his hands remembered.

The bike in the lead sped under the tripod posts, passing the massive tank adorned with an image of Noah's dove. The man, who used to stand gazing at that image, was no longer in that spot. He pedaled furiously, knowing that if he continued with the group, he would reach the main building. He would think about finding his home later. On his day off, he planned to take his child for a ride, racing together down the road.

Dozens of bicycles passed under the six enormous tanks. A moment later, a creaking bicycle called Conviction wobbled after them.

Deathbed

When we reached the funeral home located on a corner on the way to the amusement park, I couldn't help thinking it was just like my aunts. All three of my aunts were too impatient to keep giving the same directions to relatives unfamiliar with the area. They probably expected even first-timers to easily find the funeral home, since the amusement park attracted hundreds of thousands of people from all over the country during the summer months when the beach was open. The taxi driver who picked us up from the airport was worse than my aunts. Whenever the car in front didn't go fast enough, he leaned halfway out the window and either spat or yelled. After passing a sign that read "Amusement Park 5KM," we slowed to a crawl at 20 km per hour, and when the sign "Amusement Park 1KM" appeared, we came to a complete stop. Cars formed three or four lanes on a two-lane road. The taxi driver said the traffic had already been bad because of the amusement park, but had gotten worse after the funeral home opened. He lost his temper at his own reflection in the rearview mirror.

Out of nowhere, a small blue truck cut in front of us. A condolence wreath as big as a grown man was loaded in the cargo bed. The large white chrysanthemums made me think of white buns cooking in a large steamer, but I shook my head, thinking it was inappropriate to the deceased. It's not like I grew up in a bakery, but whenever I saw white chrysanthemums, I couldn't help thinking of steamed buns. On the black ribbons was the name of the company that had sent the wreath: Hanil Trading. The spelling of the Chinese characters printed on the ribbons was correct, but something seemed off, although I couldn't pinpoint what that was.

My youngest aunt's husband was sick for a long time.

"It's for real this time?" my father asked when he received the news. Every time my youngest aunt had called to say that Uncle was on the brink of death, she had wailed like a child who'd lost her father at a train station, but when he actually died, she remained composed for the first time in her life, not shedding a single tear. While waiting for the hearse from the funeral home to arrive, she massaged his limbs, which were already going stiff, and laid them straight. She said he looked so peaceful, as if he were asleep. She called the rice cake shop and ordered more than a bushel of injeolmi and songpyeon, and called her two sisters, who came wailing from their stores. My family frantically booked our flights and rushed to the airport.

At the entrance of the funeral home, a young man dressed as the chief mourner was smoking with a friend. The traditional hemp fabric of his outfit looked awkward, almost as if it were made of paper. His face was pale, and his lips chapped from lack of sleep. Even as we were confirming my uncle's name and room number on the information board, condolence wreaths came in through the door, one after another. I thought of steamed buns again, so much so that I felt full. Whenever my dad returned to his hometown, he automatically switched to speaking in dialect.

"When they build this place?"

Mother, following a few steps behind, chimed in. "Wedding halls aren't doing so well out here, so they've been converting them into funeral homes."

Beneath my uncle's name were traces of other names that had been erased. The name "Kim Miseon" was clearly visible, and beneath that, I could make out just the middle character "Bae."

I sent my parents inside and stuck a cigarette between my lips. I lit up, thinking that even with the anti-smoking trend, exceptions needed to be made in places like this. Next to me, the young man kept wiping his eyes with his sleeves, as if smoke had irritated them. The rough hemp fabric quickly turned his eyes red. His friend turned away, pretending not to notice.

Narrow streets weaved past restaurants, karaoke rooms, and clothing stores, then converged near the coast. Across from the hospital was a block of seafood restaurants that were similar both in size and their menus. Water flowed from the tanks in front of these establishments and pooled on the street, leaving a fishy stink. When a customer entered a restaurant, the owner, clad in rubber boots and a rubber apron, would emerge to scoop up a halibut or rockfish from the tank and take it inside. Behind the seafood restaurants were newly renovated motels. Every small two-pane window had an air conditioner hanging from it, and next to foreign-sounding motel names, a large hot-springs symbol was painted. The amusement park was visible between the motels. A decorative windmill turned slowly, and whenever the pirate ship swooped down in an arc, the bottom of the ship sparkled, reflecting light. Cackling, young people flocked toward the amusement park. A car pulled up to the entrance of the funeral home and a young woman, supported by others, exited the car, sobbing.

The hallway was dimly lit. Opposite the rooms, both large and small, was a reception area with a cooler bearing the logo of a beverage company. Dishwater was pooled in the hallway, as if it had flowed from the kitchen. Wilted wreaths stood crookedly in front of the bathrooms, their chrysanthemum leaves blackened and withered. The white petals scattered on the ground resembled giant maggots. People going in and out of the bathrooms trampled on them, and some petals were carried down the corridor on the soles of their shoes. The rooms were as crowded as a popular family restaurant during peak hours, with customers waiting for tables. The basement alone housed twelve rooms. As I passed one, I glimpsed a portrait of a young woman. It appeared to be an enlarged college graduation photo. Though her features were indistinct, her hair was thick and black beneath her graduation cap. In the room, only her elderly mother sat, her head bowed beneath the girl's portrait, like a doll with a broken neck.

My uncle's was the last one in the corridor. There was no need to check the name outside the room, because I saw a flash of dyed blonde hair above the low partition in the reception area and heard the rapid chatter of a rough dialect. My youngest aunt, sitting inside the room leaning against the wall, opened her eyes with difficulty and looked up at me. A hemp covering was placed on top of her dyed hair, reminding me of a yellow-haired angel with a halo from a Christmas card I remembered as a boy.

My aunts had built their entire lives around the amusement park, which was the cornerstone of their business. Back when the beach had been the only tourist attraction here, they had earned a whole year's income from just the summer sales. Carrying rubber vats filled with boiled conch and seasnails on their heads, they trekked the coastline multiple times a day. Walking on sand was harder than walking on solid ground. If someone raised their hand to flag them down, they would run, anxious not to lose a sale to another vendor. Sometimes they would trip and spill their goods on the sand. Once they started making a decent income, they dyed their hair yellow and even began chartering vans once or twice a year to visit other amusement parks.

Early September, the beach had already closed for the season. My second oldest aunt was telling my mother how she'd been just about to leave for her trip to China but had to back out last minute, blowing her trip money. Had she gotten the news about my uncle just five minutes later, she wouldn't have made it here. Even though I was now a man in my mid-thirties, my aunts took turns patting me on the bottom. My second aunt sat me down and rehashed how she'd had to miss her China trip, while my eldest aunt brought me a big bowl of rice. My aunts never sat still, due to all their years of running businesses on their own. It was second nature for them to prep, greet customers, take orders, cook, serve, and settle bills, all singlehandedly. Even at the funeral home, they checked the big pot of spicy beef soup constantly, adding water or salt as needed. They monitored the side dishes as well, letting the kitchen know if anything ran low. Even when guests arrived all at once, they handled everything efficiently, setting cutlery on the table, scooping up the rice and soup, and serving the side dishes.

Most of the guests were from the small business co-ops my aunts belonged to. It seemed these owners had found someone to watch their shops briefly while they came to pay their respects. This, too, was typical of my aunts. They'd picked a funeral home that wasn't just easy to find, but also conveniently located for their acquaintances. My eldest aunt greeted the members of her co-op who swarmed in. Whenever there was a crisis, my aunts competed over how many of their people they could mobilize. My second aunt smacked her lips.

"Everyone in my co-op's in China right now. Otherwise, they'd all be here."

It wasn't until evening that our relatives who lived scattered around the country arrived. Even the older man who'd traveled from an island found the funeral home without any issues, though everyone complained about the awful traffic. Older relatives praised my uncle for being considerate enough to pass away during cooler weather, sparing his family the sweltering summer heat. However, my youngest aunt's family remained silent, having shuttled my uncle to and from the emergency room for the past eight years, carrying him and loading him into a cab each time.

My uncle had wished to be cremated. After saying it was exhausting just thinking of his children traveling long distances to tend his grave and pay their respects, he coughed for a long time. Several relatives nodded, saying he was indeed wise and considerate. My father didn't mention he'd already bought a burial plot for both him and my mother. With that, the conversation shifted away from my uncle.

"Who's this now?"

An elderly man gestured at me with his chin as he accepted a glass of liquor. Another next to him blinked his drooping eyes and squinted at me.

"Why, he's the one who'll carry on our family line," my second aunt said.

Another elderly man chimed in, slapping his knee. "Ah, so this is him?"

I was puzzled, but my aunt looked pleased. "That's right! Works for a big company in Seoul."

An old man with white hair filled a paper cup with beer for my father. "Seems you did alright, brother."

He said he'd raised four children with just a motorboat, but now, with times being hard, he and his wife were barely scraping by. He tossed back a shot of soju.

"Hey, hey, hang on," my father said, clasping the man's arm to pour him a drink.

The man's hand shook noticeably. He wore a faded, pilling woolen jumper that seemed too warm for the season, a stark contrast to my father's formal black suit complete with a tie pin and cufflinks. Along with the other elderly men, he spewed old stories, ranging from the time ten years ago when they'd seen me at a cousin's wedding to an incident from my childhood when I spent the night at a relative's house and wet the bed, ruining a brand-new blanket. They brought up moments even I had forgotten, speaking of them as if they had happened only yesterday. One of them splayed his fingers apart and asked, "So how exactly are we related?"

At last the familiar headache-inducing question had surfaced: how many times removed were we from each other?

"Okay, okay, I got it. I'm his great-uncle."

Laughter broke out, drinks were passed, and the atmosphere felt like a family picnic, perhaps because of the nearby amusement park.

Even my youngest aunt emerged from the room and joined the other relatives. My mother seemed to be most curious about the price of burial clothes.

"We got the cheap ones. They openly admit it now, that they all come from China."

The mention of China prompted my second aunt to talk about her cancelled trip once more. Talk about timing, her brother-in-law had thrown a wrench into her plans on his way out. My eldest aunt, who had been sitting with other relatives, crawled over to my mother and dropped her voice down to a whisper. "Sehee, I heard he dropped by."

Mother seemed to understand right away. My other aunts leaned in. Mother nudged Father, who was already tipsy from the few drinks he'd had since noon.

My eldest aunt lowered her voice further. "Oppa, Muyeong showed up at Myeonghui's place."

This was news to my second aunt, who was usually the first to know everything. "At Myeonghui's house? Why?"

My eldest aunt ignored her. Normally, this would irritate my second aunt, but she remained serious.

"The doorbell rang, so Myeonghui opens the door, and there's this fella standing there who says he's Muyeong. She fixed him some lunch and then he left. Said he's tall and lanky, just like Oppa."

"That all?" my father asked, adding nothing else.

"At first, Myeonghui thought he was selling something. Figured she'd buy it if it didn't cost too much."

My second aunt cut in. "Did he ask about Oppa?"

Father was probably wondering the same thing, too.

My youngest aunt, who had been listening quietly, shook her head. "That's not Muyeong. He took after his ma, so he was real small and short."

"Hold on, when's the last time we laid eyes on him? Sixteen? Seventeen? How we supposed to know it was him?"

"Look here, you can tell a tater from a cuke by its seed. You remember his ma, don't you?"

My recollections of Muyeong were similar to those of my youngest aunt. After Grandma, I probably knew him best. From age seven until seventeen, when he left to live with his birth mom, I'd spent every summer with him. Now with Grandma gone, I was the only one who could instantly recognize him. The last time I'd seen him, he'd been shorter than other kids our age, which was accentuated when he carried a T-square in his backpack for his drafting class.

Father never called Muyeong by his name. He called him *Mame*, Japanese for *bean*, because he was short. Or he didn't bother with names at all. My second aunt cocked her head, puzzled.

"It's queer, don't you think? Why'd he drop in on Myeonghui when he hardly knows her? Should've come to us if anything . . . Is Myeonghui coming today?"

My eldest aunt shouted to the next table, "Anyone know if Myeonghui's coming?"

"She said she was," replied a middle-aged woman with a thin face and heavy makeup, chewing on a piece of squid. She was a relative, though her face was unfamiliar.

It had been almost ten years since I last heard about Muyeong. Back then, at a similar gathering, I'd heard he'd immigrated illegally to Japan. I was taking a semester off during my junior year to prepare for military service. I didn't think I could ever do something like that. *Irasshaimase! Welcome!* I envisioned Muyeong calling out to customers on the neon-lit streets of Ikebukuro or Ginza.

My youngest aunt lowered her voice, as if she'd been the one to immigrate illegally. "For crying out loud, you're trusting Myeonghui after what she's done to you? I wouldn't trust her, not for a second."

My aunts glanced at my father, gauging his reaction. The older man with the motorboat filled a shot glass for my father. My mother, who usually chided him for drinking, stayed silent. My father downed the shot and handed the glass back to the man. As the alcohol took effect, the older man's hands stopped shaking.

I stepped outside. The sun was setting, and the signs for the hot springs glowed red. I wanted to soak in water hot enough to scald. Muyeong had once pummeled me in the stomach after meeting his birth mother. Though small, his punches hurt. My knees had buckled from the pain.

"That actually hurt? I barely even swung."

He yanked me up by the collar. Although he only came up to my shoulders, I couldn't move. "My big brother? What a joke. She said you were born two months after me."

He'd discovered from his mother that his birth registration was wrong. He'd always believed he was a winter baby, but he'd actually been born in early autumn. His mother had gone into labor during Chuseok preparations, when the whole house was filled with the smell of frying food. He must have resented calling me hyeong all these years when he was the older one. He sprinted down the alley, then abruptly turned and shouted my name. Coming out of his mouth my name sounded strange. I felt as if I'd stepped on a dead mouse.

Lighting a cigarette, I suddenly realized why the funeral wreath I'd seen in the back of the truck on the way to the funeral home had looked so odd. On the black ribbon, above the Chinese characters for *condolence*, there had been an extra character: 祝. Congratulations. A worker at the flower shop must have written it out of habit.

"Maybe they're congratulating themselves for selling so many flower wreaths," I muttered to myself. I suddenly realized that talking to oneself was something Muyeong often did. Living with Grandma, who was almost sixty years older than him, Muyeong didn't have much company. She was hard of hearing, and even when you repeated yourself, she would often give an unrelated response. Out of boredom, Muyeong would ask a question and then answer it himself, as if in conversation with someone else. "He's talking to ghosts, that's what," Grandma used to say. She hated that habit of his. When I was almost finished with my cigarette, fireworks exploded in the sky above the amusement park.

Father spent most of the day, locked out, standing outside the front door. By five o'clock, darkness crept in from the end of the hallway. His hands and feet had gone numb. Normally, he would have waited for us to come home while having a meal at a warm restaurant or sipping tea in a café. But that day, he was seized by a fear—a fear that he wouldn't be able to find his way back home if he left. Mother, who'd gone out for lunch with friends, was late returning home. Lately, she preferred going out to staying home. Lunch with friends, followed by a visit to a karaoke room, made her day fly by. Father, who in his prime used to roam about town with his friends, now didn't set foot outside the house all day. When my mother rushed home to make dinner, she was startled out of her wits by a shadowy figure standing in the dark hallway.

Even after coming inside, my father couldn't recall the front door code. He knew it was a six-digit blend of our birthday months and days, but he was completely stumped.

"Looks like this man's done for," my mother blurted without thinking. Expecting an outburst, she looked at my father, but he made no reaction. With his mouth half open, he merely stared vacantly at the dark balcony. Curious, she followed his gaze. A chill overcame her and she stepped back. The thought that death was outside on the balcony struck her.

"Your father's acting strange."

I got her call during a company dinner. The tables, pushed together in a long line, were stained with stew and dried bean sprouts. Thanks to the raucous conversation of my drunk colleagues, I could barely hear my mother's voice, but she also seemed to be speaking quietly so that my father wouldn't hear. I didn't take the matter too seriously.

"To be honest, a six-digit combination's too long. Let's shorten it."

A colleague sitting next to me put his ear right up to my phone. "What's too long? You need to hem your pants?"

He stared at me with bleary eyes. I thought he had something to say, but he opened his mouth wide and yawned. The smell of semi-digested food hit me. Within a minute, another colleague sitting across from me yawned. Even before he could close his mouth, the department head sitting next to him yawned as well. Yawning spread like wildfire. A flustered female worker covered her mouth as it began to open. People started getting up from their seats. The first colleague to yawn put his head down on a wad of napkins stained with chili pepper and fell asleep instantly. As I tried to wake him, a thought crossed my mind: Could death spread like a yawn? In just a few years, my relatives had died one after another, leaving my aunts as widows. After cremating my uncle, my youngest aunt cried constantly. She cried while eating, while sitting on the toilet, even while washing her face. Her tears tell into the galbitang pot, to the point a customer complained the soup was too salty, perhaps because of her tears. According to my second aunt, my youngest aunt's face became so puffy from crying that it resembled udon noodles that had grown to three times their size.

That day, Father's body had come inside the house, but his mind seemed to be still outside, pressing random numbers on the door keypad. About a month later, a security guard escorted him home after he'd kicked a stranger's apartment door on the fifth floor. If it had been just one floor higher or lower, we could have chalked it up to accidentally pressing the wrong button on the elevator, but the floor he'd ended up on was too far off for that sort of mistake. Standing in front of a stranger's door, Father pulled out his wallet and unfolded a piece of paper where he had secretly written our door code, worried he might forget it again. He checked the numbers and pressed each digit slowly. The door didn't open. Like most keyless entry systems, after three failed attempts, he was completely locked out. Terrified and angry, he kicked the door. When it still didn't open, he opened the mail slot and reached inside. Alerted by the kicking, the next-door neighbor opened their front door and mistook my father for a thief. Security guards arrived promptly and pinned him against the wall, twisting his arms behind his back. If not for one guard who recognized him, Father would have been taken to the police station.

We couldn't understand why Father had tried to enter Suite 505.

"Mr. Shin Yeongho, why did you go there? Why #505?" Mother asked, clasping Father's hand and placing it on her knee, as if scolding a child.

My father clicked his tongue, as if still angry. My younger sister, who had just washed her hair and was dripping water on her way to her room, suddenly said, "Hey, could it be our old apartment from way back?"

Mother, usually quick to catch the meaning, didn't understand. "What apartment? What do you mean 'from way back'?" Then realization hit her, and she broke down, pinching whatever part of Father she could—ears, cheeks, arms. "Why? Why are you doing this? You're scaring me!"

We had lived in that fifth-floor apartment until I was in middle school. Back then, we burned coal briquettes for heating, which would be delivered over the course of several days in late autumn. Hauling the briquettes up to the fifth floor was no easy task, even for the experienced delivery man, who inevitably shattered one or two in the process. The long hallway in front of the entrance became a storage area for the briquettes, sometimes leading to disputes when neighbors would take each other's. As the piles of briquettes dwindled, it signaled the arrival of spring. Even after they were used up, dark smudges remained on the hallway walls throughout the year. The moment my father was about to press the seventeenth-floor button in the elevator, he seemed to have been transported twenty years back in time. Our old apartment had been at the very end of the hallway. Like dogs recognizing their owner's footsteps, we could always tell when Father was coming home, and before he could even ring the bell, we would open the door and dash into the hallway. Father always stared at the ground as he walked, only looking up when we called out to him, as if waking from a dream. The old, cramped apartment reeked of coal. I shouted in glee when I got a bicycle as a present, but soon lost interest because carrying it up and down five flights of stairs was such a hassle. What had my father liked about that old apartment? The building was redeveloped into a high-rise a long time ago. My mother often lamented that if we had continued to live there, we could have owned a spacious apartment by now.

On the first day of spring, when the temperature rose above zero, we received news of a death. I pictured the face of the old man, who had spent his entire life fishing with a motorboat. The island where the funeral was held was too far away for us to go, so we sent some condolence money along with our aunts who were attending.

"He was my cousin, the son of my ma's younger sister," my father explained, slipping into his native dialect, as though he'd returned to his hometown. "He was four years younger than me."

By my father's bedside, there was a picture frame, and next to it was a figurine I had never seen before: a pair of swans, chipped and peeling. Behind the bed, as if deliberately hidden, lay a pile of knickknacks, including grimy stuffed dolls, a plastic ashtray labeled "Bathroom Proof," and a chessboard missing the black king and white knight. The black-and-white photograph showed my father in his prime. When he was on the field, charging toward the net with the soccer ball, he would say he saw nothing but himself and the ball. He would outstrip one opponent after another, leaving them in his wake. On his good days, the goalposts appeared twice or even three times as wide, and he knew precisely where the ball should go. On his shin was a starfish-shaped scar, a memento from a kick by an opponent back then. All the soccer players in the photo have since passed away. My father alone remained. Just as he had outlasted his peers on the field in his youth, only my father has survived. At the last funeral he attended, without friends to share a drink with, he had half a bottle of soju by himself.

A man was leaning into the recycling bin at the complex, sifting through the items. I'd heard somewhere that old clothes and shoes were weighed by the kilogram and exported overseas. Once on a television program, I'd seen a little boy in Africa wearing a shirt printed with the name of a Seoul gym. I sometimes saw people rummaging in the recycling bin, so I thought nothing of it. Legs momentarily dangled in the air as he dug through the contents at the bottom of the bin. He resurfaced, wheezing, face flushed. He pulled out a briefcase, dusting it off with his other hand, and turned around. It was Father.

Because he didn't color his hair, it quickly turned white. His once-forceful strides lost their strength. His legs became crooked. Every time my mother stepped into his room, she would pinch her nose, complaining of a foul smell, even though she regularly aired out the room. She bought an air freshener that automatically dispensed scented bursts of "Dawn Forest" every hour and mounted it on the wall. Curious about the fragrance, my sister went into the room and shouted, grimacing, "Mom, I think Dad soiled himself."

Shocked, Mother ran inside the room and yanked down Father's pants. Equally shocked, Father curled up into a fetal position on the bed. Mother breathed a sigh of relief as she patted her chest. "How could you even think your dad would do such a thing?"

When I came home, my father was standing outside the front door and my mother was sweeping up all the junk my father had brought home into an oversized garbage bag. Father looked as if he was about to cry. She yelled, as if she wanted the neighbors to hear.

"If you'd done this when you were young, we would be rich by now! You used to act all high and mighty, refusing even the smallest gift, but look at you now, collecting all this trash! What am I supposed to do with this? Do you understand what I'm saying, Mr. Shin Yeongho?" At a certain point, my mother's voice had grown louder and louder.

At dinner, Father picked at his rice. When my mother urged him to take bigger bites, he shoved a large spoonful into his mouth. Rice spilled out, and soup dribbled down his lips. Frustrated by his inability to control his limbs, he slammed down his spoon. Ever since the day he forgot the door code and was locked out of the apartment, he had ceased making eye contact with any of us. He muttered something in the direction of the bean sprouts dish. No one heard him, but I understood immediately. "Mame." Even after hearing about Muyeong at my uncle's funeral, Father hadn't mentioned him until now. It was the first time he'd said anything about Muyeong.

Muyeong and I dropped the formalities and ended up not addressing each other at all. He gave an awkward grin. "Recognize me? I've changed quite a bit."

His habit of asking and answering his own questions hadn't changed. But judging by appearance alone, this wasn't the Muyeong whose head barely came up to my shoulders. His dialect was gone, too. If the café had been busy, I would have had a hard time finding him. Fortunately, the only customer was an elderly man in a fedora, reading the newspaper.

"Father wants to see you."

Instead of responding, Muyeong barked toward the kitchen, "Miss, a glass of water, please!"

A girl came dragging her platform slippers and slapped the water cup down on the table. I was brought back to our days in #505. The reason we could recognize my father's footsteps was because he dragged his heels as he walked.

"He doesn't have much time left. Go see him while you can. We can't change him, but you don't want to live with regrets."

The words came out better than I expected. Even as I spoke, I felt as though I was delivering a line from a television drama. Muyeong sipped his tea, making a gurgling sound.

"I've changed quite a bit," he said again.

I waited for him to continue, but he said no more.

I hadn't noticed in the dimly lit café, but once we were outside, I saw a scar on Muyeong's left cheek. It was shaped like a swoosh. He must have sensed my gaze, because he puffed out his cheek, making the ends of the swoosh almost touch. Muyeong thrust out his hand.

I thought he wanted to shake hands, but he was holding a business card.

"I'll go see him once."

When a taxi pulled up, he raised his arm unhurriedly. After it left, I peered down at the business card. It was transparent, displaying only his name and contact information.

It seemed Father's illness would not drag on like my uncle's. Suddenly, he refused all food, consuming only water. Mother made a thin rice gruel and held it up to his lips, but he would not open his mouth. I lifted him easily, as if he were a crate of apples, and carried him on my back down to the parking lot. He clung to me like a child, wrapping his arms and legs around me. All of a sudden, a folktale I'd read as a boy flashed across mind. An old man asks a cobbler to be carried across a stream, but once across, he refuses to get down from the cobbler's back. No matter how hard the cobbler tries, the scrawny old man sticks to him like glue and refuses to let go. Left with no other choice, the cobbler has to carry the old man everywhere. What would I do if Father refused to get down? I recalled being carried on his back long ago. We must have been walking by the sea in his hometown. He sang a song by Bae Ho: "I have no regrets. I don't cry. After you left . . ." The words from that night rang in my head, as if he were singing it again.

The nurse jabbed the same spot twice while trying to insert the IV needle. She said the veins were hard to find. Although he ate nothing, Father kept soiling himself. The patient sharing the room turned away, unable to bear the smell. I brought a basin of warm water and washed his bottom. My father, more lucid than on other days, wept quietly. His wrinkled, lopsided testicles were difficult to clean.

The path behind the hospital led directly to the funeral home. Muyeong and I stood outside the hospital's rear entrance and smoked together. I had started smoking before him. The memory of secretly stashing a pack of 88s in my school bag and offering one to Muyeong came to mind. While we smoked, three funeral wreaths made of plump white chrysanthemums paraded past us to the funeral home. As soon as I saw them, I couldn't help thinking of steaming white buns. I peered up at Muyeong's face. He was also looking at the wreaths.

Even as she gave me cousin Myeonghui's number, my youngest aunt had warned me. "Remember, nine out of ten things that come out of her mouth are lies. Got it?" Despite living out in the country, Myeonghui didn't speak in dialect. When I asked for Muyeong's number, she gave it to me right away, as if she'd been waiting for me to ask.

Muyeong strode ahead of me, his long limbs filling out his suit nicely. How did Muyeong know cousin Myeonghui? As I trailed behind him, I blurted, "Hey, don't you wear glasses?"

"My vision's the one thing I've got," Muyeong said, not bothering to turn around. "Perfect 20/20."

My aunts arrived in a chartered van, as if they were going on another one of their trips. Even when they were near the hospital, they called over ten times for directions. They stepped into the hospital room, complaining that the driver didn't know Seoul at all.

Father's lips trembled, as if he wanted to speak. His body was stiffening. My mother glanced at my aunts as she dabbed her eyes with a handkerchief.

"If you've got something to say to him, say it now. He can't speak, but he understands everything."

My second aunt hesitated and then blurted, "The apple . . ."

"What on earth are you talking about?" my eldest aunt snapped, glaring through her tears.

My second aunt exhaled deeply. "Oppa, you're on your way out, so listen up. I've got something in my heart I've been carrying for a long time. Fact is, I was sore at you. Being a boy, you got yourself an education and plenty of good jobs. I know you looked down on us." She was crying. "When you were nineteen and I was thirteen, you always got the best food. Mama gave you an apple that time. I wanted it, God, I wanted it, but you gave it to some girl from our neighborhood instead. It was cruel what you did. But I'm letting it go now. So long, Oppa. Make sure you find us a good spot, okay?"

My father stretched out his hands and clawed at the air. It looked as though he were brushing something away or trying to grab it. When his hands grazed my second aunt's face, she gasped and burst into tears. Muyeong, who had been standing in the back, strode forward and clasped Father's hands. Father suddenly grew calm. Only then did my aunts notice Muyeong.

"Who's this? That you, Muyeong?"

My two oldest aunts gripped Muyeong's hand, but my youngest aunt narrowed her eyes.

Father's eyes were open, but they appeared to see nothing, covered with a thin film. Muyeong wept silently, his tears dropping onto the back of my father's bony hands. My aunts threw themselves at Father's chest and wailed. From behind, their dyed heads were indistinguishable from one another. Mother put her ear close to Father's lips, trying to catch his last words. I stood back, as if at the funeral of a friend's father. No tears came to my eyes. At the funeral of a friend's father, no matter how sad, you shouldn't cry more than your friend. Muyeong had visited the hospital three times. Given that I barely recognized him, how could my father, who only saw him once a year back when we were boys, recognize him? Even so, Father studied Muyeong's face as he held his hand, as if searching for any resemblance. Father had wanted to hide Muyeong. Back then, my father had been in the prime of his youth, eager to kick every ball that came his way. If the typhoon hadn't kept his boat moored to the island, he would have never made such a mistake. Now, it didn't seem to matter to him if this man was actually Muyeong or not. What he wanted was to embark on his final journey with no regrets, a fitting closure to his life. My gaze drifted to the scar on Muyeong's cheek. Who was he, really? The Muyeong I'd known had bad eyes. So bad that he'd mistaken chrysanthemums for steamed buns. Because of him, I thought of steamed buns every time I saw white chrysanthemums.

The machine connected to Father's body began to sound an alarm, signaling the end. Father began to pant. Muyeong gripped Father's hand harder. What had happened to Muyeong? My second aunt shouted at my father's fading consciousness. "Go now, Oppa! May you find eternal peace!"

The light left my father's eyes, and his slightly open mouth grew rigid. It was the peaceful end he had yearned for.

A Hotel at the End of the World

The Polar Hotel was built on a sandbank. The balconies of over a hundred rooms faced the South Sea. Sunlight streamed in through large protruding windows, waking guests early and prompting the dining area to open at dawn. A handful of islands, as tiny as pebbles, lay scattered on the shimmering horizon in the middle of the window. Each day, loudspeakers blared from the pier, enticing tourists to go on island cruises. Every two hours, when a cruise ship sounded its horn and left the pier, a flock of seagulls took flight and trailed behind the stern. It was a monotonous scene that repeated itself. On foggy days, none of this was visible, but you could guess by the muffled horn that a cruise ship was passing somewhere outside the window.

The can-can team rushed into the dressing room of the Moulin Rouge after their performance. As they hurried in, holding up their tiered ruffle skirts, they collided briefly with the acrobats going on stage for the next act. Breathing heavily, the dancers cursed as they undid the laces of their tightly cinched bodices and tossed off their skirts.

They said performing high kicks in high heels while repeatedly shaking their skirts caused them to lose all sensation in their limbs. After a performance, their entire bodies, including their faces and necks, would become slick with sweat. Every time they flapped their skirts, their body odor wafted over to the woman sitting at the vanity table. Makeup, sweat, and mold. These sweat-soaked costumes had to be dried in the sun, but the dressing room didn't have a single hole where a ray of sunlight could come in. Mold grew on the costumes, and a few of the dancers developed skin diseases.

A makeshift dressing room had been created by blocking off one side of the hallway. A long vanity was fitted along the hallway, and light bulbs were strung across the ceiling. Costumes hung on the clothes rack set up along the opposite wall. The end of the hallway, technically an emergency exit, was piled high with props used in the show, like fans and drums. It had been a long time since anyone other than the dancers had come in here. Boxes of imported whiskey and canned ham were stacked to the ceiling on the staircase leading from the emergency exit up to the first floor. The door barely opened enough for a single person to squeeze through.

A dancer threw her leg onto the vanity where the woman was sitting and began to remove her stockings. Sweat had caused her mascara to smear, leaving dark smudges beneath her eyes. Perhaps the strain of stretching had brought tears to her eyes. Judging by her long, slender neck, the woman suspected the girl might be Kyeonga, the one who said that by the end of the show, she felt like a puppet whose wrist and ankle strings were being manipulated by someone above. Or given the constant blinking because of the false lashes, maybe it was Jenny, who felt only relief at the finale when she lifted her skirt and flashed her backside to the audience. Dancers at the Moulin Rouge all had slender faces and long necks, and once they were styled with identical updos, fake lashes, and red lipstick, it was almost impossible to tell them apart.

They took off their ruffled skirts and tops, stripping down to bras and knickers. Dressed this way, they killed time before the second act, sometimes sneaking into the kitchen across the hall to snatch some of the appetizers meant for customers, or sitting on dusty beer crates to smoke. Before stepping back onto the stage, they changed into their sequined costumes and pinned up their hair with bobby pins, touching up their makeup to hide the bags under their eyes. Their thinning hair, gathered up, hardly amounted to a handful, and sometimes words or saliva slipped through the gaps in their teeth. Because their throats grew parched from cigarette smoke, they popped a candy into their mouths and rolled it around with their tongues. Having a private dressing room was out of the question. Their six-month contract with the Moulin Rouge was almost over, and there had been no word from management about renewing it.

Whenever waiters came down to the kitchen to fetch food and drinks, loud stage effects and applause leaked through. Not many guests appeared to be present today since the servers weren't coming down to the kitchen often. There were rumors that the Moulin Rouge was knee-deep in debt. The waiters, even when they came down to pick up the appetizers, lingered to joke with the dancers. Neither the dancers nor the waiters felt embarrassed about the dancers being in their underwear.

The woman snatched a cigarette from a dancer, dragged deeply on it, and handed it back. Smoking was particularly damaging to the voice. She experienced a head rush, and the plastic crates loaded with glass bottles seemed to be tilting toward her. She staggered forward and heard a dancer yell, "Good luck, Mama!" She waved without turning around. It was impossible to tell if it was Kyeonga with her long neck or Jenny blinking her constantly tearing eyes. All the dancers were smokers, with raspy voices.

The Polar Hotel started where the sandbank ended. In the garden, trees that the gardener tended with the same attention as he would give his children endured the sea breeze. From early spring when the flowers started to bloom, guests flocked to the Sky Lounge where the window seats remained occupied throughout the season. The garden, thoughtfully designed, offered captivating views from both ground level and the Sky Lounge. Violets, daffodils, lilies of the valley, daisies, hollyhocks, peonies, hydrangeas . . . From above, one could appreciate how the annual and perennial flowers blended harmoniously with the carefully pruned trees, shrubs, and grass. The garden resembled a handkerchief embroidered with a large star or a starfish.

On the three sides of the Polar Hotel that didn't face the sea, mosaic windows of glass fragments adorned the walls. The sun, rising from the direction of the balcony windows, set toward the main entrance where there was a tourist shop and a Korean restaurant. Regardless of where the sun was, the hotel lounge was bathed in sunlight until late afternoon. The sunlight coming through the windows pooled and rippled near her ankles, like water in a stream.

The hotel had restaurants that featured fresh seasonal dishes, and the lounges, stairs, and hallways were covered with thick, burgundy carpet. All spring, strawberries simmered in sugar for the Strawberry Festival, their smell lingering in the lounge.

On stage at the Moulin Rouge, a human tower was being erected. At the far left of the stage, Kim, the heaviest, stood at the bottom, while his cousin stood atop his shoulders. There was a seesaw at the center of the stage, and at one end was Kim's wife, Park. The band created suspense with a drumroll. A big acrobat ran full speed and jumped onto the seesaw, sending Park flying into the air. She did a somersault mid-air and managed to land on the shoulders of Kim's cousin, adding another level to the human tower. Scattered applause broke out.

From the waiting area beneath the stage, the audience wasn't visible, but it was easy to gauge the size of the crowd. Guests were likely spread throughout the hall. There had been times when she had sung to a packed house, with those unable to find seats filling the aisles. The temperature of the theater rose from the crowd's breath and body heat. At such times, the audience became a large, solid mass, overwhelming her.

The human tower continued to rise, but the scattered applause soon stopped. The trick had lost its allure. A spectacle like an acrobat flying off course and plummeting headfirst into the audience would certainly have captured their attention. Kim's lips turned blue from the strain of supporting five people on his shoulders. His muscles bulged, and the seams of his leotard appeared ready to burst at any moment. Gritting his teeth, Kim walked around the stage with his burden. The human tower disassembled with a collective cry, and the acrobats bowed their heads and raised them in unison. The team exited the stage on the opposite end and the host cracked some jokes, but there was no reaction. In the past, he would have had the audience in stitches, even with a little stumble. He quickly called the next act, the woman, onto the stage. Having shared the stage with her many times in the past, he still called her "Miss," though she'd been middle-aged for quite some time. The dancers called her Mama. The acrobatic team had left sweat patches everywhere on the stage, causing it to be slippery like ice, so she needed to tread carefully. A misstep could cause her to plop down on her bottom or tumble off the stage. As soon as she stepped onto the stage, the band started playing. She needed to grab the microphone at center stage before the intro ended, but it was too far. She waddled awkwardly across the stage, triggering laughter from somewhere in the audience.

The dressing room was thick with smoke from the cigarettes of twenty dancers. A pot of kimchi stew, delivered from the Korean restaurant next door, sat atop a beer crate. A few dancers huddled around it, having a late dinner. "Mama! Come join us," invited a dancer with lips stained from the stew, thrusting a spoon toward her and making room for her to sit. In the large, shallow, stainless-steel pot were chunks of kimchi and tofu mixed with swollen glass noodles. She sat down but had no appetite. She felt cold sweat run down her back. She'd narrowly avoided falling on stage, saved by the host who had caught her. He refrained from the slapstick antics he was once known for. He was the one who had told her about the financial state of the Moulin Rouge. The Moulin Rouge was indeed deep in doubt.

The dancers quickly cleared away the food, and passed around cigarette packs in perfect order, like when they were performing. A lighter was tossed through the air. Vendors made their way right into the dressing room, where several performers squatted in front of a vendor's rubber tub, munching on rice cakes and kimbap. The second part of the show was going to start soon. Although they left the emergency exit open, the room didn't get proper ventilation. The first-floor door that the emergency exit was connected to was locked from the outside. The smell of cigarettes and food rose to the top of the stairs and was forced back down into the dressing room. The heat from the stage lights had caused the dancers' makeup to melt around their noses, and sweat created pale streaks on their cheeks and foreheads. They dabbed their faces with powder puffs.

The performers were all on contracts ranging from three to six months. If they managed to get their contracts renewed, they could enjoy peace of mind for a little while. Some dancers spread out a blanket and played cards, cigarettes dangling from their mouths. Turnover among the dancers was high. Fewer than five members of the can-can team had been there when the woman began singing at the Moulin Rouge a year earlier. As long as the Moulin Rouge stayed open, the can-can team would continue, but the dancers couldn't rest easy. They noticed more foreign dancers in amusement park parades and at other venues. Those dancers didn't need to powder their faces as much to appear fair, and were favored by employers for demanding lower salaries than Korean dancers. They were also less likely to complain, at least until they became fluent in Korean.

As closing time approached, not only Jenny's but also all the other dancers' eyes became bloodshot from the lash glue they used. As they continually touched up their sweat-streaked faces, their makeup grew thicker, making them look as though they would shatter like Chinese porcelain dolls if they fell.

The coastline began behind the Polar Hotel and gently curved to the opposite shore. She walked aimlessly along the shore, which led to a breakwater and a hill formed by stacks of small and large rocks. She hopped between the rocks, the water below appearing deep and dark. Two female divers in loose rubber suits were diving for abalones and sea cucumbers. A flock of seagulls swooped in and pecked at the crevices in the rocks with their bent beaks. Her manager had brought her to the very end of the mainland and told her, "Just lay low for two months. Everything will blow over by then." The divers took a deep breath and plunged into the inky water. She tried to hold her breath for as long as they did, but she couldn't manage it for even twenty seconds, probably because she smoked. A strange silence ensued. The only things bobbing on the surface were the two yellow Styrofoam floats to which the divers hooked their nets. She hurried down the hill, slipping on the rocks and banging her shin several times. Peering into the dark water, she felt her mouth go dry. After what seemed like an eternity, the divers resurfaced, their heads poking out next to the yellow floats. They laughed when they saw her ashen face.

"Oh, did we scare you?"

"Afraid we'd drowned?"

From a distance, the hotel resembled a tropical botanical garden, towering above raw fish restaurants, karaoke bars, and indoor gaming arcades. She wandered along the coast for some time. Standing at one end of the shore, the hotel on the opposite side had seemed close enough to touch, almost within swimming distance. She dipped her toes into the sea and found the water shockingly cold.

There was no message from Seoul. She'd gotten into her manager's car as though they were fleeing in the dead of night. That had been the last of it. Drunk, she dozed on and off, slumped in the back seat. Each time she opened her eyes, red streetlights whisked past the window. She felt nauseous. The manager was nervous, fretting she might spoil his freshly reupholstered seats. With reporters camped outside her lodging, she'd had no time to pack. She arrived at the hotel early in the morning, wearing a tracksuit with white vertical stripes and sneakers without socks. In the darkness, the sea was invisible. The hotel lounge was empty, except for a tall male employee in a black suit stationed at the front desk. His hair was neatly slicked back. He glanced between her manager and her, who stood a few steps behind, surveying the lounge. When their eyes met, he seemed to recognize her instantly, despite her disheveled appearance. He even seemed to know the reason why she'd come to this remote place at such an hour, all the way to the farthest tip of the mainland.

A waiter hurried down to the dressing room. Responsible for ushering guests at the theater entrance, he was the best source of news.

"He's here?" one of the dancers asked, craning her neck out of the dressing room. She then yelled into the room without bothering to wait for his response. "He's here!"

The waiter sped down the hallway. Park from the acrobatic team, who had been knitting, jumped up. "Did you let the men know?"

Male performers didn't have their own dressing room. Some arrived just in time for their acts and left immediately afterward. Occasionally, famous celebrities who performed at the theater went straight up to the VIP room on the second floor. Male performers affiliated solely with the Moulin Rouge were likely asleep in a van in the parking lot.

"Yeah, just now," the waiter said. "Mr. Kim yelled at me, asking what difference it would make for them to know he's here." Park seemed like she wanted to inquire further, but the waiter had already vanished up the stairs.

They said the owner of the Moulin Rouge would suddenly drop by the theater to watch the show. Such rumors began circulating one or two weeks before the contract period ended. He was supposedly scouting performers for the next production. A dancer, in the midst of shuffling cards, threw down the deck. She folded the blanket without gathering the cards and shoved everything into a corner. The dancers stood and dusted themselves off nonchalantly. They placed a leg on the vanity to stretch, touching up their makeup where needed. The can-can team, the Moulin Rouge's main attraction, wasn't safe either. They faced the possibility of losing their act to foreign dancers with fair skin and long, slender legs. Despite grumbling about how tired they were, once on stage, they would raise their legs higher and shake their hips more enticingly. Acrobat Park tried to resume knitting, but soon gave up. She had a talent for fitting her whole body into a small box. When she tucked her last remaining leg into the box, her tangled limbs resembled a ball of yarn. This trick had sustained her for fifteen years.

Two dancers squabbled over a missing stocking. "I know you hid it on purpose," one said, hopping up and down in anger with a stocking on just one leg. "You'd better hand it over right now!"

"On purpose, huh?" the other one said, jutting out her chin and placing her hands on her hips. "You're right, I hid it just to give you a hard time. What do you want me to do about it?"

In a different corner, an argument broke out when a dancer accidentally kicked another in the face while stretching. "Where do you think you're putting your dirty feet?"

"Dirty? Who are you calling dirty? Come over here and let's see if your feet don't stink." She tripped the other girl, making her fall.

Turnover among the dancers was high. Many considered their time at the Moulin Rouge as something to experience briefly in their twenties. Though the emergency exit door had been left open, the smell of smoke and food remained trapped inside the dressing room.

Even before the can-can started, word came that the owner's black car had left the Moulin Rouge. He'd been at the theater for a mere half-hour, during the set of a young comedian who deejayed at the Moulin Rouge every week. The fact that he didn't watch the whole show could mean he planned to renew all the performers' contracts. However, the host had said that the Moulin Rouge was buried in debt. So it could mean he might not renew any contracts at all. The dancers returned to the dressing room, their ruffled skirts flapping, while the acrobatic team exited to perform. One dancer rifled through her bag for a cigarette, not bothering to change out of her costume before lighting up. Her whole body was glistening with sweat. Her corseted chest heaved and there were dark smudges under her eyes. She couldn't tell if it was Kyeonga or Jenny.

The Polar Hotel stood on a sandbank at the southernmost point of the mainland. In the peak of summer, the beach attracted over a hundred thousand visitors. As she walked along the beach, she got sand in her sneakers. She sat in the garden's shade, spending a long time shaking out the sand. Sipping from a mini bottle of whiskey she'd tucked into her sweatpants pocket, she eyed the beachgoers. At night, the waves glinted like razor blades. Drunk, she went back to her hotel room and fell asleep without washing up. Despite sleeping for hours, it always seemed to be night. In the morning, she discovered grains of sand in her bedsheets.

"The sea breeze ruins all the electrical appliances. Know why beach-side rooms are so expensive? It's because appliances depreciate so quickly," said the hotel gardener. He propped a ladder against a Hollywood Juniper and began pruning its branches. His shears were so large that he needed to grasp one handle with each hand. Except for the gleaming blades that looked as though they'd just been sharpened, everything else was covered in red rust. When the blades came together, they snipped easily through branches as thick as fingers.

"It doesn't matter if the appliances are behind double, triple doors. Give it a week and the entire hotel will be covered in sand. Fine grains, almost like fog, get in machines and break them down. The salt from the sea doesn't help either."

A milky sap oozing from the freshly cut branches smelled like super glue. The sea breeze damaged more than just machines and appliances. The gardener's skin resembled traditional changhoji paper, which had been soaked in bean oil and dried multiple times. Legend had it that not even arrows could penetrate changhoji.

The gardener moved with urgency, as if he were being pursued by someone. When he finished pruning the trees, he staked new saplings for support. Weeds emerged from the meticulously trimmed grass and flowerbeds. He prepared a sodium chlorate solution, dipping the ends of the weeds into the mix. As they absorbed the toxin, the weeds yellowed and shriveled. It was also the gardener's responsibility to drag a long hose around, watering the garden. He watered the flowerbeds daily and quickly removed any wilted flowers, replacing them with fresh ones of the same color. When he yanked out the wilted flowers by the roots, he seemed almost ruthless. It was hard to believe he'd been the one to tend to the flowers with so much care. "Once they wither, they don't bloom again," he muttered, tossing the withered flowers into a wheelbarrow. "It's because of this damned sea breeze. Everything fades too quickly." Because the gardener always removed the wilted flowers right away, the garden looked unchanged from the Sky Lounge.

Gold and silver foil from the magic show lay scattered across the stage. The woman performed three songs twice a day at the mostly empty Moulin Rouge. The emptiness of the hall lent an unusual chill to the spring night. The waiters complained that customers nursed their drinks, ordering only the minimum—a few bottles of alcohol and a basic appetizer. According to the host, the era of theater shows had passed. Gone were the days when the 10,000-foot theater was packed with guests. The venue had been operating at a loss for over a year now. The host was angry, because his comedy no longer had the same impact, but he still refrained from performing slapstick. Appearances by famous celebrities had also dwindled. The host blamed the decline on the government. Standing there, listening to the host's diatribe, the woman didn't know whether to laugh or cry, and was uncertain which expression to make. It was clear that if the shows were as popular as they had once been, she wouldn't have been singing there at all. The heat of the stage lights was intense. Her scalp began to sweat. She wondered if the lights would scorch her eyebrows.

Musicians played their instruments half asleep. As the music flowed, disco balls suspended from various points on the ceiling spun. The dance floor remained empty until she reached the midway point of the first verse, when a couple emerged from the audience. They embraced and started dancing. Soon after, several couples rushed out from different corners of the room to dance.

The second song was an old hit called "Goodbye Forever." Some people still recognized her face from this song. A few even claimed to be fans, thrusting their beer glasses toward the stage. She couldn't help flinching as she looked at their deeply lined faces and dark gums. A commotion erupted in the back of the room. The stage lights were blinding, but it seemed a drunk guest had stood up and fallen, knocking over a table. The fall caused the next table to topple as well. She heard bottles break. All eyes turned to the back of the room where the tables had fallen. No one paid attention to her singing anymore. The dancers stopped dancing as well.

The man who had fallen got up. He was tall. Swaying back and forth, he staggered across the hall toward the stage. The couples who had been slow-dancing stepped aside and watched. The stage was only about a meter high—easy for even a drunk person to jump on. The waiters huddled together and whispered among themselves, neither righting the fallen tables nor stopping the man. She glanced at the band, but they seemed unfazed, as if used to such customers, and continued to play.

"Can't you sing better than that?"

It seemed the man would jump onto the stage and grab her hair at any moment. She stepped back, holding the microphone.

The man stared up at her with surprise, his drunkenness suddenly gone. He shook his head vigorously. The woman continued to sing, ready to flee at any moment, but the man listened meekly. During the last verse, he even joined in: "I'm letting go of your hand, goodbye forever, goodbye forever."

He extended his hand, as if for a handshake. She hesitated, uncertain whether to take it. He shook his hand again, and she shuffled toward the edge of the stage. His hair was neatly trimmed, as if freshly cut. As she reached out to shake his hand, she noticed tears glistening in his eyes. She was so surprised her mouth dropped open. A few men, who appeared to be his companions, rushed to the stage and dragged him away by the arms, leading him out of the hall. They stumbled, laughing. The man lost one of his shoes as they dragged him away. He tried to shout something at her, but the band drowned him out. His lone shoe got kicked around by the people on the dance floor.

It was a bespoke shoe with laces. If their paths ever crossed again, she wanted to ask him why he'd cried. She grabbed the shoe and dashed outside, but neither the man nor his group was in sight. A large windmill adorned the neon sign of the Moulin Rouge. The stage lights switched off. From outside the theater, she could hear the waiters sweeping up the broken bottles and rousing customers who had fallen asleep at their tables. The dancers swarmed out and split up to board two vans that were waiting in front of the theater. They had only changed their clothes, leaving their makeup and hair intact. Though it was a spring night, the early morning air still held a chill. Through the window of the darkened van, the faces of the dancers resembled the heads of rag dolls made from white fabric. The van exited the alley and turned onto the main road. The other van started to follow but suddenly stopped. A dancer jumped out, blinking. It was Jenny. It seemed she had forgotten something in the dressing room. The van drove away, leaving Jenny behind. Jenny waved at the retreating van and, once it had disappeared, rushed back into the theater, her hands shoved in her coat pockets.

Though all the performers had left, a warmth still lingered in the dressing room. The woman tucked the man's shoe under the costume rack. She removed her sequined dress, placed it in a shopping bag, and took off her high heels. A purse sat on the vanity. It was most likely Jenny's. The emergency exit was open. Despite being open all day, the smell of smoke never cleared. Jenny, who'd come back into the Moulin Rouge before her, was nowhere in sight. The kitchen lights were off. No doubt the waiters had spotted Jenny as she came in, and she was now chatting with them. The woman closed the emergency door and locked it by pressing the button on the doorknob. She left the lights on in the dressing room for Jenny. Sure enough, on one side of the empty hall, waiters sat around a table, laughing and drinking beer. There was no chance these young men would let Jenny slip away so easily.

She saw the fire at the Moulin Rouge on the afternoon news. Having woken around eleven, she was about to take her first spoonful of rice mixed with water when heavy black smoke billowed out beneath the Moulin Rouge windmill sign. Though it was dark, the flames illuminated the sign. Flames leapt out of the windows, licking the walls like massive tongues. The fire had started around 4:10 in the morning and was extinguished three hours later. On the television screen, fire trucks kept spraying water, but the flames seemed to evade the water only to flare up again. The hoses wriggled in the firefighters' hands like enormous snakes. The cause of the fire was suspected to have been either a discarded cigarette or an electrical fault. Fortunately, the theater was empty at the time, so there were no casualties.

The Moulin Rouge was unrecognizable, burned beyond repair. Thankfully, the other shops in the alley were spared. Water pooled heavily on the scorched, blackened floor of the hall. Performers hovered around the site. Beer bottles had exploded in the flames, and plastic crates were stuck to walls like melted taffy. Canned goods had swelled as if ready to burst, their wrappers charred black. Only the vague outlines of the stage and hall were distinguishable. Waiters, out of uniform, murmured together. "Jeez, it freaks me out just thinking about what could've happened. If we'd had a few more bottles like you said . . ." Suddenly, the woman thought of Jenny. She hadn't seen her among the dancers, who were watching the wreckage from a distance, shaking their heads with their arms crossed.

"No, not yet. She's always late. She's probably still asleep and hasn't even heard about the fire."

"I know Jenny well," a waiter said, looking at the woman with confusion. "But we drank on our own last night. If we'd seen Jenny, we would've invited her to join us."

"Jenny?" said another waiter, chiming in. "Nope, didn't see her. If she'd come back in, we would have seen her for sure and convinced her to join us. We didn't see a single dancer."

The woman distinctly remembered seeing Jenny go back into the theater. She also remembered a bag someone had left on the vanity table.

She had returned to the dressing room, changed out of her costume, and locked the emergency door that had been left ajar. She shook her head. Boxes of whiskey and ham were stacked behind the emergency exit, a door rarely used and opened only for ventilation. If Jenny had been there, she would have known. Jenny would have screamed when she closed the door. The woman rushed into the theater, water splashing onto her clothes. She located the stairs leading to the basement dressing room, but couldn't go down. The stairs were half-flooded from the water used to extinguish the fire.

Could there have been a reason Jenny couldn't make a sound when she closed the emergency exit? The first-floor door connected to the exit was padlocked from the outside. Just as she was about to run toward it, a waiter stopped her. "She's here! Jenny's here!"

As if she'd just found out about the fire, Jenny was making a fuss, staring at the wreckage. In broad daylight, hser face seemed unfamiliar. She blinked less, perhaps because she wasn't wearing her false lashes. The dancers all looked the same once they donned identical costumes, pulled their hair up in buns, and applied false lashes and red lipstick. Plus, it had been late, and the neon sign had been off. Was it Jenny who'd darted back into the theater? The waiters claimed they hadn't seen her. The woman felt dizzy, as if she'd experienced a headrush from inhaling cigarette smoke too quickly. The false lashes caused Jenny to blink a lot, but now she wasn't even sure if it was Jenny or Kyeonga who blinked incessantly.

"He's here."

The performers gathered around a black sedan that had just pulled into the alley. The acrobat Kim, who'd been chain-smoking, stubbed out his cigarette with his shoe and stood up.

The woman didn't recognize Kwak at first. It was only when he mentioned he played the bass guitar that she vaguely remembered him.

"Famous celebrities are performing, too. And the pay's much better than at the Moulin Rouge . . . Why not give it a try until they rebuild?"

Kwak seemed to know quite a bit about her. He had a habit of emphasizing his sentences with, "You trust me, right?" He was in his early thirties, with pockmarks etched on his face. She felt a pang of guilt for not knowing more about him, despite having performed alongside his guitar for the past six months. When Kwak mentioned their destination, she had no reason to hesitate. Two other band members who'd lost their jobs due to the fire also joined them: Lee, the drummer, and Park, the keyboardist. The trio seemed to know each other well, and they knew quite a bit about her too.

In the car and during a brief stop at a rest area for some udon, the conversation revolved around the Moulin Rouge fire.

"Does the name invite fires or something?"

"Oh yeah, I forgot the original Moulin Rouge also burned down."

"The current one in Paris was rebuilt after the fire. It's a Parisian landmark, after all."

"There's no way they're going to rebuild Seoul's Moulin Rouge."

They had known for a long time that the Moulin Rouge was mired in debt.

"The owner profited from the fire. Who would take over a rundown theater? He was hemorrhaging money, so in a way, it all worked out for him. Hey, you think he started the fire?"

Kwak, frequently glancing at the side mirror, squeezed into the next lane. His driving was fast and restless, weaving impatiently through traffic and frequently honking the horn. Lee and Park seemed used to Kwak's driving style.

"The place was doomed from the start. Sure, there were fewer and fewer customers, but the staff were the problem. They sold the alcohol and canned food on the black market at discounted prices. Only the boss didn't know. Everyone was in on it."

On the morning of the fire, she'd seen Jenny go back into the theater. The waiters denied seeing her, or any other dancers.

"Remember the whiskey we had on your birthday?" Lee said, chuckling.

Kwak swerved into another lane, causing the car behind them to flash its headlights and lean on the horn.

It was clear that Kwak had been duped. He paced the lobby, smoking cigarette after cigarette. The three people who had trusted and followed him found themselves in the same predicament. On the walls, promotional posters were displayed in a row. In one poster, under the headline "The Singer of 'Goodbye Forever,'" there was a photograph of the woman taken seventeen years earlier. Her face was smiling brightly, framed by bangs and a bob. The famous celebrities slated to appear were impersonators, who used humorous, slightly altered names of real celebrities. The event, billed as a "local singing contest," was merely a front for peddling medicinal products. In a large rubber tub at the base of the stage, snails as large as adult fists squirmed.

Her sequined costume looked cheap and garish in natural light. Kwak looked carefully at the other three and reasoned that since they had come all this way, it was better to perform half a day for some compensation rather than leave with nothing. The singing contest contestants, along with their families, relatives, and friends, made up the audience.

A man, bearing resemblance to a famous trot singer known for his sideburns, mimicked the original performer down to the slightest gestures, placing a hand on his waist or biting his lower lip, eliciting laughter from the crowd.

"And now, back from America just for this singing contest, give it up for Patti Kim!"

As each act was introduced, the crowd, ever gullible, craned their necks, half-expecting the actual celebrities to appear. Some impersonators had gone as far as to receive forehead injections and nose jobs to look like the singers they were portraying. Several elderly members of the audience stood up and swayed awkwardly to the music, waving their arms at the same speed, whether the song was fast or slow, while their faces remained oddly vacant.

Between acts, the host would pluck a snail from the rubber bin, letting it crawl on his arm as he extolled its medicinal virtues. It left a trail of mucus behind. A drunken man stood up, shouting, "It's all a scam! Where's the real Jo Yong-pil? Bring him out!"

Following the woman's performance, the same man clamored for a more upbeat number. Two burly figures appeared and dragged the man away. People laughed, thinking it was part of the act. Snails escaped the rubber bin, crawling across the stage in all directions. The host stopped and scrambled to collect the snails, causing people to laugh again. At the end of the contest, contestants received prizes like cosmetic sets containing gold dust, or soaps touted to eliminate freckles and blemishes. Satisfied with their winnings, people eagerly purchased boxes of medicine containing snail extract and herbs.

Their payment was different from what had been initially promised, with snail extract making up part of the compensation.

"What the hell? This isn't what we agreed on!" Kwak protested.

The host grinned, flashing his yellow teeth. "We never said we wanted genuine stars. Seems like you misunderstood. Acting all high and mighty because she isn't an impersonator . . . Should have been friendlier, shaken a few hands, you know? A lineup of young girls would have been better."

Kwak was about to argue, but stopped, catching sight of the burly men who had been eyeing him the whole time. The band loaded the boxes of snail extract into the trunk of the car themselves.

When they left the sushi bar, they were already drunk. They debated what they should do with a trunkful of snail extract but couldn't come to a decision. Kwak said he knew just the place and led the way. The woman wanted to take her share of the money and go home. They veered off the coastline and climbed a winding road up a hill. Kwak seemed familiar with the area. They passed some low-rises and eventually arrived at a basement café in a commercial building. Its neon sign was turned off, and the door was locked. Kwak banged on the door. Footsteps approached and the door opened. Kwak and the man skipped all pleasantries, exchanging only essential words, as if they had seen each other recently.

"Say hello!" Kwak said to him.

The man peered at the woman, and then exclaimed in surprise. "What's all this about?" he muttered, rubbing his hands together.

Kwak mixed whiskey with beer and passed the glasses around. Lee and Park gulped theirs down. There was a drum set in a corner of the café.

"Have a drink, sis," Kwak said, offering her a glass. She figured she could manage half a glass. The beer was lukewarm, but she was thirsty. The spicy soup they'd eaten with the sashimi had been salty. She took another gulp. The café owner sat at the drum set and began to pound out a rhythm. The sound faded and her vision grew blurry.

"Hold on, don't tell me you're already drunk!" Kwak's voice floated to her from a distance.

"Is she alright?" the drummer asked, sounding concerned.

"Hey, this is nothing for her," Kwak said. "She's performed high as a kite. Incredible singer, but crippling stage fright. The police raided her boyfriend's house, you know. The entire backyard was full of poppies. Seriously. You trust me, right? He won't be getting just fifteen years this time."

A finger prodded her cheek. "Hello? Hello? Don't tell me you're done already."

A giggle slipped out—poppies? Kwak knew more about her than she'd realized. Then her head hit the table with a thud.

She woke to the sound of crying. Lee, the drummer, was crying like a child, his gaze shifting back and forth between his stomach and the floor. It looked like he'd spilled something. Suddenly, he scraped the floor with his palms, as if gathering something and pretended to shove it back into his belly. He looked at the floor again, cried, and repeated the same actions again. "I ripped open my stomach climbing over the barbed wire," he sobbed. "My intestines spilled out. If I lose even one, I'll be in big trouble."

The café owner was still drumming away. Park was sprawled on the sofa, and Kwak lay on the floor beside another sofa. The lower part of his pants was wet, as if he'd had an accident. Her temples throbbed. When she slapped Kwak's cheek, he slowly opened his eyes. His face, marked with pockmarks, was ashen, and his eyes seemed to be veiled with a blue film. She took some money from Kwak's jumper. She made her way to the main road and hailed a taxi.

"The Polar Hotel, please."

The driver peered at her through the rearview mirror. "First time here, huh? The hotel's just over there. You could walk there, especially if you're in the mood for a stroll."

Relief washed over her. "So it's still standing. It's been a really long time . . ."

As she had done years ago, she followed the coastline, her heels sinking into the sand. She took off her shoes and carried them. She smelled the sweet aroma of strawberries simmering in sugar. Drawn by the scent, she found herself outside the rear entrance. A gardener hurried between the shrubs, a bucket in each hand, water sloshing onto his legs with each step. Above the hotel entrance, a sign announced: "Strawberry Festival: Festival of Love."

She saw the dining area through the glass window. A waiter placed a strawberry mousse cake on a table, eliciting a cheer from a young woman. The scent of strawberries filled the lounge, where a Filipina singer crooned to percussion rhythms. A group of tourists, seemingly Japanese, were busy taking pictures, their luggage piled up on one side of the lobby. Each held a camera or camcorder. A short, elderly man handed his camera to the woman, asking if she could snap a group photo. He then joined his companions, posing in front of a fountain. As she turned around after taking the picture, she locked eyes with a tall staff member behind the front desk. Recognizing her, he offered a timid smile.

"You said you'd be back next spring, but here you are. It's been sixteen years and sixty-nine days."

She approached the front desk to check in and noticed he had aged as well. The lighting was glaringly bright, making her self-conscious about the wrinkles her makeup might not be covering. Recognition dawned. "Oh! Are you perhaps . . . the guest who cried for me?"

He nodded. "Yes, at the Moulin Rouge. I never dreamed I'd see you there. Gosh, I was so thrilled. Your song that day was magical. It suits you now, especially with your husky voice. 'I'm letting go of your hand. Goodbye forever, goodbye forever.' I couldn't help crying. To be honest, your voice from when you were young was almost too pure."

"I couldn't find your shoe. The Moulin Rouge burned down."

"Ah, so that's where it was? I had no clue where I'd lost it. Don't worry, I tossed the other one."

Sunlight streamed in through the window, shimmering around her ankles. The light was shockingly cold.

"It's March, so the water's still very cold. Come up here."

She glanced down at her feet, submerged in the frigid water. The water lapping around her ankles was so cold that the skin below was flushed red like a monkey's.

"Believe it or not, it's high tide. You've read all about it in the papers, haven't you? Global warming, rising sea levels. If you stand on this sandbar, you can watch the water rush in during high tide. Come up here before your feet turn to ice."

A headache made her temples throb, and a fake eyelash was stuck to her cheek. The drummer had dozed off, revealing a surgical scar on his belly. Paler than the surrounding skin, the wound looked like the fossil of a large millipede. The room was dim. In the hallway, she stepped on something soft. It was Park, the keyboardist. Her foot had landed on his thigh, but he didn't stir. The café owner lay next to the drum set, grimacing as if he were still drumming in his dreams. The bottom of Kwak's pants was wet. She slapped him on the cheek, but he didn't wake up. She pulled some money out of his jumper. Unable to find her heels, she took off his sneakers and slipped them on. She headed for the main road and hailed a taxi.

"The Polar Hotel, please."

The driver peered at her through the rearview mirror. "First time here, eh? The hotel's right over there. It's a short walk if you're in the mood."

The beach was teeming with people and seagulls. Tourists tossed shrimp crackers into the air for them. With every toss, flocks of seagulls swooped in. If you held up a cracker, they even snatched it right from your fingers. Kwak's sneakers were too big, causing her heels to slip out repeatedly. Loudspeakers blared from the pier, enticing people to go on island cruises. People cast curious glances at the woman in the sequined dress.

The Polar Hotel no longer shone. Its glass façade was cracked, as if someone had pelted rocks at every pane, exposing the skeleton of the building. Seagulls had nested in the crevices. Where the hotel sign had once been, only a large outline of dust remained. Beyond the front gate, the hotel's garden was visible. A "No Entry" sign was posted at the entrance to the garden.

The stone bridges, where she used to shake sand from her sneakers after returning from the beach, were now buried in weeds. It was clear the gardener had long since abandoned the hotel. Where hydrangeas and cannas once flourished was now completely overrun with clover that bloomed white, and the grass on the sunny side was scorched. A towering fir tree, transplanted at some point, stood three stories high beside the hotel's outer wall, its looming shadow snuffing out the clover. The untamed tree resembled an angry, feral giant, and other trees, once meticulously cared for, now had branches bent and twisted, reaching desperately for sunlight.

She placed one foot up on the iron gate that led into the hotel. Years ago, she'd vaulted over it in a single leap. This time, the hem of her dress snagged and ripped, scattering sequins on the ground. Weeds had grown knee-high, hiding the stone bridges, but the path to the hotel was as familiar as ever. The fallen placard by the hotel's back door was trampled with muddy footprints. It read: "Strawberry Festival, Festival of Love."

In the dining area, the grand piano, the crystal wine glasses, tables, and chairs were all gone. Also gone was the souvenir shop, where battery-powered traditional dolls that would bow at ninety-degree angles lined the shelves. A faint aroma of strawberries simmering in sugar hung in the air, making her mouth water, as if she'd taken a bite of strawberry mousse cake. Laughter and the clinking of ceramic dishes seemed to echo in the empty dining room.

White sand had settled thickly on the red, plush carpet. Despite the posted warnings, many had trespassed, evident from the jumble of human and animal footprints. The elevator was out of service. The fountain seemed to have dried up a long time ago and was now filthy with sand and seagull droppings. Sand covered not only the stairs, but also the front desk and even the gaps between the glass windows. The hotel was now a house of sand. She walked past the rooms where seagulls waddled freely about. Through the balcony window, a cluster of islands the size of pebbles hovered on the horizon. A cruise ship cut across the sea, blaring its horn, and a flock of seagulls took flight, trailing behind the stern. She went into the bathroom and turned on the tap, half expecting sand to pour out, but rusty water trickled out instead.

Seventeen years ago, she'd spent a spring at the Polar Hotel. As she checked out, a tall hotel employee had said softly, "Please visit us again next time." She'd promised to return the next spring. The scent of strawberries simmering in sugar followed her even as she dragged her bulky suitcase through the lounge. Her manager walked hurriedly, a men's clutch dangling from his wrist. "What on earth is in that suitcase? Did you set up house or something?"

She exited the hotel and got into the company car that had been waiting out front. Instead of taking her back to Seoul, the car took her to the airport.

"Hey, don't think it's unfair," her manager said, even though he'd been the one to assure her that the rumors would subside in two months. "After all, you dug your own grave. This country's too small. There's no place for you to run anymore. Go abroad, lay low for a year or two. People will forget."

Seventeen years had passed since she'd promised to return for the Strawberry Festival. From the Sky Lounge, she could see the hotel's garden, a secret garden of clover and trees. Glittering in the sunlight between the weeds were sequins that had spilled from her stage costume.

A Baffling Mistake

In a literary journal, he came upon a short essay by a poet he liked—K—in a column called "Whatever Happened To." He hadn't read K's work in almost two years. Through the essay, he learned that earlier this year, K had wrapped up his thirty-eight years in Seoul and moved into a wooden ranch house he'd built outside the city. The essay mostly detailed his life there: the snail he'd almost trampled on the veranda, which he found climbing the Benjamin planter in the corner of the living room three or four days later; the poisonous snake he'd struck with a shovel when it came into his yard. These tales captivated him. K's essay had a certain charm that was different from his poetry. The magazine was in color, featuring large and small photos of K posing by a window full of light or in front of a flowerbed of hydrangeas. The backs of his white rubber shoes were caked with mud.

Even from the pictures alone, one could guess that K's eyesight had deteriorated. K had written about his eyes before. Referring to the story of the cobbler in the *Arabian Nights*, he said his excessive greed would blind him one day. Enticed by an old paralytic who claims he can see all the treasures buried in the earth, the cobbler applies a magical ointment to one eye. When that eye goes blind, he begins to see every hidden treasure in the earth and sea, and burns with a desire to see more. Convinced he'd be able to possess all the riches of the world if he goes blind in the other eye as well, he begs the old man to apply the ointment to his remaining eye. Once the ointment is applied, all the treasures disappear, leaving only darkness. The old man then climbs onto the cobbler's back, tightening his bony legs around the cobbler whenever his pace slackened. However, what the man knew about K's story had nothing to do with greed. The deep lines around K's mouth seemed to be evidence of the hardships he'd endured.

K mentioned that although it wasn't visible from the house, the West Sea lay behind the mountains, and the smell of seaweed washed in on rainy or overcast days. He added that after moving to this place, he found himself more in awe of things he couldn't see. None of the photos included a view of the wooden rancher that K himself had designed. A part of the ceiling beam was visible above a close-up of K's face, and suspended beneath this dark beam, which resembled a railroad tie, was a small view of the outside, no larger than an adult's fist. Did the trail lead to the beach? Is that why his white shoes were covered with mud? K's prose, just like his poetry, stirred the man's thoughts.

Near the end of the essay, a sentence made the man's heart sink. "I get dizzy on this lonely path where my child goes before me. Even the sunlight is sad."

He'd seen K for the last time eight years ago. K had married later in life, and his eldest son, born when K was nearly forty, would have finished college by now and entered the workforce. There was also a daughter, who was five years younger. Wondering if he'd misread the sentence, the man read it aloud once more. "I get dizzy on this lonely path where my child goes before me. Even the sunlight is sad." He then read the sentences before and after, but he couldn't find any clues to help him understand that statement.

When he visited K's apartment in Gaepo-dong, his sixth-grade daughter had opened the front door. K had been wiping the floor with a wet rag. He got up and offered his other hand, the one not holding the rag. The old apartment was cramped and poorly lit. The girl, with big eyes and hair braided in pigtails, stared at him with her hand on her father's knee. Was her name Yoon or Yeon? It had been a single syllable. K's wife, an elementary school teacher, wasn't home. The girl clattered about in the kitchen and brought out a tray with two glasses of orange juice and two moon pies. The soles of her white socks were black, as if she'd gone outside shoeless.

"What Ever Happened To" was a column dedicated to tracking down luminaries who had been out of the public eye for some time. The man examined K's face. He even examined the mud-stained shoes that K was wearing. K's gloomy eyes could be due to aging, but perhaps constant crying had wrinkled the soft skin around them. His tightly pursed lips appeared as if he was gritting his teeth to endure a heavy burden. He had seen K for the first and last time eight years ago, and it had been five years since the occasional phone calls ended. The New Year's cards, which he sent out at the start of the year, also stopped three years ago when they came back with a "return to sender" stamp. K hadn't appeared in the press for over two years. What on earth had happened to him? The man glanced out the window. It was eerily quiet outside, with no breeze. The sky, peeping out from between the blossoming apple trees, was dark, as if railroad ties had been woven together.

Through the small window that opened into the kitchen, large pots were visible. Every time the soup boiled over and fell on the blue flames, the bottom of the pot turned black. The air conditioner was out of order. A technician, in coveralls with the company logo embroidered in gold thread on his chest, inspected the air conditioner, with various parts scattered beside him on the restaurant floor. The wall-mounted fans made a grinding noise every time they changed directions.

While waiting for the beef tendon soup he'd ordered, he began to talk about K's essay he'd read that morning. The editor-in-chief kept mopping the sweat streaming down his flushed face. The yellow stains under his arms were growing bigger. Every time he wiped his face and neck with the wet towelette, the man could see his hairy armpits. "Aigo!" the chief cried, dropping his towelette, as if he, too, hadn't known about K's recent affairs.

Chung from the editorial department crunched on the pickled radish banchan. "Gaepo-dong? Oh, the real estate there's been on fire lately. Getting your hands on anything earlier this year would have been tough . . . 'We met like migratory birds.' That's the poet, right?"

They continued to talk about K as they slurped soup from the earthen pot, scooped out the meat, and dipped it in sauce. The technician, with his hands on his waist, peered at the dusty air conditioner filter. He barely looked twenty and seemed as if he'd just completed his training. His neck was blotchy and red where it had chafed against the crisp seams of his uniform, while sweat also trickled down from his scalp. The chief wiped his face with the towelette again, saying he couldn't understand how such a scandal had subsided without any rumors. He then nodded, saying they'd probably held a small, private funeral just with family, since the child passed away before the parents. Chung kept confusing the poet K with the poet H. She mused that K's two-year hiatus might have been related to this incident, chewing the meat as an old woman might, gnawing with her gums. The folds of his skin were slippery with sweat. Big men stepping into the restaurant were stunned by the stifling heat and promptly retreated outside. A bustling four-lane road was visible through the restaurant window. Above the car taillights, heavy clouds were gathering. The chief put on his shoes and stepped outside, a toothpick in his mouth. "Mr. L might know something. I heard they're close."

The man felt a little embarrassed at the sentence: "The woman spread open her legs to him." Despite the writer's poor handwriting, it was clear those were the words. The man typed up the sentence without making any changes. Maybe because of the heat, Chung, who was sitting across from him, was staring into space with her mouth half open. Her thin hair, damp with sweat, clung to her forehead, making her look tired. Her makeup had worn off, revealing her blemishes. When their eyes met, he looked away, as if he'd accidentally touched a hot pot lid. She narrowed her eyes at him. Whenever he glanced up, he found her watching him suspiciously.

"Even Mr. L doesn't seem to know anything," the editor-in-chief said, taking a cigarette from the man's pack and putting it in his mouth. "He asked me if it was true. Not only has Mr. K quit writing poetry for the past two years, but it seems he's cut ties with his friends as well." He glanced up at the ceiling and formed his lips into an O. Smoke rings slowly dissipated.

The man called the magazine that had published K's essay and was given his phone number and address. He'd thought the magazine editor would know more about K's recent affairs, but the staff who answered the phone said the editor was currently away from his desk and didn't know when he would return.

He picked up the phone but then put it back down. Five years ago, while getting K's poetry collection ready for publication, he'd talked with K every day over the phone. He thought maybe a letter would be better than a phone call this time. "Dear Mr. K . . ." After writing down the first line, he was at a loss. Several times he tried to continue by saying that Typhoon Rusa was heading north, but crumpled up every attempt. It had been three years since he last sent K a New Year's card. During this time, he had changed jobs twice. He wrote that he was now too old to change jobs again and quickly erased it. Despite having set the air conditioning to a lower temperature than usual, Chung fanned herself, saying the room felt humid. Smoke rings floated above the chief's cubicle. Somewhere in the building, a toilet flushed. He asked for forgiveness for his long silence since he last got in touch.

As he wrote, the face of K's daughter, with her big eyes and dirty socks, grew clearer in his mind. He wrote that the roofline of the house he glimpsed in the magazine photos was lovely. He also wrote that he'd like to visit before the hydrangeas in the flowerbed faded. These weren't empty words. But for some reason, he didn't want to mention the mud on K's shoes. Nor did he want to mention K's daughter, who'd watched him spill crumbs as he ate the moon pie, or her grimy socks, the soles blackened from having played the rubber game outside without shoes. All he said was that he was sorry. He didn't say the wooden house, as dark as railroad ties, seemed ominous. He kept beating around the bush. Was it because he'd met her then? Of K's two children, it seemed the girl was at the center of the tragedy. But he only wrote that K's essay had made his heart ache that morning.

The man barely made the last bus. While he ran to the bus stop, sweat oozed from his pores. Catching his breath, he glanced up at the Seoul sky. Scattered rain clouds were slowly gathering. At two in the morning, he and a young couple sitting at the very back of the bus were the only passengers. The bus had good air conditioning, and as his sweat dried, he felt cold. The bus left the city center and started to speed along the dimly lit road. From time to time, the driver glanced at the inside of the bus through the rearview mirror. He couldn't shake off K's words he'd read that morning. He pictured K wandering over the mountains to the mudflats every night like a wild beast, his eyes bloodshot and swollen. The boy at the back of the bus seemed to be tickling the girl in the armpit. She shrieked like a seagull.

The girl had kept her hand on her father's knee the entire time they were talking. Mid-conversation, K took his eyes off the man repeatedly to look at his daughter. It was apparent that the mother was away. Faint traces of a child's scribbles remained on the worn wallpaper, and bookshelves lined every wall of the cramped living room. Books that couldn't fit on the shelves were stacked precariously on the floor, resembling cairns. Though it was broad daylight, the sun didn't come in through the balcony window. He saw through the living room window that the iron bars of the balcony were red with rust. A sour smell, which he'd noticed from the moment he first stepped into the apartment, wafted in from the kitchen with the stained ceiling. As the moon pie melted, his fingers became sticky with chocolate.

Eoshim Sushi Train, Hwaseong BBQ, Gangnam Silk Goods, Café Olive, Gugu Pharmacy, Astro Boy Comics . . . There were many days he wanted to walk down this narrow street in a drunken stupor. But he would sober up on the bus ride home, so by the time he stepped into the street, his mind was at its clearest. The street, stretching for about a hundred meters, hasn't seen any change in the past decade. The redevelopment boom, which had made headlines for some time, came to a halt across the street. People who'd come hoping to secure a new apartment settled down in the old houses behind the shops. The store signs went dark, and signs of life disappeared from the street.

The menu items that had been stuck on the window of Eoshim Sushi Train for the past ten years have remained untouched. Every summer, the water-soaked parts fell off, leaving fewer and fewer letters intact. All day long, the restaurant owner-chef was clad in a yukata printed with ink-colored bamboo. The conveyor belt stopped running a long time ago. Soy sauce stains covered the belt between the plates, and rust had set in. Though the menu boasted over twenty kinds of dishes, the owner now only made rice topped with assorted sashimi or simple sushi rolls, mostly for the workers from a nearby construction site who came in for lunch. The men ate, sitting around the stationary conveyor belt. The signboard that had been put out to attract customers was swept away in the first flood. Even the letters on the restaurant sign have fallen off one by one over the past ten years. For a while, outlines of dust remained where the letters had been, but the wind and rain erased even those outlines. No one replaced the signs.

The store awnings sagged like wet laundry. As he walked down the street, he started sweating again and the hem of his pants stuck to his bare skin. There was no breeze. Soaked and dried repeatedly, his clothes smelled like dried fish. A woman had once come to this street to meet him. He'd been sleeping in one Sunday morning when he'd received her call. She'd gone to church, decided to get on a train while she was out, and arrived at the station about ten minutes earlier. She asked where she should meet him. He jolted awake, stuttering. The woman laughed.

"Go straight from the station. If you keep walking along the tracks, you'll see a sign for Eoshim Sushi Train."

But she wouldn't be able to find the restaurant, since almost all the letters in the sign had fallen off, leaving only *Eo, Su*, and *in*.

"Then could you wait for me at Café Olive?"

But the Café Olive sign was the same, with only *Ol* and *vi* managing to stay up. "Actually, why don't you wait at the station? I'll be right there."

He ran, following the tracks. He slipped on the gravel several times, putting out his hands to break his fall. She was sitting in the waiting room of the new station. He watched her through the window without entering. She tapped her feet, glancing at her watch and the people passing through the turnstiles. He didn't go inside. While walking back, he called her again, saying something urgent had come up and he wouldn't be able to make it. She said nothing. All he heard was the crunch of gravel. After a few minutes, she was the first to hang up.

There was a time when this street bustled with life. Now when the sun sets, all the stores rush to close their doors, but there used to be many places that stayed open late into the night. Before the apartment complexes came in, this area was one of the hottest date spots on the weekends. Couples poured out through the gate of the small, shabby train station. Bars hoping for the weekend boom opened in front of the station, along with gift shops and entertainment centers, like air-rifle shooting ranges. There weren't any special attractions. Couples walked aimlessly along the tracks. The shop-lined street was situated halfway along the date route. Plates loaded with different kinds of sushi went around the conveyor belt in the sushi train restaurant. Singing close to screeching came from karaoke rooms until dawn. On Monday mornings, the ground was strewn with vomit, hairpins, earrings, sanitary pads, empty wallets, and coins. His mother still longed for those times. She said she'd squandered all the money she'd worked so hard to save.

In his essay, K had said that after moving, he found himself more in awe of things he could not see. Eight years ago, when the man had visited K in his Gaepo-dong apartment, they had gone for a walk to the temple on the back mountain with K's daughter. A large magnolia tree stood in the middle of the entrance, forcing visitors to walk around it. The magnolia was in full bloom. People preparing for the forty-nine-day ritual moved busily around the temple yard. However, the backyard was empty. From somewhere inside the temple, the soft weeping of an old woman could be heard. He peeked inside a shrine. Among the memorial tablets crowding the altar was a picture that seemed to have been taken recently of a young woman with dark eyebrows and hair. Below the woman's picture was a Minnie Mouse plushie with a red ribbon. The doll's yellow gloves were a little worn and dingy.

K said he would slowly walk down with his daughter after fetching some spring water, so they said goodbye in the temple yard. As the man walked down the mountain, he looked back and saw K standing under the magnolia tree, watching him. He bowed again to K, who waved back. This happened a few more times until the man rounded a bend and could no longer see the temple yard.

The sign of the butcher shop, which had been named after the man, was turned off. In the alley next to the store, a metal door led to the living quarters attached to the shop. The light was still on in his mother's room, which meant that his father had not yet come home. As if sensing his presence, a groan came from her room. Whenever his father came home late, his mother would sigh and complain. "Your dad's going to end up dying on the road, I know it." Her words flew at the back of his head as he was going into his room.

The window was open, but the breeze couldn't make it through the screen. His sweaty skin kept sticking to the linoleum floor. He wanted to visit K, but he did nothing about it. Counting on his fingers, he realized K's daughter would be twenty-one by now. Suddenly, the picture of the young woman he'd seen in the temple shrine, when he'd gone for a walk with K, crossed his mind. The woman's hair and eyebrows had been strikingly black. The face of K's daughter became superimposed over the picture. The same girl who had laughed at him, when he'd been flustered about his chocolate-stained hands, would have grown into a young woman by now. If she were still alive, that is.

He heard a man's drunken singing coming from the end of the street. It was his father.

In 1992, his house flooded for the first time. If not for the chaos outside, he would have kept sleeping and suffered a bigger disaster. The rainwater that seeped through the walls made the linoleum floor bulge. His mother ran around the yard, shrieking his name. As soon as he opened the door, water flooded into the room, rising to his ankles. When he passed by an electrical outlet, his feet tingled, as if an electric eel was swimming in the water.

Though all the stores were closed, their signs were lit up. It almost felt as if the good times were back. But not long after, the power went out, and the street turned pitch black. People stumbled into each other, fell, and hurled insults. Water gushed to low-lying areas. Sewage flowed backward up the drains. Shop owners didn't know what to do. Someone wailed. Someone else cried out their child's name, as if they'd lost their mind. All the children burst into tears at the same time. A few men ran into their shops to scoop out water, but eventually, they threw down their buckets and sank to the floor. The plastic chairs from the chicken shop floated on the water. The current was so strong that it almost tipped people over.

Two days after the rain stopped, the water drained, leaving behind red clay in every building. They spent all their time sorting what was usable from what wasn't. Broken appliances, mud-stained books, and clothes were heaped up everywhere on the street. Women laughed and cried. Water trucks sprayed the sediment away, while water delivery trucks arrived to distribute clean water. Kids, holding kettles and plastic bottles, stood in a long line in front of the truck. Once a day, disinfectant trucks sprayed white smoke over the street, trailed by a band of screaming, half-naked children. The streets turned into a giant laundry yard, with blankets and clothes that had been washed over the course of a few days fluttering in the wind. Inside the large refrigerator at the butcher shop, meat began to rot, attracting swarms of flies. Stray dogs appeared in front of the shop, but they couldn't be given the spoiled meat, of course. His mother threw stones to chase them away. He felt bad about having to throw all the meat away, but the sight of all the comic books at Astro Boy Comics turning to pulp is what made him curse. He had learned how to read through those comic books.

The weather agency forecasted that Typhoon Rusa would make landfall on the southern coast of the Goheung Peninsula in South Jeolla Province before three in the afternoon. It was moving north at a speed of 30 kilometers per hour, and as it headed north or north-northeast, it would pass through North Jeolla and Gangwon Provinces, bringing rain to the southern regions. The man saw a picture of the clouds in the newspaper. Typhoon Rusa looked like a donut, similar to the smoke rings the editor-in-chief had blown. They said that the eye of the typhoon was so clear that from inside it, one could even see the constellations. Occasionally, tropical birds were carried into the eye of the typhoon. The man looked out the window as if stargazing. The leaves of the crab-apple tree shook a little.

That summer, after the first flood, the houses flooded again. People speculated it was due to the apartment complex built right behind their street. The complex, located on higher ground, couldn't handle all the rainwater, resulting in water coursing into the low-lying areas. Although the power was cut off and it was dark, people weren't as flustered as before. They could make out each other's faces in the dark, thanks to the glow of their white underclothes. They even exchanged greetings, asking each other if they were okay. Once again, they could only watch helplessly as water gushed into their homes. They took their pre-packed bags to the elementary school auditorium, which had been designated as a shelter, and then headed back home when the water receded. They grew skilled at scooping out sludge. The women's association from the apartment complex came and distributed instant cup noodles to the disaster victims. This time, they didn't peel off the wet wallpaper to repaper it. Even after the water drained and the walls dried, water stains remained. The women stroked the stains, recalling how high the water had risen. They no longer laughed or cried. With their lips pursed, they washed the blankets and hung them to dry and wiped the muddy plates with dish soap, occasionally shouting at the kids, "Make sure you don't drink the tap water! You have to boil it first!"

Once the garbage truck carried away all the broken appliances, the houses filled again with second-hand items. The area was labelled a flood hazard zone after experiencing two floods. The elementary school building, which had served as a refuge, made the news two years in a row. After that, visits from real estate agents came to a complete halt.

On his way back from lunch, the man dropped the letter he'd written to K into the mailbox. Just then, he felt a drop of rain.

The sound of the rain was so loud they had to raise their voices to be heard. The rain tore the leaves off the crab-apple trees outside the window, and the wind sent the green fruit flying. Employees returning to the office stepped on the fruit, spreading bits of apple everywhere. Their sweet scent mixed with the smell of rot. Pedestrians clutched their umbrellas as they hurried along, some women shrieking and on the verge of tears, as they wrestled with inside-out umbrellas. Others scrambled to retrieve umbrellas snatched away by the wind, while signs rattled and signboards were knocked over, carried more than a meter away. A woman in a wedding dress walked along the street without an umbrella, soaked up to her knees in dirty water. A tuxedo-clad groom chased after her, holding a large golf umbrella. The bride's makeup was smudged. She shouted toward the groom. Her tears weren't visible because of the rain. The wind lashed the skinny trees lining the street. Suddenly, he recalled his father mentioning that he was attending a wedding that afternoon.

Luckily, they caught the mistake before the book went to print. The editor-in-chief tossed the proofs on the man's desk. It was the second page of a novel titled *Red River*, which was soon to be published. The chief had a habit of calling the staff by their last names.

"Hey, Kang! From now on, I'm calling you Spread-open-her-legs!"

Bewildered, the man examined the proofs, marked up in red. The corrections were clearly in his handwriting. Chung had come up behind him at some point and was peering at the page over his shoulder. She read the marked-up sentence aloud: "The woman spread open her legs to him . . ." Chung erupted into laughter, smacking him on the shoulder. "Get your mind out of the gutter!"

Frantically, he found the original text, running his finger over the words. He lost his place repeatedly and had to start over. No matter how many times he checked, the sentence "The woman spread open her legs to him" was nowhere to be found. Instead, there was only the sentence: "The woman spread open her bags to him."

Chung kept teasing him. "So, is this why you couldn't even look at me that time? You dirty dog . . ."

Since their office was so small, the entire staff quickly caught wind of the incident. For the past few days, the man had been plagued by thoughts of K and his daughter. The editor-in-chief perched himself on the edge of the man's desk and lit a cigarette.

"When you work in editing for a few years, you can't ignore any typos. You find yourself proofreading bathroom graffiti. But after about five years, a typo starts to feel human. But do you know what happens after ten years? You start writing your own novel."

Even the new employee from accounting seemed to know about the incident, quickly darting back into the office when she encountered him in front of the elevator.

Later, on his way home, the man found the road had vanished, replaced by a large pool of reddish water. Muddy water filled the ditches along the road. The bus was forced to make a U-turn. Some passengers took the bus back to town, while others got off and stood in the rain. Gazing at all the water, he thought of K's words. "I find myself more in awe of things I cannot see." He wondered if the water flowing across the road had simply reclaimed its original path. He seemed to recall hearing the sound of flowing water under the asphalt during bus rides home at night. As always, K's writing lingered in his head for a long time.

Because of the rain, both he and his mother had to shout on the phone. She said their street had flooded. The toilets had overflowed, and the sewage had backed up. "But what can we do? Your dad isn't even home yet," she lamented, starting to say something else when the call was disconnected. He tried to call back, but the phone lines were down. The man took the bus back to town, where the storm had also caused damage. Uprooted trees blocked paths, forcing pedestrians onto the roads. Every time a car passed, they got soaked. A man in his forties was reported to have been fatally electrocuted while crossing the street.

He spent the night on the office couch. The rain continued until morning. A man in his sixties, who'd gone to inspect his fields, was swept away by the torrent. A landslide caused a park cemetery to collapse, resulting in the loss of over a hundred graves. In the morning paper, he read about the death of an unidentified man, also in his sixties. The estimated time of death was Saturday afternoon. Dressed in a light green suit, he was approximately 170 centimeters tall. He'd been found by the back fence of an all-boys' high school. The name of the school sounded familiar. He seemed to recall seeing its name on the uniforms of students at the bus stop every morning. His father had said he would be attending the wedding of the daughter of a business association member that Saturday. His father had only one summer suit, and it was light green. A dark alley, a playing field behind a slate wall about two meters high. The students who'd stayed after school for supplementary lessons chatted loudly, playing soccer. His father could have been mistaken for a homeless man, as he was known to fall asleep anywhere when drunk. By the time he left the wedding hall, he would have been so drunk he would have had trouble walking.

It had started pouring when he put the letter for K in the mailbox. The newspaper carrier didn't recognize his father lying by the side of the road. The darkness and the heavy rain would have obstructed his view. A bicycle ran over the back of his father's hand. No, no, that wasn't right. He shook his head. The print in the newspaper was too small. He read the article once more. The description of the deceased man turned out to be completely different. He was reported to have been wearing a Hawaiian shirt with a sailboat pattern and cotton shorts, and was found at a school he'd never even heard of. The woman spread open her bags to him. The woman spread open her bags to him. It was nothing serious. Lately, he'd had been preoccupied with thoughts of K.

The road home remained closed until Monday afternoon. His street was still flooded. The muddy water carried a mix of rank smells. He rolled his pants up to his knees and waded through the foul water. He found his mother at the elementary school, chatting with the other women. She smiled at him, saying she'd already packed all their important things. His father was nowhere to be seen. She said he'd called, saying he was at a friend's house, drinking, since the road was closed.

Clearing away the sludge and piling up the soaked items on the street seemed to have become an annual ritual for those in the area. A street sweeper was dispatched to clean up the garbage, and a water truck arrived to distribute clean water. Even the children helped, using dustpans to scoop up the mud that had seeped into their rooms and dumping it outside. They had grown stronger from scooping out mud and water. Each year, the water level inside the house rose. As the man took down the wet calendar from the wall, he thought about hanging it higher next time. While sweeping away the water, he discovered a crack starting in the room's floor, large enough to fit his index finger. Each flood eroded the house's foundations, exposing its roots. In a few years, it wouldn't just be plastic chairs, dustpans, and small appliances floating in the water, but entire houses. Flies started to swarm. A disinfection truck drove down the street, spraying a white mist with a familiar smell. Amid all the chaos, he heard drunken singing. Though the mist obscured the end of the street, he knew it was his father.

"Do you know who's here right now? In the chief's office?" Chung asked, rubbing her palms together in excitement. "A ghost, that's who. There's a ghost in the office right now! Hey, what's the matter with you these days?" Chung swatted the man's shoulder and gestured toward the editorial department with her chin.

A young woman with big eyes was standing by the door. He didn't recognize her. "A ghost!" Chung mouthed to him. The woman seemed to recognize the man instantly.

"We've met once," she mumbled.

Suddenly, the face of K's daughter in braids came to mind. "Mr. K? Then are you Yoon?"

Only then did a small smile spread across her face. "It's Yeon. Yoon's my older brother . . ."

Just as he'd suspected from the magazine photos, K's vision started deteriorating two years ago. Now Yeon had taken on the task of typing his poems and delivering them to his publisher.

"He became a little difficult after his eyes went bad. He says everything's cloudy, like the time he played with a white plastic sack over his head as a boy."

Did that mean tragedy had befallen not the daughter but the eldest son, Yoon? Yeon took an envelope out of her bag and put it on the table. It was the letter he had sent K.

"My dad was happy to receive your letter, Mr. Kang. But I couldn't read it to him. All our mail got wet in the typhoon. I couldn't make out your writing, because the ink had run. I barely made out your name."

They said goodbye in front of the building. Yeon turned and gazed up at him. Her dark pupils still gleamed with the playfulness of the sixth-grade girl, who'd found it amusing to watch a grown man fret over his chocolate-smeared hands.

"I hope you can come visit before the hydrangeas fade, Mr. Kang. For some reason, friends he's lost touch with have been calling lately . . . After his eyes went bad, my dad's only joy has been to go for walks with my brother and me."

The man flipped through the literary journal and found the "Whatever Happened To" column. In the photo, K looked much older than he'd appeared eight years ago. L must have called K to see how he was doing. No matter how many times he has read K's essay, it felt fresh. He found it easy to immerse himself in the snail's journey of several days, in the story of having to strike down a snake with the end of a shovel, fearing it might bite his heel. He didn't doubt that K could spot a snail with his dim eyes or accurately strike the head of a snake. K had written that since moving, he found himself more in awe of things he could not see.

The man finally arrived at the sentence that had troubled him for days. It was just as Yeon had pointed out. "I get dizzy on this path where my children go before me. Even the sunlight is sad." An entirely different picture unfolded before his eyes. K's grown-up son and daughter stride forward. The poet slows down deliberately to watch his children go. The sunlight hanging over his children's shoulders is dazzling. Why had he misread the sentence in the first place? It was a mystery, a baffling mistake.

Button

Every Friday night, H and I went out. The streets were so packed with cars and people we could barely move. People stood outside buildings and shops, checking their watches or stamping their feet, waiting anxiously for their friends. If we weren't careful, we risked getting our feet trampled on. We kept walking to avoid getting our shoes dirty and ended up going in circles. It wasn't unusual to run into the same person more than once. "Hello again," we'd say, laughing. A sign at the entrance of a parking lot announced it was already full. The road practically turned into a parking lot, causing traffic jams on nearby connecting roads. That was Friday night.

In the alleys, tall young men huddled together, smoking and catcalling any woman who passed by. Under the streetlights, it was hard to gauge anyone's age. Maybe we wanted to hide our age in the darkness. We were thirty-two, perhaps a bit too old to be roaming the streets at night. When we mixed in with the crowd, our breathing naturally quickened. Girls on the street laughed freely, showing their teeth and cackling at the smallest things. Friday night fever. That's what H called it.

During the day, we bought things we normally wouldn't give a second glance. More than half of our paychecks went to these useless trinkets—stuffed dolls, strapless dresses, sandals with ten-centimeter heels, eyelash curlers. With shopping bags in both hands, we jaywalked, just like everyone else. Finding a cheap bar got us excited like teenagers, but we didn't think of going back the next Friday. Friday night fever. Inside these bars, people were excitable. They spat wherever they pleased, and fights erupted for no reason. We clinked beer glasses with the men sitting next to us, shouting to make ourselves heard over the loud music. We barely caught their names. As the night wore on, the bar floor became filthy with peanut shells, cigarette butts, and spit.

When we stepped outside around three or four in the morning, our ears still rang, so much so that H and I had to shriek at each other. Our skirts were wrinkled and stained with drink and food, giving off a sour smell. We avoided looking too closely at each other's faces. Exhausted, we looked ten years older. The crowds that had filled the streets were gone, and shops had lowered their shutters and turned off their signs. Friday night was over, and Saturday had already begun.

We walked slowly through the streets. A few stragglers remained. A girl sat outside a dark store, sobbing like a child who had lost something. A drunk man urinated, casting a large shadow on the wall. Whenever he moved, urine fell on his own sneakers. Black garbage bags discarded by restaurants lined the streets, filled to bursting. Trash spilled out from a bag a cat had torn open. The smell of rotten melon peels and chicken bones was nauseating. Vomit gleamed beneath electric poles. Once, we even stepped on the thigh of a man passed out on the sidewalk. He didn't move. It seemed someone had already rifled through his pockets and taken his wallet. He lay in a posture of surrender, as if he had nothing left to offer. H, feeling mischievous, stepped on his thigh again and snickered. I stepped on his other thigh. He groaned and shifted. I was sure he was one of the men we'd encountered in an alley.

Giggling and chattering, we either returned to H's room or mine, and passed out without removing our makeup. The room filled with the smell of fish jerky, flat beer, stale cigarette smoke, and a perfume we couldn't identify. We would wake but pretend to still be asleep, ignoring the shopping bags full of trinkets beside us. After all, it was Saturday.

The woman ran out of the apartment complex and headed straight for the main road. Though she hadn't run in years, she was amazed by how fast she still was. Her handbag slid off her shoulder and dragged on the ground. Sweat made her blouse cling to her body. Her stockinged feet slipped inside her shoes. She nearly lost her balance and dropped the bundle in her arms when she stumbled, but recovered just in time. She cut in front of a car entering the complex. The driver screeched to a stop, rolled down the window, and yelled at her, but she ignored him. She flagged down a taxi, and as soon as she jumped in, shouted, "To the terminal!" Her one thought was to get out of the city.

At the terminal, she was the only woman in proper clothes. Summer was almost over. Girls dressed for the beach chattered away, and young men walked by, dragging along their flip-flops. People kept bumping her legs with the corners of their suitcases as they wheeled them by. Children ran around the waiting room, bouncing colorful beach balls, and babies wailed incessantly.

She picked the farthest destination, somewhere she'd never visited. Although she hadn't traveled alone since getting married, her thoughts had been straying from home for a while now. She muttered the destination several times to herself. It soon felt as familiar as home. Buses left the terminal every five minutes, but the next tickets to where she wanted to go were already sold out. She waited at the terminal for over an hour. A noisy group disappeared through one set of doors, while sunburned, exhausted travelers left through another. She kept her gaze on the ground to avoid unwanted conversation. She jumped every time someone bumped into her.

The bus made a wide turn and exited the terminal, merging with other buses en route to various destinations. The familiar cityscape gave way to an industrial area dotted with large storage tanks. Black smoke billowed from towering smokestacks. She adjusted the baby in her arms. The baby slept well without fussing. The bus passed arid fields. A thin, middle-aged man in a white tank top and wide-brimmed straw hat stood watering a field. The water flowed, darkening the red earth and making the hose squirm like a snake. The sun moved to the other side of the bus, its setting rays shining in her eyes. The baby, as though irritated by the light, scrunched his face in his sleep. H's face came to mind. Right about now, H would be enjoying her South Pacific-island vacation, probably eating some chilled melon for breakfast at the hotel buffet. She recalled H complaining over the phone that the black bikini she'd gotten last year had become too tight.

H's housekeeper had kept yawning. Her disheveled hair lay flat against the back of her head. It seemed she'd just woken up. Her head shook slightly, as if affected by tremors.

"I've raised four grandchildren. I've seen them all, but this one's different. His nights and days are completely mixed up."

To cure his habit, she had even pinched his cheek when he slept during the day, but he wouldn't stir. She tapped his mouth with her fingertips. "Don't tell Mommy, okay? She might get the wrong idea." She said she was sore from holding him all night. Wide awake, he'd wanted to play.

The woman must have dozed off. She almost dropped the baby, but she quickly adjusted him in her arms. His round eyes were watching her. When she clicked her tongue, he cackled with glee, revealing new teeth sprouting from his pink gums.

When she got off the bus, she saw college students in matching T-shirts sitting in a circle on the terminal floor, engrossed in a game. The baby tensed whenever they clapped loudly, and startled when they burst into laughter. Apart from the students, the waiting room was quiet. A couple of elderly people sprawled across several seats each, dressed in traditional summer clothes. A middle-aged man entered the terminal and greeted them with a deep bow. The smell of urine wafted out of the public restroom and filled the waiting area.

Cafés, supermarkets, and restaurants lined the streets around the terminal. Perhaps because there were no customers, owners perched on platforms outside their stores, fanning themselves. Taxi drivers, their pants rolled up to their knees, sat at the stand, smoking. She stopped by a market and bought water, formula, and diapers. She wasn't hungry, but the baby needed a diaper change, so she entered a small restaurant with private rooms. The sign outside said "Open 24 Hours" in large letters. A large cauldron was boiling in a shed outside the restaurant, spewing steam from the side of the lid. Dried bits of bean sprouts and red chili pepper flakes were stuck on the table, and flies buzzed around, attracted by the sticky food residue. Flypaper dangled from the ceiling, the bottom half black with flies. A middle-aged woman, with a large belly and eyes so puffy her pupils were barely visible, set the side dishes on the table with a clatter. The melamine bowls were scorched at the edges, and water pooled under them, as if they hadn't been properly dried.

The baby's diaper was soaked. She wondered how he'd managed to sleep in such discomfort. He clearly didn't take after H. Even so, H often complained over the phone about how demanding he was. A red rash covered his groin area. Lying on his back, he swatted at the flies buzzing near his face, his eyes crossing whenever one came close.

"That's why you should use cloth diapers," the restaurant woman muttered, setting a clay pot of soup on the table. "Young people these days just want convenience over what's best for the baby. He must have felt so uncomfortable. And he can't even let you know. Here, let me."

She scooped up the baby with one arm. He dangled from her sturdy arm, his bottom marked by his blue Mongolian spot. She gave his bottom a firm pat. "You need to eat. You're just skin and bones," she said, and left the room with the baby tucked under her arm.

The soup tasted bitter, likely overcooked.

The owner scolded her for not finishing her meal. "No wonder you're not producing milk. You need to eat."

When the woman lost weight, her chest had flattened. She mixed some formula and tried spoon-feeding the baby. Used to a bottle, he struggled, licking the spoon but fussing when he couldn't get enough. The owner seemed to be cleaning up in the kitchen. She heard the clang of stainless-steel bowls and utensils falling onto the tile floor.

The guesthouse, converted from an old home, was surprisingly clean. The room was so tiny that a mat took up most of the space once it was spread open. Still, it had a small vanity and a TV. The bedding seemed to have been freshly washed and dried in the sun. She sat at the vanity. Her hair, which had been damp with sweat, was now dry and tangled, and her makeup had faded, revealing her freckles. She stared into the mirror as if seeing a stranger.

Down the hall was a communal sink with two faucets. The wooden floor creaked with each step. The soap was so soft the baby left an imprint when he grabbed it. The baby took up the whole sink. He squirmed the entire time. When she soaped him, he was so slippery she almost dropped him. Water splashed onto her blouse.

He crawled around the cramped room, trying to stand by pulling himself up using the corner of the vanity, only to plop back down each time. A flush spread across his nose whenever he failed. He pressed every button on the TV remote, startling and falling back on his bottom every time the screen flickered on. When the people on TV laughed, he cackled, too. He knocked over a cup, and the TV channel kept changing.

The bedding smelled of sunshine. When she'd run with the baby in her arms, he'd felt as light as a feather pillow. She pulled him close, laid him down beside her, and switched off the light. She held the squirming baby tightly. He kicked, flailed, and began to wail. When she turned the light back on, his eyes were surprisingly dry.

Not a single breeze came in through the small sliding window. A fan mounted on the wall spun tirelessly, merely stirring the lukewarm air. She could see the terminal square and the hangover soup restaurant where she'd eaten. The trees in the square stood motionless, as though there was no wind. A taxi was parked with all its doors thrown open. The driver seemed to be sleeping with his feet on the steering wheel, his white socks dazzlingly bright. Her husband should have gotten home by now. The hangover soup restaurant was empty, and the owner reclined on the raised wooden floor, watching TV. With each breath she took, her large belly rose and fell, completely hiding her legs from view.

The baby stayed awake until dawn, eyes twinkling with mischief. He crawled over the woman's stomach, causing her to cry out in pain. He yanked her hair, poked his finger into her ear, and then brought it close to her nose. Each time he leaned in, she caught the sweet scent of his breath. When he lay on her stomach, she could hear the thumping of his heart. His constant movements turned his skin slick with sweat. The rustling made her smile, even in her sleep. She heard a woman shriek. Dishes clattered and rolled on the floor, and a case of bottles crashed and shattered. Memories of Friday nights with H came back to her. Although she heard it all, she couldn't open her eyes. She sensed the baby moving. There was a rustle near her head, her waist, and then near her feet. She woke up to the sound of the first morning bus leaving the terminal. The TV was on, and the baby was sleeping near the door.

At the hangover soup restaurant, the owner was filling the cauldron with water. Her nose was bruised and swollen. "Taste buds age, too, you know. That's why everything gets saltier."

She scooped up some soup with a plastic ladle and offered the woman a taste. It was a bit salty. The owner added more water.

"Restaurant food needs stronger flavors than homemade food." She smiled when she saw the sleeping baby in the woman's arms. "He's a handful, that one. Noticed your lights on all night."

The woman walked toward downtown, carrying the baby. Downtown was a 200-meter strip beginning at the terminal, with shops, a post office, and a library. When a bus pulled up, folks climbed out slowly with bundles and rubber tubs so big that they struggled to maneuver them through the narrow door. Those who reached the sidewalk first claimed the best spots. Some even tripped in their rush. They unpacked and displayed their wares. A cart blaring trot music passed by, loaded with cassette tapes. The baby was sound asleep. The woman had to stop every few steps to readjust her grip. Although it was only morning, the heat was already intense. An elderly woman hawking small peaches shaded her eyes with one hand and called out to those passing by. Her face shone like a bronze bowl. Beside her, another old woman opened bags of cooked herbs, releasing steam. The woman walked past carts selling tteokbokki and soondae sausages. A man, dressed as a clown, sold taffy, dancing to the snips of his large scissors as he cut the taffy into pieces.

She stepped inside a baby goods store. Though the sign said, "Baby Goods," women's underwear dominated the displays, while baby items were pushed to the back. Unsure if a carrier would work for her, she opted for a stroller recommended by the young salesperson. She liked the canopy, complete with a plastic window for the baby to peer through when it was pulled down. The stroller also had a large storage basket at the bottom. She settled the baby in. He smacked his lips as if nursing. She also bought two bottles, two sets of clothes, and some baby powder for the diaper rash, placing them in the stroller's basket, along with the diaper bag she'd been carrying around. The basket quickly filled up.

Despite the clamor of loudspeakers and trot music, the baby slept soundly. She went into the hangover soup restaurant, boiled some barley tea, and poured it into a bottle. As soon as she held the bottle to the baby's mouth, he latched on instantly like metal to magnet, sucking so forcefully that the liquid level dropped noticeably. She pushed the stroller through the market, pausing to pick out four hairpins for a thousand won. She pinned back the baby's sweaty bangs. Shoppers couldn't resist lifting the stroller canopy to peek. "Oh, she's a big girl," they exclaimed. "Look at those big, round eyes!" With a pin in his hair, he was easily mistaken for a girl.

She bought a peach and sat in the shade to eat it. She kicked off her shoes. Her swollen feet were blistered and red. Juice from the peach dripped onto her creased, stained skirt. After she changed into lighter, wide-legged pants and tennis shoes, walking became easier. She didn't think she'd need her black heels again, so she tossed them into a trash bin. She felt as if she'd lived here for a long time. It seemed that if she continued down this new road, she'd come upon a house where white cloth diapers flapped in the yard. The town was small, but it seemed to have everything she needed.

She spotted a photo studio. She would need to get the baby's portrait done for his first birthday in the fall. The studio was modest, but she liked the photos displayed in the window. The photographer, a man in his sixties, sported a brown beret angled jauntily to one side. H would have a fit if she found out—H had already picked out a studio before the baby was even born. The photographer lifted the beret off his head and used it to fan himself.

Two young mothers came pushing their strollers and sat next to her. They struck up a conversation about babies. “So, is yours a girl?” they asked. She remained silent. H would be looking for a boy. She figured it was safer to let them assume the baby was a girl. After asking how old each other’s babies were, conversation naturally turned to the experience of their deliveries.

“She was almost four kilograms. I was in labor for two whole days,” she said. Once she started, the lies came easily.

H had indeed been in labor for two days. It was her first pregnancy, and she was at full term. H’s husband was away on a business trip. The woman sat in the hospital waiting room, watching a basketball game. H had called in the middle of the night. Annoyed at being woken just as he’d managed to fall asleep, her husband, A, turned and faced the other way in bed. She rushed to H’s apartment, nearly hitting a black dog that darted into the alley, its back arched like a bow in the glare of her headlights. Nearly invisible in the darkness, it tucked its tail between its hind legs. Afraid she might hit it, she honked her horn, but the dog merely glanced back and refused to move.

H was annoyed she’d taken so long to arrive. Despite how she’d sounded on the phone, H appeared well enough that she could have driven herself to the hospital with her overnight bag. Then suddenly, she doubled over in pain, startling the woman. Two expectant fathers sat in the waiting room. One was drunk, though it was only noon, and the other seemed to be there solely to watch the basketball game. He stood up abruptly at one point, miming a free throw with an imaginary ball so large he looked like Atlas holding up the sky. He swore at every mistake on the screen, though it was clear he wasn’t rooting for either team. She wondered what H’s husband would have been like in the waiting room. What about A? One question led to another.

H's newborn had round eyes and hair so long it seemed you could tie it back, even straight out of the womb. At the flash of the camera, he opened his eyes wide and stared at the woman.

"Oh, he just looked right at me!"

The nurse holding the baby laughed. "Sorry to disappoint you, but he can't see anything yet."

H's damp bangs clung to her wide forehead. As soon as she saw the woman, she started complaining about her husband. "He sticks to me like glue when I don't need him, but when I actually do, he's AWOL."

When the woman raised the camera to take a photo, H waved her arms and shouted, "No, no!" She'd done a complete turnaround from when she'd first entered the delivery room. The woman pushed H's hair back from her forehead.

"Oh man, I thought I was going to die," H moaned. An unpleasant smell wafted from her.

It wasn't until H was moved to a regular room and had her bowl of post-delivery seaweed soup that her husband finally arrived. He was holding a single rose with only a few petals remaining, as if he'd run with it all the way from his business trip. Although she'd done nothing but complain about him, she cried as soon as she saw him. That was H.

One of the young mothers began to unbutton her shirt to nurse. When she touched the corner of her baby's mouth with her finger, the baby turned toward it as if by magic. Her breast was pale and full, blue veins spiderwebbing through her flesh. When the baby's small mouth latched on and began to suck, she giggled as if being tickled. The milk leaking from her other breast created a wet circle that spread on her shirt.

I once heard a story about a woman who was dying from illness. When her husband went to work, she was left alone in the empty apartment. The husband was still young, at an age when he preferred to go out rather than stay home. He played sports whenever he had the chance and cared about how he looked. She believed he would keep living his life, even after she was gone. She was already halfway there, due to all the medications and treatments. A foul odor came from her armpits, as though she were rotting away, and chemotherapy had claimed all but a fistful of her hair.

When they were first married, her husband used to say, "I can't live without you. If you die, I'm going to follow you." She knew he was joking, but still she liked it. But these words only hit her much later, years into their marriage. The couple fought a lot around that time. She hurled her favorite dishes and screamed.

One day, she waited for her husband to return from work. It was summer, so everyone kept their windows open. As soon as he walked in, she removed a button from his suit and led him to the balcony. "Remember when you said you'd die too, if I died?" she asked. He appeared confused. She leaned back against the balcony window. As he stepped toward her, saying it was dangerous, she stretched her arms toward him. But instead of taking his hands, she pushed him away and fell backward, tearing through the screen and plummeting below.

The police speculated that he had pushed her, especially since she held a button from his suit in her hand. Maybe, in her final moments, she had grabbed his jacket in desperation, tearing off the button. How did the story end? I can't recall. All I know is that sometimes, I'd find myself clutching a button from A's suit, and it would be slippery with sweat.

She could tell it was the woman from the hangover soup restaurant. Old ladies selling vegetables jumped up, hurling curses at the man. The man was much smaller than her, yet he easily kicked her down. Her floral workpants became covered in dirt. His face reddened with rage as he glared at the woman, sprawled on the ground. She didn't try to fight back. Still furious, he grabbed a fistful of her hair and dragged her along. Her purple plastic slippers flew off.

"Why does she put up with it?" said the young mom, offering her other breast to the baby, who sat facing her. "She's stuck to that cauldron all year round, never takes a day off, while he gallivants around town. If only she could handle him the way she handles that pot. I couldn't live like that."

Several men from the market intervened and separated the couple, ending the fight. The woman slowly got up, dusted off her pants, and ran her fingers through her hair. A clump came loose. She hopped on one leg to retrieve her slipper, her belly and buttocks jiggling.

As evening fell, trucks packed up and left the market. Elderly folks with empty rubber tubs boarded buses or hopped into the backs of trucks, disappearing down the new road. Store lights came on. Summer nights. The woman from the hangover soup restaurant drank soju with a side of kimchi. The drought had cut off what little tourist traffic remained. A sour smell wafted from her armpits each time she took a shot. Her eyes were puffy, as if she'd been crying. After emptying her glass, she offered it to the woman. The baby was crawling around the spacious floor. He was so fast that one moment he was on one side and before she knew it, on the other. She took a gulp. It had been a long time since her last drink. Fearing she'd spill her secrets if she drank, she'd stayed away from alcohol. When the soju went down her throat, she let out an "ahh." The owner chuckled. They exchanged more drinks. She gestured at the baby with her chin.

"So where's the dad?"

The woman didn't answer, but the restaurant woman nodded as if she understood.

"Yup, that's life . . ." She wiped her eyes with her thick palms. "It wasn't always this bad, but everything kept going wrong, you know?

Maybe life was already going wrong for him before we got married. He wasn't the kind of man I could respect. I guess I just wanted more."

The owner picked up a piece of radish with her fingers and chewed noisily. The woman couldn't remember the details of their conversation, only fragments—the owner slapping her knee, saying, "Oh my!" while clicking her tongue. She worried she might have said too much, but the next morning, the owner merely asked her to taste the soup seasoning.

I don't like the way I look in my first birthday photos. My mom shaved my head, hoping my hair would grow in nice and thick, but it hadn't grown back in time for my first birthday. In the photo, I look like a servant boy in a lace dress. Isn't it hilarious? A boy with a buzz cut, wearing a white lace dress. I still don't have much hair, but at least I don't have a buzz cut anymore. It's grown out now, enough to look somewhat feminine, though I don't obsess over its thickness. I have bigger things to worry about. I can't help thinking of H's hair—jet-black and glossy, spread on a pillow like gleaming seaweed.

In those birthday photos, my lace dress sports five metal buttons. My mom had attended La Sa Dressmaking Academy in Seoul when she was younger. That's why I'm wearing a dress instead of the usual multi-colored hanbok everyone wears for their first birthday celebration. My mom had cut the fabric herself. She was incredibly busy, juggling all the household chores, preparing for the celebration, and making my outfit, which she finished the night before the party. As she was sewing on the last button, she realized one was missing. She scoured the floor but couldn't find it. Struck by an uneasy feeling, she grabbed my ankles and turned me upside down, fearing I'd swallowed it. My face reddened as blood rushed to it, and then paled. I was too scared to cry. Mom smacked my back with her palm. At one point, she even started pounding it with her fist. The breastmilk I'd had that morning flowed out from my mouth and nose. If you look closely at my photos, the top four buttons are different from the one at the bottom. The four big round buttons are regal, engraved with crowns that resembled something the Queen of England might wear. I don't know where she got those buttons, but my guess is they must have been moved from one piece of clothing to another many times. Back then, buttons were valuable. But the bottom button is engraved with a university name encircled by laurel leaves. That was from my father's college uniform. Mom's sewing box was filled with all kinds of buttons, but only the button from my father's uniform matched the size of the crown buttons.

Fast forward to second grade: I was catching my breath after running the hundred-meter dash. No matter how much time passed, the sharp pain in my side didn't go away. I spent the rest of the class clutching my side before returning home. The doctor said I had appendicitis. Fortunately, I didn't need surgery, and an anti-inflammatory shot did the trick. I didn't say anything, but what would have happened if the doctor had said I needed to have surgery? Could he have removed the button lodged inside me? During science class in the fourth grade, I was pulling magnets out of a box when they were mysteriously attracted to my belly. Afraid someone might notice, I quickly put them back in the box. Years later, when A and I got married and we went on our honeymoon, the metal detector at the airport kept beeping. I went through multiple times, but the beeping continued. The line behind me grew longer, and people started staring. Still, I never spoke of the button, and neither did my family. Even now, I can feel what seems like rust seeping inside me. It's barely noticeable, but I can feel it.

The new road snaked its way through the mountains, its end shimmering in the heat, inducing dizziness. Pushing the stroller, she walked under the shade of roadside trees. She paused occasionally to sit and gaze at the fields and paddies across the way, or to offer the baby a sip of barley tea. The wind was hot, and the fields were parched and cracked. Soybean and perilla leaves curled at their tips. The baby had been up all night, crawling around the room. When she woke in the morning, she found him snuggled against her, using one of her legs as a pillow. Despite frequent baths, he seemed to attract dirt. Grime accumulated in the folds of his neck and arms. She spread his fingers and wiped away the dust. Though his days and nights were mixed up, he was an adorable baby, eating and sleeping well.

Though she kept to the shade, she was sweating. Her pants clung to her legs. Sweat trickled from her forehead into her eyes, causing them to sting. The baby, too, seemed listless in his stroller. She offered him the bottle, but he wouldn't take it. At the far end of the new road, a crowd materialized as if from a mirage. They approached slowly, finally passing her after what felt like an eternity. Leading the procession was a man in a traditional mourning robe, trailed by sun-darkened pallbearers in robes of coarse hemp. Some kept scratching their necks, as though the fabric chafed at their skin. Their garments sagged, and their chanting turned into murmurs. The weight of the bier seemed to press heavily on their shoulders, as though the bier carried two bodies. Yellowish stains marked the pallbearers' shoulders. A little girl about seven, her head covered with a hemp shroud, followed some distance behind.

She veered off the road onto a side path. A rusted sign, no larger than a license plate, lay hidden in the undergrowth. The word *orchard* was the only legible text. As she climbed the hill, an abandoned lot unfolded before her eyes. All that remained of the orchard were dead, uprooted trees scattered haphazardly. In the middle of the lot, beneath the shade of a big persimmon tree, stood a small house. It had two rooms, one large and one small, along with a tiled bathroom and modest kitchen. Its doors were barely hanging on, and the wallpaper was tattered and full of scratches. Strewn around the house were everyday items like plastic basins, aluminum pots, and toothbrushes. A heavy chain lay coiled in front of an empty doghouse. The branches of the persimmon tree sagged as if about to break under the weight of the fruit. She parked the stroller in the shade and pulled back the canopy. The baby's nose was beaded with sweat. She pictured white diapers flapping in the breeze, hanging across the yard. Time seemed to flow quickly, punctuated by the soft thuds of ripe persimmons falling to the ground.

Even when she seasoned the soup lightly, it would reduce down and become salty by evening. The baby, his belly full of milk, crawled around the restaurant, eyes brimming with mischief. They said the orchard on the new road had been producing juicy peaches for over a decade. But the land was arid now, and the peaches, no bigger than a baby's fist, were hard and dry. Since the land was idle, she was told she could rent it for a low price.

"You really think you could do it? Aren't you scared?" asked the restaurant owner.

As long as she had the baby, she felt she could do anything. The owner set down the knife she'd been using to trim the bean sprouts and wiped her hands on her pants. "Might as well go and ask," she said, standing up.

Though she'd been vigilant, the baby had somehow slipped away. Even while boiling and cooling the barley tea in the kitchen, she'd kept an eye on the dining area. The baby wasn't outside the restaurant either. The streetlights on the new road were sparse, casting a dim glow. She figured that if he'd wandered into the street, he would be drawn to the light. Sprinting toward the terminal, she saw a dark figure dart behind the supermarket. When she went closer to look, it was just a large black cat. She kept walking, gaze fixed on the ground, even jumping at the sight of garbage bags on the street and inspecting them to make sure he wasn't there.

Passengers lounged in the terminal, watching television as they waited for their buses. She scanned the floor. There was no sign of the baby. Her legs weakened, but then she heard his laugh. A young woman was holding him. Snatching him back into her arms, she learned the young woman had picked him up because he'd crawled into the terminal crying. She waved as she walked away. "Bye, bye!" The baby suddenly stretched both arms toward the young woman and burst into tears. She looked startled. A young man pulled her toward a Seoul-bound bus. As she passed through the ticket gate, the baby's cries grew more sorrowful. The woman patted and cooed at him, but he remained inconsolable. His knees were scraped from crawling all the way to the terminal, and his bottom was dirty. The young woman cast a final glance back at the baby. She resembled H a little.

Though he'd stopped crying, his chest still heaved. He pursed his lips. He wasn't cooing.

"What?" the woman said, bringing her ear to the baby's mouth.

"Um, um."

Whenever H went to work, he would stretch his arms toward his mother from the arms of the housekeeper. H never held him, instead waving and saying, "Bye, bye!" The baby clearly remembered H. With great effort, he uttered, "Umma!"

H complained I'd brought A along. Didn't I realize how easy it would be for three people to get separated in a crowd this size? I felt bad and became antsy. A looked as though he hadn't been out to a place like this in ages. I was worried he'd heard H complain, but he was too busy gawking at everything to notice. Just as H had said, we kept losing A. Whenever that happened, we'd duck out of the crowd and wait for him in front of a store.

We took the elevator up to the top floor of a skyscraper. We could see the whole city sprawled below us. It was quiet and peaceful from up high. H pressed her nose to the glass and shook her head. "Can you believe we used to go around like that?" The streets squirmed with people. A laughed, drawing a sharp glance from H. He was far from H's type. He was too skinny and older, with hair that was already beginning to thin.

At the bar, H sulked when we ordered drinks. Even when we pushed the menu her way, she didn't cheer up. A seemed amused and kept laughing. At first, I wondered why he was laughing so much, but looking back, H had her endearing quirks. As the drinks kicked in, H gradually warmed up. Every time she cracked a joke, A laughed. Neither seemed to notice when I stepped away to go to the bathroom.

You know when you're drunk, there are moments that are choppy, like slides in an old projector? Just a few scenes remain in my mind. I saw H and A sitting at the bar, their backs to me. I was about to squeeze in between and throw my arms around them when I saw A's hand hovering above my empty seat. And then slowly, H's hand lifted to meet his. They held hands. Their entwined fingers were long and pale. I don't know who made the first move. Their interlocked fingers were beautiful.

In the elevator, I acted like I hadn't seen anything. H and A seemed to buy it. We joined the crowd on the streets once more. People kept stepping on my feet. My black velvet shoes became covered with marks. A group of drunk men broke into rowdy song, coming from the opposite direction. The crowd scattered to avoid them, and just like that, I lost H and A, who'd been walking beside me. I waited for a long time, but they never showed up.

I didn't tell them. After all, it was Friday night, and we often caught that Friday night fever.

The housekeeper let me in right away. After all, she knew me well. H had left the baby with her housekeeper while she went on vacation. That was just like H. The baby had a thick head of curly hair.

"His days and nights are completely mixed up," the housekeeper said. She then peered at my face. "By the way, why haven't you had kids yet?"

She said she hadn't been able to sleep a wink the night before. She started snoring the second she lay down. I picked up the baby. He fit perfectly in my arms, as if he were mine. Once I picked him up, I didn't want to let go. So I just put on my shoes with him in my arms. I don't remember anything after that.

A once described me as an "intellectual," and said that he wanted the mother of his children to have that quality. I married A, and remained best friends with H, just like before. So that's what you wanted—an intellectual?

After that Friday night, I hated the sight of people holding hands, fingers intertwined. Some nights, the pain was so unbearable I'd writhe on the bathroom floor like a worm. Then I'd seep into H's house like water. I'd crawl into her bed while she lay asleep. H hasn't aged a day. Her nightgown was unbuttoned so that she could feed her fussing baby at night. The baby's mouth, small as his mother's nipple, was stained with milk. One breast caught the light from a nearby security light. The red threadworm opened its mouth and sank its teeth into her breast. After that Friday night, the next five years were a mess. I started running, carrying the baby in my arms. It's something I'd wanted to do ever since.

Daytime to Daytime

The rundown restaurant in the old town was one of the stops on the tour. Ten tourists gathered around a guide holding a travel agency flag. As the guide talked, their eyes traced the windows and roof of the plastered building that was marked with clear trowel prints. Through it all, an old man with glasses kept his video camera trained on the scene.

Earlier, while waiting for a connecting flight at Incheon International Airport, this same old man had filmed the airfield bustling with trucks and stair cars that weaved in and out between the planes. When the boarding time was announced, he'd recorded the group as they headed to their gate.

The group included elderly people, a middle-aged couple, and a young man. As if no attention had been paid to the seating arrangement, they sat scattered around the cabin near the woman. The interior of the plane was cold and dim, with all the sunshades pulled down to block out the harsh sunlight. They were flying from daytime to daytime. During the thirteen-hour flight, no one reclined their seats or wandered the aisles. Their conversations were inaudible over the hum of the plane. The only sound that pierced the quiet was the distant wailing of a baby from the rear of the plane.

The package tour covered several Swiss sights in a short time. After the guide's talk, they took turns posing for pictures in front of the restaurant in groups of two or three, each using their own camera. Everyone seemed reluctant to exchange contact information or make plans to share photos later. They all stood in the same spot, each striking the same pose, while a young man in the group took the pictures.

The tourists didn't look like they were from the city. No one seemed concerned about their appearance. Their hair was disheveled, as if they hadn't bothered to brush it, and their hats were crumpled. Their skin, peeking out from drab-colored coats, looked dull and chapped. Even the young man in the group was wearing stained jeans and dirty sneakers. When the guide waved the pennant flag and led the way, the group filed toward St. Peter's Church. Just as he had back at the airport, the old man trailed a few steps behind, leisurely filming the buildings of the old town.

"These Japanese tourists are on another level. I once went on a trip with someone who'd lived in Japan for five years. We barely got to see anything, because he kept telling me to stand here and there for photos. Can you imagine traveling with someone who was born and raised in Japan?"

Choi, who had come to the airport to pick her up, hadn't dropped the honorific throughout their entire conversation.

The restaurant, once an armory during the Middle Ages, wasn't all that different from a family restaurant in Seoul. Wooden tables, covered with red-and-white striped tablecloths, were placed around the building's columns. Though the window shutters were open, sunlight barely filtered into the dark interior. Weapons used by knights some five hundred years ago adorned the walls above the windows, while the air was thick with the stale smell of cooking grease. In the smoking section, clouds of cigarette smoke lingered near the blackened ceiling beams. A wheeled cannon stood near the entrance to the kitchen, and waitresses in Swiss costumes bustled through the restaurant, balancing up to ten plates in their arms.

Starting Thursday morning, after concluding his official business in the city, her husband had explored a few nearby cities. He began with a walk through the old town, choosing to travel by train and foot, instead of renting a car. After three nights away, he returned to the city, spending half a day in the Bahnhofstrasse shopping district, pausing for a simple lunch of a sandwich and sparkling water in the park with the Pestalozzi statue. He stopped at a few shops on his way back to the hotel, purchasing two scarves and some handmade chocolates. He was scheduled to return to Seoul on Tuesday on a direct Korean Air flight.

During his time in the old town, he dined at one of the restaurants and jotted down a review of it in his journal.

Roast lamb w/ buttered potatoes. Taste ★☆☆☆☆ Price ★☆☆☆☆

He was somewhat stingy when it came to evaluating food and people. He loathed additives and artificial flavors. It had taken her a long time to get used to the taste of additive-free food.

Noise from the kitchen interrupted her conversation with Choi. Dishes clattered, and food sizzled in frying pans. The waitresses' thick German accents became more pronounced when taking customers' orders. She ate only half of her roast lamb and potatoes, but Choi didn't urge her to eat more as he once did or drag the dish toward him to finish it himself. He didn't seem to like the food either. Just like her husband's review said, the food was overpriced.

"It must be the middle of the night there. I'm so sorry for waking you."

After apologizing for calling late, Choi had remained silent. Then instead of calling her hyeongsu-nim, since she had married his senior, he'd called her by name, as he once had. Before she got married, he used to phone her occasionally, only to say her name and fall silent, causing her to blurt, "Hey! You been drinking again?"

They had started at the company in the same year. Though Choi was three years older, they didn't bother with honorifics and spoke informally to each other, a common practice among colleagues who started at the same time. If she got too drunk at work parties that stretched into the early hours, he would carry her home on his back, even patting her back as she threw up in an alley near her house. During a company mountaineering club trip to Bukhan Mountain, when she needed to relieve herself midway, it was Choi who stood guard with his back to her. She tried to be careful, but urine ended up trickling down the slope, wetting the soles of Choi's hiking boots. "You better not turn around!" she'd warn, while he smoked a cigarette and admired the view of the city below, but she knew he wouldn't peek. Their colleagues often teased them, asking when they planned to tie the knot. Her husband was among those who'd teased them.

She was glad to hear Choi speak casually to her again, and she laughed, while several scenes from the past flitted by. But her laughter soon faded. As his silence stretched on, she couldn't help thinking of the blazing August sun, the seething sea, and the loud arguments and swearing of country kids darkened by the sun.

She and Choi walked together toward the lake. Most of the buildings on this corner had stood for over five hundred years. The crypt in the cathedral dated back to the late eleventh century. Her husband, too, must have strolled through these streets flanked by sixteenth- and seventeenth-century houses and guildhalls on his way to the lake. A line from his journal came to her. "For some reason, whenever I'm around old buildings, I get drowsy."

As the afternoon wore on, the temperature rose, making her sweat beneath her sweater. The benches along the lake were occupied, leaving them with no place to sit. Grimy-looking swans glided across the murky lake where wads of tissue paper floated. On the benches, young couples embraced and kissed openly, oblivious to those around them. Choi, stationed at the Swiss branch for the past two years, seemed unfazed by the sight. He put a cigarette between his lips and then, as if suddenly remembering, offered the pack to her. In the past when the office was empty, she would snatch the cigarette from his mouth and sneak a drag or two, making him burst into laughter if she coughed. At some point, she had started buying cigarettes again, hiding them in sacks of onions, or shopping bags with tofu or fish. When her husband left for work, she would crouch down in the narrow laundry room on the balcony for a smoke. Since it was just once a day, she managed to keep it a secret.

On the way back to the hotel, they came across many people walking their dogs. They had to stop repeatedly as large dogs beelined for roadside trees or security lights, sniffing vigorously and marking their territory. They said goodbye on the street across from the hotel. Standing on the other side of the tram tracks, Choi motioned for her to go in first, the same way he had years ago in front of her house. "A man should never turn his back!" he joked. It had been seven years since she'd last heard him say that.

This hotel seemed to have kept its historic exterior while completely renovating the inside. There were old chairs, glass bottles, and plates in the lobby and hallways, with labels indicating they were artifacts from several hundreds of years ago. The hotel itself was like a small museum. She was given the room where her husband had stayed, free of charge. It was an upscale establishment, rich in tradition, situated only a block from the Central Station. The police had already searched the room, but were unable to find any note left by her husband.

The handles of the oak wardrobe gleamed, worn smooth by countless hands. Inside, her husband's suit, down parka, and casual clothes were neatly hung. The collars and cuffs of his dress shirts were stained, with yellowish half-moons under the arms. Memories of his hairy armpits, the strength in his arms as they encircled her waist, and the firmness of his thighs pressed against her body came flooding back.

She found his suitcase under the bed, its contents sliding and bumping against each other. The suitcase, which had accompanied her husband on his business trips, bore luggage stickers from airports across the world. It was only when she was staring at the suitcase that she thought about its combination lock, something she'd never pondered before. She tried the first four digits of her husband's social security number, but it didn't open. She tried the last four digits of their home phone number, as well as his cell, but neither worked. She remembered that men who'd served in the military often used their service number, but she had no idea what his was.

Her husband's journal lay open in the middle of the desk, surrounded by his passport, gum, pens, and a stack of documents. He was a habitual note-taker, and the numerous pen markings on the pages made the journal bulge. Appointments were scheduled for the upcoming months of November and December. However, as she scanned the pages, she found no number that resembled a military service number.

FRI

09:00 Left Zurich.

09:40 Arrived at Rhine Falls.

People are fascinated by things that fall.

Waterfalls, autumn leaves, shooting stars, bungee jumping, roller coasters . . .

14:00 Arrived in Lucerne. Saw the Chapel Bridge, Hofkirche, Lion Monument.

The bravery of the Swiss Guards and a male lion seem at odds.

Don't they know a wild lion is a symbol of laziness?

Tourist Hotel (Tel 041 410 24 74; touristhotel@centralnet.ch)

St Karli Quai 12, private bathroom, CHF 134

The hotel manager sat with his back perfectly straight. A thin man in his early fifties, his years of experience in the industry were evident in the stiffness of his posture. Choi spoke to him in brisk, assertive English, while she struggled to understand the manager's German accent, leaving her to rely on Choi's intermittent translations. It was a hotel employee who had first found her husband, yet all inquiries were being redirected to the manager. A witness had thought her husband had fainted while jogging.

The declared cause of death was a skull fracture. He had fallen from the thirteenth-floor gym, clad in shorts and a T-shirt, his hand still clutching a towel embossed with the hotel name. The hotel staff had ruled it a suicide.

When Choi challenged the lack of a suicide note, the authorities shrugged, offering no further comment or explanation. The manager's voice dropped to a whisper as he shared his fears about the news spreading to other guests. He urged them to collect her husband's belongings and leave as soon as possible. But Choi wasn't one to back down so easily. He thrust a sheaf of papers at the manager. The manager, taken aback, shook his hands. It was a photocopy of her husband's journal, which Choi seemed to have already read.

While the manager flipped through the pages, Choi leaned in and whispered, "He's insisting it was a suicide. Acknowledging it as an accident would mean compensation, which is a major inconvenience for them. I mean, consider this city. Tourism is Switzerland's third largest industry, and one-sixth of the entire population's livelihood is tied to it. A young man with a bright future fell to his death from their hotel gym, but they're refusing to take responsibility. Something's fishy here. They keep denying everything."

The news that an employee had committed suicide while on a business trip would send shockwaves through the company. Something her husband had written in last Friday's entry flashed across her mind: "People are fascinated by things that fall. Waterfalls, autumn leaves, shooting stars, bungee jumping, roller coasters . . ." Perhaps her husband had wanted to write down another word. A fascination with things that fall. Suicide by jumping.

The gym was furnished with a collection of fitness equipment, including a treadmill. The floor-to-ceiling windows offered a view of the entire city of Zurich. The gym had remained closed after her husband's accident, and a musty smell lingered, trapped by the sealed windows. She looked down to the spot where her husband had been discovered. A small yellow car was parked there now. The thirteenth floor wasn't as high as she'd thought. It seemed she could almost touch the objects below if she stretched out her hand. If there was any relief, it was in knowing that he hadn't feared death for more than a few seconds.

She arrived at Rhine Falls after one in the afternoon. She had expected a rustic train station, but was greeted instead by just two benches and a sign bearing the station's name. The sound of the waterfall came over the trees. She walked toward the noise. Standing at the edge of the rock, she saw the river stretching hundreds of meters below, with observation decks close to the waterfall. The steep steps were muddy from the shoes of previous visitors. Those coming up from the waterfall were soaked. They shook water droplets from their hair, appearing exhausted from the spectacle they had just witnessed. As she descended the stairs, the roar of the waterfall grew louder. The spray created puddles on every deck. Nearby, a German couple was shouting at each other to be heard. Various decks offered different angles of the falls. The water pooled at the top, crashed down onto hollowed rocks, twisted, and split into two streams as it passed over a boulder in the center. The rapids, changing directions with each turn, cascaded in diverse shapes and sounds. The lower deck jutted out like a balcony over the water, facing the direction of the flow. A massive stream of water seemed to engulf those standing there. The tourists were speechless and awestruck, overwhelmed by the ringing sounds and smell of water.

Her mother-in-law had writhed, foaming at the mouth, and finally fainted. Her sisters-in-law, who were much younger than her husband, broke into wails, more shocked by their mother's collapse than by the news of their brother's death. Her mother-in-law soiled herself, filling the living room with a foul odor. In the hospital, she remained unconscious, even during treatment and after being transferred to a regular room. Her father-in-law came running, having received the news late. He appeared remarkably healthy for a seventy-year-old, enough to be mistaken for a young man from behind. Her husband had taken after his father, rather than his mother, who was short and stout. Whenever she had imagined her husband as an older man, she'd naturally pictured her father-in-law. "Maybe it's a mistake? Are they sure it's him?" he asked, his hand starting to shake. He thrust his trembling hand into his suit pocket and stared out the hospital window for over an hour.

She had stretched out on the cot next to her father's bed, but she hadn't been able to sleep. The August sun beat down on her eyelids. Outside, the waves kept rising, and the sun-darkened children skipped over the waves, holding hands. The waves crashed over their heads, and they coughed and spluttered, swearing in dialect. A smell of decay came from her father's body. She opened the window and turned the fan to high. The popsicle in her hand melted, dripping down to her wrist. She frantically licked at the stickiness as she looked down at her father's face. He had driven his motorcycle drunk, zigzagging down the road before getting sucked in under the wheel of a bus.

Relatives came to the hospital to see her father one last time. Over ten of them slept in chairs outside the room. Her mother had gone with them to the restaurant across the street to have a late breakfast, repeatedly saying to come get her if anything happened. Flies clung to her father's face. A foul smell came from a nearby kiln yard, a place that was always swarming with flies. She shooed them away, even managing to catch a few with her hands, but it made no difference. Suddenly, her father's eyes flew open. His bloodshot eyes stared at some point on the ceiling. She leaned in close, but he didn't seem to recognize her. He kept moving his lips, as if trying to speak. The machine attached to his body started to beep urgently. The hallway was empty. He suddenly arched his back, then crashed back onto the bed with a thud. He heaved, as if blowing out cigarette smoke, and convulsions started in his chest, quickly spreading throughout his whole body. Life lingered on the tip of his big toe for a long time, like a butterfly that had lighted on a blade of grass. It was from this point that that the woman started to believe that the soul, responsible for animating the human body, might be small and light, like a butterfly. Soon the spasm in the big toe also stopped.

She stood next to her father's bed until her mother and the relatives returned from the restaurant. Her popsicle had melted completely by then, dripping down her elbow to pool on the hospital floor. She was still holding onto the popsicle stick. Her mother wailed, shaking her father. His brothers, who'd been standing with toothpicks stuck in their teeth, sobbed loudly. The roar of the waterfall sounded like wailing. While lying on the cot, she'd felt a wave of anger sweep through her. She'd clenched her teeth to stifle her moans. Her shoes were wet from the water spray. A few meters below at the bottom of the waterfall, the water turned calm.

After leaving Rhine Falls, her husband had arrived in Lucerne at two o'clock in the afternoon and toured the city. Because she stayed too long at the waterfall, she missed the train. She had to wait a long time. By the time she arrived in Lucerne, it was dark, and she couldn't see the lake. She realized she'd forgotten to call Choi.

She looked through her husband's journal by the light of her night-stand. Even his entries were tinged with sarcasm. The business meeting had been a success, and the outcome largely positive. They had indulged late into the night, and everyone had gotten drunk, yet there had been no incidents, not even the accidental breaking of a glass. Choi had driven her husband back to the hotel that day. There was a distinct voice present in the journal, but it seemed to belong to a stranger.

As soon as her mother-in-law regained consciousness, she frantically put on her shoes, causing her IV needle to fall out. The woman ran into the hallway to get a nurse. Moans from an ill patient echoed through the hallway. Her mother-in-law fought off the nurse who was trying to reinsert the needle. "I'm going to dig up that grave! It swallowed my child!" She was amazed by the strength her mother-in-law possessed. Two nurses, attempting to restrain her mother-in-law, were flung back.

Relatives came to visit. Some shook their heads, worrying they might have another death in the family. Someone started to mention a temporary grave, but quickly shut their mouth. Her mother-in-law lay weeping like a child. Though it was night, the August sun pierced her eyes. The sleepless nights continued. Her unwashed body smelled. Even in the middle of the day when there were no visitors, she lay in the cot next to the bed. When hunger pangs struck, her empty stomach twisted and her insides chafed. She went down to the hospital snack bar and gulped down a bowl of instant noodles, but the water from the dispenser wasn't hot enough to cook the noodles properly. As she was setting down the plastic bowl, she saw her reflection in the window and saw a face that looked twenty years older. She started feeling sick while inside the elevator that took her back up to the room. She ran to the bathroom and threw up what she had just eaten.

As soon as her mother-in-law saw her father-in-law, she charged at him, scratching his face. As if her anger was far from spent, she leapt up to strike his face.

"So you like outliving your son? You think you'll get to live another thousand years?"

Her meek mother-in-law, known for using only organic, high-quality ingredients in cooking, for diligently taking care of the children, for never talking back to her husband, had transformed into a completely different person. Grinding her teeth, her bony arms grabbed her husband's collar and a shirt button popped off.

"I'm going to dig up that grave right now!" she shrieked, foaming at the mouth. He glanced at his daughter-in-law and cleared his throat, embarrassed.

After turning seventy, her father-in-law had become obsessed with his health. He found himself attending more funerals of friends, and he often had nightmares of being buried alive, of concrete being poured over his grave. He went to bed with his mouth closed, but it drooped open naturally, causing saliva to pool under his pillow. While sleep was sweeter, waking up proved challenging. Were it not for his internal clock, attuned to waking at six for seventy years, rising would have been difficult. He felt that his sphincter was always a little loose, and although he wasn't a smoker and had exercised moderately for over thirty years, he became breathless whenever he climbed the stairs. He would gaze vacantly at young people who bounded up the stairs two or three steps at a time. Once, a molar fell out during a meal. To him, sleep was no longer rest, but a rehearsal for death. His wife, sleeping next to him, was often struck by his flailing limbs. He made a grave for himself halfway up a mountain, burying an empty coffin and erecting a tombstone with his name, hoping to deceive death into believing he was already dead.

Choi believed her husband's death had been an accident. So did her husband's family. She'd called Choi to ask what had happened that day, but he hadn't picked up.

SAT

11:00 Arrived at Gruyères, Gruyères Castle, cheese factory tour.

Jerry's favorite food, bought some Gruyère cheese.

Waterfalls, church, castle. Nothing excites me.

Only a block of cheese stimulates my appetite.

Why such an obsession with this life that's as nauseating as cheese.

14:00 Arrived in Montreux, toured Castle Chillon.

Saw Byron's name carved on the third pillar.

My Mary, to Love once so dear . . .

I remember the hour, She rewarded those vows with a Tear . . .

"The Tear"

Yes, I remember.

Villa Germaine (Tel 021 963 15 28)

3 Ave de Collonges, private bathroom, CHF 105

When she first left the hotel, she had planned to follow her husband's travel route. She wanted to know what he'd seen and felt on his last few days. However, she hurried past the Lion Monument and the Musegg Wall. Feeling impatient, she practically ran across the two-hundred-meter-long Chapel Bridge. She hardly noticed the woodblock prints hanging on the ceiling. Even when she boarded the train to Gruyère, her impatience didn't subside. She felt as if she were chasing someone aimlessly, as if she were trying to catch up to a friend who'd left earlier by bus. Impatience overcame her. Her husband had followed various routes featured in package tours. He hadn't climbed Pilatus or Titlis in Lucerne, as he had set his sights on the Matterhorn.

Passing Bulle station, she saw fattened cows grazing in a vast meadow. They wore Swiss bells around their necks, the size of their heads. As they ran, their sagging rumps jiggled. It seemed there was a festival. Men dressed in traditional red Swiss clothing walked in pairs toward a large building. Tourists were crossing the meadow. Their hair was disheveled, and their hats crumpled. They walked slowly, following a guide carrying a pennant flag. She'd only glimpsed them for a moment, but she knew they were the same Japanese tourists from the Incheon airport.

The smell of cheese followed her all the way up the alley to Gruyères Castle, wafting out from several fondue restaurants along the way. The interiors of these restaurants were dim, with candles on the tables. She kept slipping on the cobblestone path. Old buildings, converted into shops, sold handmade butter candies, cookies, and identical-looking ceramic plates. A middle-aged woman with rosy cheeks motioned her over and pointed at handknit baby clothes. The tourists at the castle were all female. Apart from the woman selling tickets at the entrance, there seemed to be no other staff. She wandered in and out of rooms, following the sequence in the brochure provided at the entrance.

The train sped around Lake Geneva. The sunlight reflecting off the water was so bright that she had to close her eyes. About to draw the curtain, she flinched, remembering her husband's dislike for blackout curtains. In the end, they had settled for vertical blinds. It was always the sunlight, not the alarm, that woke her. She saw her husband's face up close, his cheeks and chin stubbly, despite having shaved the morning before. He turned and fidgeted in his sleep. The fine lines running from his nose to the corners of his mouth disappeared after washing, but would etch deeply into his cheeks one day. There would also come a day when the wrinkles on his forehead, appearing when reading or faced with serious questions, wouldn't fade. Naturally, her father-in-law's face came to mind. Her husband would become an old man, health-obsessed like his father. Whenever she had a bad dream, she peered at her husband's face. She was determined to be at his deathbed, unlike her mother, who had missed the moment her father passed because of a late breakfast. Even after the funeral, her mother asked, still dazed, "Did your father leave any last words?"

She thought they would be stopping at Chillon after Montreux station, but the train continued on. When she inquired, girls in heavy makeup told her the train stopped at Chillon station only if someone pressed the buzzer, adding that the number 1 bus would drop her off right in front of the castle. She waited at the station, but the bus didn't come. She started walking. The rain began to fall, and water seeped into her clothes. The number 1 bus passed by, completely empty.

Tourists milled about in front of Castle Chillon. Those without umbrellas took shelter under store awnings and trees. An Asian woman handed her a brochure in Korean, noting it was now five o'clock, and asking if she still wanted to go inside the castle, given only an hour remained for the tour. The woman's blunt bangs made it difficult to gauge her age. The Korean brochure was full of mistakes. Castle Chillon was bigger than Gruyères Castle, and there were many rooms she had to skip. If she didn't check the numbers above each door, she would have easily gotten lost. With the castle soon closing, only a few visitors remained. As she moved through the rooms, loud voices and camera flashes came from the next room, but upon entering, she found them empty. From every window, Lake Geneva was visible, its surface appearing to boil under the heavy rain.

The underground dungeons were connected by narrow passages. The walls were partially in ruins, lined with torture instruments, red with rust. She stood in front of the third pillar, but she couldn't find Byron's name amid all the scribbles. Walking past the dungeons, she came upon several passages. As long as she followed the numbers, there was no fear of getting lost, yet she suddenly grew afraid. The passages narrowed, forcing her to crouch over. Then the space abruptly widened into a chapel, adorned with a crucifix. Muffled voices echoed nearby. When she exited a passage, hunched over, she glimpsed someone slipping into another one. She'd caught just a glimpse of his back, but she was sure it had been the elderly Japanese man with the video camera. The drone of voices faded. Had all the remaining tourists left? The rain made the dungeons even gloomier. She hurried, expecting to reach the third passage, but found herself back at the pillar where Byron had carved his name. A sharp pain struck the back of her head. She ran toward the third passage in an awkward hunch. Her hands grew damp. The third passage led to a large hall on the second floor, filled with knights' coats of arms, but it was empty.

Outside, the ground was slippery with rain. All the tourists had left. The castle gate was shut, only a small side door left open for remaining visitors to exit. The Asian woman at the ticket window was gone, likely finished for the day. The shop was closed, and those who had taken shelter under the trees and awning were also gone. Across the lake, she could see the more cosmopolitan Montreux. The number one bus didn't come.

SUN

10:30 Arrived in Zermatt, toured Matterhorn.

From a height of 4,478 meters at the Matterhorn, I think about things that are 4,478 meters below.

If I go down 4,478 meters, I'll probably think about things that are 4,478 meters above.

Confirmed Zurich hotel reservation, Monday night, late checkout.

Goldenes Schwert (Tel 01 266 18 18; Fax 266 18 88; hotel@rainbow.ch)

Hotel Bahnhof (Tel 027 967 24 06; Fax 967 72 16)

Across from train station, no breakfast, CHF 76

Her husband's parka was too big, and the sleeves came over her hands. Chalets huddled together at the bottom of snow-covered mountains, and carriages carrying tourists creaked past. The Matterhorn peak loomed, visible from anywhere in the village. Once she passed the Gornergrat railway station, a souvenir shop, and a shoe store, a quiet rural village unfolded before her.

A middle-aged woman in casual clothing, who was sitting at the front desk, had a message for her from Choi.

"I didn't know where you would be by now, so I called every hotel. I finally caught you in Zermatt."

Since Choi also had a copy of her husband's journal, he had guessed her location. She heard the sound of flipping pages over the phone. "So I guess you'll be heading back tomorrow?"

It would take half a day to go up to the Gornergrat observatory and back. "You're not going on the hike, right? In that case, it should take about three hours at most. I guess you'll be back in Zurich by tomorrow afternoon. I'll come to your hotel then."

Her hotel room was too big for one person. It had two double beds and an additional bed in the loft. There was even a balcony, and when she stepped out onto it, she saw the Matterhorn towering above colorful rooftops. She tried each bed, but she couldn't sleep.

She saw them again when she was coming down from the observatory and walking to Zermatt station. They stood at the station square while their guide spoke about Zermatt, gazing blankly at the Matterhorn rising above the shops in front of the station. Disheveled hair, flaky faces, and wrinkled, worn clothing—they looked exactly the same as they had in the old town of Zurich, except now they were shivering slightly from the cold. She recognized them, not only because she kept running into them, and not just because of the odd elderly man who was constantly filming everything. Although they looked like strangers who had come together thanks to the travel agency, they also resembled members of the same family—a family that seemed to be missing something vital, one that had recently endured something terrible. Their clothes had become more crumpled in the meantime, and the young man's dirty sneakers, as if stained by spilled food, now bore the marks of a red sauce. They followed the guide with the pennant flag in single file, the old man with his video camera and the young man with his hands jammed in his jeans pockets. He briefly glanced at her, shook his head if he'd been mistaken, and continued walking.

MON

09:35 Left Zermatt.

13:20 Old town tour. For some reason, whenever I'm around old buildings, I get drowsy.

15:30 Bahnhofstrasse tour. Bought two scarves and some chocolate. Underneath this street, there is a vault full of gold bars. I feel dizzy walking down it. One false step and you'll get sucked into the vault forever.

The trip is over and I'm still bored.

The trip was over, and she was back at her starting point, Zurich Central Station, but she felt just as angry and exhausted as she had when she'd first arrived a week ago. Everything felt surreal. Choi was waiting in the hotel lobby.

"I don't understand why he wasted so much time on the road," Choi said. "You probably noticed, but it's like he didn't even consider the route. Heading east one moment, then west."

But the Japanese tourists had followed the same route as well.

"A travel agency would never plan a route like that. You must have gotten them confused with a different group. After all, Japanese tourists are everywhere." Choi didn't believe her.

The hotel manager was polite, but his expression remained cool and unmoved. He was a stubborn man. Choi lowered his voice.

"They've backed down now. What they said in the beginning was complete nonsense. According to the police investigation, the window in the gym was the problem."

The casement windows in the building were old and the hinges rattled. The window where her husband had fallen was the same. As it was the off-season, there weren't many hotel guests, and her husband was the only one in the gym that early morning. His body quickly became sweaty. He must have wanted to open the window to breathe in the fresh dawn air. He approached the window, turned the handle, and pushed it open. Suddenly, it swung back, and her husband, his hand still holding the handle, was flung out the window. This was the police investigation's conclusion. Only the tasks of collecting his belongings and transporting his body remained. The process was complicated. Choi told her that his body had been moved from a hospital mortuary to a funeral home. "It's unfair. He went too soon . . ." Choi trailed off.

She gathered her husband's belongings, but she still didn't know the combination for the suitcase. Suddenly, she became very curious about its contents. It seemed that everything would become clear once she opened the trunk. She tried various combinations of his 13-digit resident registration number, but the trunk wouldn't budge. Growing impatient, she brought over his journal and tried out any numbers that she saw, but it remained locked. An hour passed. She paced around the room, looking for something she could use to break open the trunk, but couldn't find anything. She attempted to pick the lock with a pen, but the pen quickly snapped.

As they were saying goodbye in front of the hotel, Choi had said, as if he'd just remembered, "I almost forgot, your birthday's around Christmas, right? Did you know he'd already made a reservation for two at a hotel restaurant, even though your birthday's more than a month away? I saw it in his journal. The police called the hotel to confirm there was a reservation, and that turned out to be a crucial piece of evidence."

She tried her birthday on the lock. Unexpectedly, the trunk clicked open.

Inside were a box of handmade chocolates and two identical scarves, presumably for her and her mother-in-law. She searched the trunk, but there was no note. The cheese from Gruyères, which he'd mentioned buying, had blue mold growing on it.

The mortician was a Caucasian woman around her age. She unzipped the body bag to show her his face. It seemed that a prosthetic had been inserted into the part of his head that had caved in when he fell. Looking closely, she saw needle marks all over the body, apparently where the chemicals had been injected. His nose and ears were sealed with cotton.

A gurgling sound came from behind the folding screen where her father's body had been placed. Her mother, thinking he had come back to life, opened the coffin lid, only to find that the sound was from his organs rapidly decomposing in the August heat. The funeral procession wound through the small town where her father used to ride his motorcycle. It followed the seaside road and climbed up the mountain, with her mother trailing behind. The mourning robe chafed at her neck. Though it was only morning, the heat was sweltering, and the sun pierced her eyes. The waves were rising, and children, dark as coal, laughed as they rode them. Fluids leaking from the coffin dripped onto the shoulders of the coffin bearers.

Her husband's face was clean, as if he'd just shaved and washed. He used to smack his lips when coming out of the bathroom after brushing his teeth. As though he'd been cringing when he fell, a deep line was etched into his brow. Every morning at dawn, her husband had gone jogging around the lake by their apartment. His pulse had quickened, his muscles had swelled, and his blood had pumped through vessels long enough to circle the Earth two and a half times. But all that stopped in twenty-two seconds. When she fell behind, he'd grab her hand and pull her along. His lungs, that had once expanded and shrunken repeatedly, ceased to move. He could cause the family to laugh out loud with a sudden witty remark. The brain that had come up with clever words and innovative ideas had stopped functioning after four minutes without oxygen. His knowledge became useless, and his memories were erased. To load her husband's body onto an airplane, she needed an embalming certificate from the undertaker. His body had to be loaded via a different route, costing triple the regular airfare, and separated from the other cargo. His body went back into the freezer. Through a small crack, she saw another stainless-steel bed below, with luxuriant golden hair strewn across it.

She called Seoul. After the phone rang for a long time, her sister-in-law who was still in high school answered. "Mom's been crying nonstop since she got home from the hospital. She won't eat or sleep and she's acting really strange. She's laid out all his photos in her room."

An ambulance had to be at the airport when the plane arrived, along with people to transport the coffin. "But I don't know his friends' numbers! But eonni, it's really him? He really died?" Her sister-in-law sobbed.

"Mother knows Park Seong-gu's number. If you call him, he'll get in touch with the others. We need at least six people. Okay, repeat what I said."

"At least six people, I got it. Because my brother's really heavy."

The casket needed to be enclosed in an outer container. The mortician had explained that a wooden casket should be placed inside an aluminum container, with dry ice filled in the space between. She recalled her sister-in-law as an elementary school girl, clinging to her mother's skirt when she'd first gone to his house. She made her sister-in-law repeat what she had said, and her sister-in-law stuttered as she went through each point. "He's going to be buried below Dad's grave. Right in front of Dad's fake grave."

In a shop at the airport, she spotted the young man with dirty sneakers browsing through magazines. On their way to the airport, Choi had said several times that it had been an accident. The old man with the video camera was sipping coffee at a café, seemingly reviewing his footage, although he wouldn't find himself in it.

"Hey, did you know that I— Well, the thing is, I used to . . ." Choi mumbled.

She nodded.

"You did?" Choi asked, raising his voice. At the sound, the old man glanced their way. "You knew all along but pretended you didn't?" Choi mussed her hair, just as he used to.

When she looked back after passing through the checkpoint, she saw Choi waving at her. She may never see him again. In time, she would probably hear about his death from someone else. That is, if she lives until then. She was about to gesture at him to leave, but she didn't. He wouldn't listen to her anyway.

Again, the Japanese tourists sat apart from one another. Announcements came on, signaling takeoff, and the engines' roar grew louder. She thought about her husband who was in the cargo area. It had been eighteen days since his accident, and he was finally returning home.

TUES

Airport Choi Seungwu 18:00 pick up.

Korean Air (KE918) Zurich 20:05 → Incheon International Airport Wed 15:05

16:30 Home.

HA SEONG-NAN is the author of five short story collections—including *Bluebeard's First Wife* and *Flowers of Mold*—and five novels. Over her career, she has received a number of prestigious awards, such as the Dong-in Literary Award in 1999, Hankook Ilbo Literary Prize in 2000, the Isu Literature Prize in 2004, the Oh Yeong-su Literary Award in 2008, and the Contemporary Literature (Hyundae Munhak) Award in 2009.

JANET HONG is a writer and translator based in Vancouver, Canada. She received the 2018 TA First Translation Prize and the 2018 LTI Korea Translation Award for her translation of Han Yujoo's *The Impossible Fairy Tale*. She is a two-time winner of the Harvey Award for Best International Book for her translations of Keum Suk Gendry-Kim's *Grass* and Yeong-shin Ma's *Moms*. Other recent translations include Kwon Yeo-sun's *Lemon* and Kang Young-sook's *At Night He Lifts Weights*.